The
Adventures of
Natalie Bloom

BROOKE STANTON

COCO
— *and bee* —

The Adventures of Natalie Bloom by Brooke Stanton

ISBN: 0-996851437
ISBN-13: 978-0996851435

FOR MY MOTHER,

SUE CHIRONE

One

I bend my neck back and glide my eyes up, up, up the mirrored façade of the towering building that houses Kennedy Media and all its publications. It's an impressive structure with all its chrome, steel, and colossal opaque windows. Hundreds of faces could be looking out in the offices above, glamorous people I can't see.

Pushing the silver frame of the revolving door, I swing it around until I'm deposited into the vast lobby. I feel minute as I look across the sprawling white marbled floor to the large security desk with only one guard sitting on his perch. A couple of young women, in heels and outfits that look fitting more for a night out than a morning at work, push through the turnstiles after they swipe their badges. The *click-clack* of their heels disappears around the corner, and I'm left alone.

It's just before noon, and the lunch rush hasn't begun. There's an internal shift in people's brains as soon as the first hand strikes twelve. They suddenly have a Pavlovian response and rush to the nearest deli counter or restaurant. I've seen it again and again from the many restaurants I've run as a sous chef and then head chef, but now I'm finally opening my own restaurant.

"Catelyn Bloom's your sister?" The security guard frowns at the driver's license I hand him.

One day, I better be known as more than Catelyn Bloom's sister.

Quickly, the middle-aged man's scowl transforms into a bright smile. The sun coming in from the slanted skylights high above him reflects off his balding scalp. "That lady's all right. Last night, I made her pumpkin cheesecake from that TV special she did in November. My wife and me didn't even need to wash the dish. We licked it clean." He laughs boisterously.

"Did you make the praline topping?" I ask, unable to keep the eager tone out of my voice.

"Yeah. It was damn good." The man chuckles again as my eyes widen. "Sorry for the language, lady."

My cheeks hurt from the smile that has spread across my face. I created that recipe, I want to tell him, but I don't. I've kept my involvement in my sister's career a secret for the past four years—what's one more day?

"I'll let my sister know you liked it," I say as I pass through the security turnstile and walk around to the elevator bank. My sensible Frye boots (a gift from Catie—the beauty editor at one of the fashion magazines in the building gave them to her, but Catie only wears boots with at least a three-inch heel) don't make the intimidating *click-clack* like the heels the other girls wore. My shoes have the very unimpressive sound of mediocrity.

A bell dings, and one of the eight elevator doors opens. *Simply Chic*, the lifestyle magazine my sister writes for, is on the tenth floor. When I arrive, I walk straight past the doe-eyed receptionist—who yells out a small protest—and wind my way past desks and work tables to Catie's office. The blinds are drawn across the large glass windows that face the outer office, hiding her office behind them.

"Doesn't anyone at your work get suspicious that the

Queen of Clean's office is such a pigsty?" I ask, entering.

Last year, *The New York Times* called Catie the "Martha Stewart for a younger, hipper generation." As far as her readers and fans are concerned, she's the go-to domestic goddess, gourmet chef, and perfect wife and homemaker.

Except it's pretty much all a lie. She's a complete slob, doesn't have a husband, and burns toast. But I'm helping her change that. We were both almost outed two months ago when she filmed a special on national TV. Catie's quitting the magazine soon to pursue a more honest career in interior design, and I'm opening my own restaurant. Finally.

Looking around, I'm reminded of her true talent—interior design. Her office is impeccably styled with only the hottest designers' furniture and décor—none of which I can name—but it's impossible to see the beauty of it with the piles of magazines, design books, loose papers, a white Christmas tree overdue to be put away, and multicolored boxes stacked on and around every empty space. She can design the hell out of anything, but that's where her domestic talents end.

Catie's lucky I fell in love with cooking while helping our mom run her catering business. At the first sign of a spatula, Catie fled our kitchen. But she loved designing and putting together the centerpieces and table settings for the parties. So we each found our calling.

Catie looks up from her computer screen, where she's watching a how-to video on the differences between chopping, dicing, and mincing. I almost laugh at the intensity with which she's watching it. I've been sending her videos to study and then coming in and practicing with her in the test kitchen as she hones her skills. I don't expect her to become a master chef, but she needs to at least know the basics as she transitions to a more authentic work life.

In the meantime, I suggested she use readers' recipes instead of her own (i.e. my own) in the magazine for now. The new column has been a big success. The recipes are also posted online, and readers get to vote and comment on their favorites.

"Should we go to the kitchen?" Catie asks, pausing the video.

"After my meeting," I say, already inwardly cringing as I think of watching Catie nearly slice her perfectly manicured fingers at every chop.

"I thought the meeting with your contractor was this afternoon?"

"No. It's in ten minutes. Thanks for letting us do it here. The electricity was shut off at the restaurant site when I stopped by last night. I don't know why, but I left a message with Con Ed." I stand, double-checking I have my binder of all-things-restaurant. "It's as frozen as Susan Lucci's face out there. The restaurant would have been an icebox."

"I know. My nipples almost fell off on the walk from the subway." Catie turns back to her computer, clicking the video back on.

"Any word on the book?" I ask, pushing her door open. Catie waves me away, and my mouth purses at her dismissal of my question, which means she hasn't followed up with her publisher like she promised.

Last year, Catie wrote a best-selling lifestyle book called *Catelyn Bloom's Guide to Living Simply Chic.* I secretly provided all the recipes for her book. Now her publisher is eager for a follow-up, but I'm not going to help Catie unless my name is on the cover too. Catie's waiting to hear back from them, but I'm not sure how hard she pushed the issue. It's not that Catie would mind having me coauthor it—she did give me half the profits from the last book, which is how I got the seed money to open my own restaurant—but she's been distracted by the amount of work it takes to actually write about cooking in her columns instead of waiting for me to give her the content.

The main cooking column, which used to feature complex

recipes for the more advanced readers, has now been changed to "Cooking 101." It's being promoted as a column for her readers who are newbies at cooking, and Catie regales them with tales of her early mishaps when she was learning to cook. Little do they know, these mishaps are happening just days before she writes the column.

I want to press Catie more about the book, but I only have a few minutes until the meeting. Jim, the contractor for my new restaurant, was cagey on the phone when I asked him about the permits we've been waiting for weeks to be approved. The budget is tight, and the last thing I need is delays with the permits. They are taking longer to get than a taxi at 4:00 p.m.

When I arrive, Jim is already in the small conference room, looking out of place in his paint-splattered pants, workman's boots, and ratty backpack against the sleek, modern room.

"I hate to sound like your father, but I'm disappointed in you," Jim says before I can offer a greeting.

The owner at the French bistro I worked at recommended Jim, and we hit it off when I discovered his wife is a huge fan of Catie's. From the start, our relationship has been open and honest, and he guides me in the right direction when he feels my ideas are too intricate or overreaching, even if it means less money for him. He's helped renovate and build a dozen restaurants and businesses in the city, and I look to him as a beacon in this new world of business ownership.

I was involved in a restaurant venture four years ago that turned into a financial and permitting mess, all because of me. So I am eager for any guidance that is offered to me. My father died when I was twelve, and my stepfather, who is a wonderful man, didn't marry my mother until I was out of the house and in culinary school. My formative years were lacking a male role model, which didn't bother me until I began this endeavor. Jim's guidance has been a great relief. If it weren't for him and my business partner, Luke Hawker, I would be drowning in second-guesses and self-doubts.

"I know I don't know you that well," Jim continues, and I cringe under his gentle scrutiny, "but I have two daughters around your age, as you know." He strums his hands on the desk, and I stare at him. I don't mind that he's overstepped the boundaries of our relationship. Because I didn't have a father during my adolescent years, having a man looking out for me almost endears him to me, but I have no idea what he's talking about. So far, everything has run smoothly. I found a landlord who rented me a beautiful space for a reasonable price located on the border of Williamsburg and Greenpoint, Brooklyn. The spillover from the now gentrified and overpriced Williamsburg has made the demands high and the rents higher in Greenpoint, now an up-and-coming neighborhood. I was lucky to sign a deal with the landlord on the cusp of the boom.

Jim has been fast and efficient with his work so far. I visit the restaurant several times a week to check on the progress, but so far, all we've done is gut the insides and discuss design and function as we wait for the remaining permits to be approved.

"I wondered if you were even a part of the operation anymore." He threads his fingers and leans forward; a whiff of sweat and paint drift under my nose. "I speak to Luke more than you these days."

Luke is my first and only investor and my unofficial accountant and business adviser. He used to be a managing director at Morgan Stanley, which meant he oversaw a lot of rich people's money. I was surprised when he offered to invest in my little restaurant, but I eagerly accepted, since he knew far more about handling money and running a business. I'd already failed once at opening a restaurant, so his insights and expertise were a blessing. And we'd become close friends by the time he offered to invest, so I felt less pressure accepting his money.

"Sorry. I've been busy helping my sister."

"The big star," he says, referring to his wife's starry-eyed admiration of Catie, and smiles.

I laugh, but it comes out more like a groan. "Kind of."

"My wife is redecorating every bedroom in the house thanks to her book." Jim frowns, momentarily distracted. "After Catie signed it for her, she wrapped the damn thing in plastic so it won't get a spot on it." Jim rubs the five-day growth on his chin, shaking his head, but there's a small smile on his lips that suggests he likes that it makes his wife happy.

"My wife DVRed that special where Catie hosted that travel journalist, Max something-or-rather, who almost died saving that little girl in Greece," Jim says. "She watches it all the time. She wants our house to look exactly like Catie's."

At the mention of Max, my heart leaps excitedly in my chest, like a puppy trying to reach a treat.

"It was a fun shoot." I resist telling him that Catie almost didn't do it, since it meant she had to fake knowing how to cook and find a man to pretend to be her husband for the special. Luckily, Sam Harding, her knight in shining Armani came to her rescue. She barely made it through the filming with her job, dignity, and heart intact.

"Anyway, I'm sorry to be blunt, but do you have the money I'm owed?" Jim's eyes dart away and back at me.

I furrow my brow, trying to recall if Luke mentioned a payment that's due. Pulling up the calendar on my phone, I scroll through it, but the last payment was paid a week ago.

"Didn't Luke give you a check last week?" I ask.

"No. And I still need the payment for the last two permits I filed. Plus the demo work in the cellar." Jim takes out two invoices with the word *overdue* stamped across them in red ink. Why does it always have to be red ink? It takes me back to the days in school when the teacher passed graded papers back, and everyone could glaringly see when you failed. It was humiliating, and that's how I feel now looking at the invoices.

"He told me he paid you. He sent me texts confirming it was done." Quickly, I search through my phone and find them. I show my phone to Jim.

"He lied."

A cold sweat breaks out across my forehead. "There must be some misunderstanding."

Jim takes a deep breath and temples his fingers. "Check your bank account."

"Why?" My stomach clinches.

"It's just a hunch. Do me a favor, and log into your account."

My fingers fumble as I tap in the password. After the fourth attempt, my account screen flashes before me.

Checking: $5.07 glares back at me.

"It…it must be a mistake." My voice barely makes it out of my throat. I bend over, the blood rushing back into my brain. But I can't think. There should be over forty thousand dollars in that account.

"How well do you know Luke?" Jim asks. His voice is calm, and there is no judgment in the question, but my ears begin ringing as the implication hits me.

I gave Luke complete access to my business account two months ago. Unless I'm a victim of identity theft, which I highly doubt, he's the only person who could have taken the money. But I know Luke. We've been friends for over a year. He's a very successful banker. He doesn't need my money.

But even as I think it, I doubt myself. How well do I really know him? I met Luke when he moved into the newly renovated lofts across the street from Chez Bella, the restaurant I ran. He was hard to miss when he first walked in. He was tall and broad with a mop of blond hair and tan skin and looked more like a surfer than a banker, even in his tailored suit, his silk tie loosened at the end of the day. Every weekend, he'd come in with a different beauty on his arm, ordering cocktails, three-course meals, and expensive bottles of wine. He was the ideal customer. He always came back, never complained, and tipped the waiters generously. Sometimes he was gruff and came across as entitled, but in New York, that's run-of-the-mill. Then one day, he asked to speak to the chef after ordering the steak tartare. He wanted to compliment me on the preparation. He said he'd never tasted a more flavorful tartare outside of France. His red-haired date—stunning in a Mason Hosker tiered dress—looked impressed, and I applauded him silently for his guile, realizing he only brought me out to impress her. But it worked. I saw them walk past the restaurant during brunch service the next morning—him in jeans and a Thomas Pink blue-and-white-striped button-down and her still in her backless dress, a bit more rumpled than the night before.

After that night, he frequented the restaurant several times a week with his stunning dates, but sometimes he'd come alone, for a postwork nightcap or a drink with colleagues and clients. He began asking for me regularly to discuss the specials or my recommendations. Then one night after the restaurant closed, he sauntered into the kitchen, swirling his Glenlivet 18, and rested against one of the stainless steel workbenches, chatting with me as I prepared ingredients for the following day's lunch.

We chatted, and then he was rolling up his sleeves, assisting me with the prep. As he chopped, sliced, or sautéed, he asked me dozens of questions about working in the restaurant industry and asked how I became a chef. He confided in me that he was burned-out from banking and wanted to try something new, something he could be passionate about, like I was. He knew I was going to start my own restaurant and offered to be an investor, which isn't unusual. Many young professionals become investors in restaurants and bars in the city, mainly because it looks good on their social résumés, not because it makes a killing in profits.

BROOKE STANTON

Luke managed millions, if not billions, of dollars of other people's money for a living; his investment in me was tiny in comparison, so I accepted his offer. Once it was official, I picked his brain about the financial side of owning a business, and he actively participated, coming with me when I looked at spaces, meeting with contractors, and offering me accounting and business tips. He soon became more than just an investor—he became my partner.

"I'm sorry to say this, but I'm stopping work until I get paid." Jim's battered, black workman's boots shuffle under my lowered gaze as he places his hand on my shoulder to soften the blow. "Be careful who you trust. You wouldn't be the first gal to be taken in by a pretty face like his."

What is he saying? I look at my account again—$5.07 swims in my head, muddling my thoughts.

"Don't worry, Jim," I finally say, giving him a weak smile. "I'll figure this out."

He's quiet and then says, "Take a few days, talk to Luke, and give me a call once it's sorted. I want to continue working with you, but I have a family and bills I need to pay too." There's a *swoosh* as the glass door opens and slowly shuts behind his retreating form.

In a daze, I walk back to Catie's office.

"How did it go?" she asks, not looking up from her computer, where she's typing rapidly.

The mention of the meeting sends tingles into my hands and feet. I shake my head but can't utter the words. Catie slips around her desk and ushers me into one of the two armchairs, moving stacks of books from both. "You're shaking. What happened?"

"Oh, Little Bee." My chin quivers, and I suck in a deep breath. "The money's gone. I think Luke...I don't know. But it's gone."

There's a pause, and I look up to see the same shocked expression I felt on my face when I first saw my empty bank

10

account. "How?"

"Jim says he hasn't been paid in two weeks, and when I looked at my bank account there was only five dollars left. Five dollars!" I yell, the realization of what it means hitting me.

"Calm down," Catie coaxes. I take a deep breath, and she continues. "How did Luke get a hold of the money?"

"I gave him full access to the account," I admit.

Catie gasps. "Oh, Natalie. How could you?"

"He's practically my accountant," I shoot back defensively. "He has tons of money. I've seen his office at Morgan Stanley. It's huge. Or it was huge."

"Didn't he quit his job?"

"Yeah. He was burned-out and wanted a change. But he has plenty of money and wanted to invest in a passion project. Something that was more exciting than managing other people's money." My head drops. "I thought he was a godsend. Especially, after what happened to me last time…"

Taking my hand, Catie waits until I look at her; my eyes fill with tears at my stupidity. I'm usually the one taking care of Catie. She was nine when our father died, and I slipped into the role of her protector, which is why I was so willing to take a back seat and help her with her blog, which turned into her career. It feels strange for the roles to be reversed. "Are you sure he stole it? What did he say when you talked to him?"

"I haven't." I pull out my phone, realizing I should have called him the second I saw my dwindled bank account, but I was too stunned to think clearly. "I came straight here after the meeting." Opening my contacts, I tap his name, calling him. It goes straight to voice mail, and I leave an urgent message telling him to call me but not mentioning the money. "I haven't talked to him in weeks. We've exchanged dozens of texts and e-mails, but that's it. I've been so busy with the designer and experimenting with the recipes for the menu and helping you transition and spending time with…with

Max." I look away sheepishly, realizing I've been so swept up in other people's lives that I may have let a thief run away with all my money.

"I thought you said Max ran off when you tried to kiss him." Catie means no harm, but the words sting.

"He did, but...I've still been helping him with Bailey."

Catie looks at me in disbelief. "Okay. We are so going to talk about that later. For now, you need to go to his apartment."

"Whose? Max's?"

"No, Luke's. You know where he lives, right?" Catie brushes her dark hair out of her face and waits for my answer.

"Of course. Well, I know the building. I don't remember the exact apartment number."

Catie looks at me with a disbelieving look. "How can you not remember? You were at his place a few weeks ago."

"Two months ago. And it was late, and I was a little drunk. I can't remember exactly."

"Hold on." Catie leans across her desk, knocking over an overflowing pink paisley jar of colored pencils and picks up her phone, pressing speed dial. "Patrick, get in here."

A moment later, Catie's editor, Patrick Simon, walks into her office, his reading glasses pushed into his thick brown hair, making pieces stick up sporadically like a cactus.

"Catie, I'm the one who's meant to yell for *you* to come into *my* office," Patrick says without conviction.

Waving her hand, Catie brushes off his comment. Catie treats him like her kid brother, but he secretly loves it. He'd do anything for her. "Can you get your assistant to find an address for Luke—" She looks at me.

"Hawker," I say.

"He used to work for Morgan Stanley." She looks at me for confirmation.

I nod.

"Patrick's assistant is a master sleuth," Catie explains.

"It's okay." I look up at Patrick's tall frame. "I can do a search online. It's not hard to find an address. It'll cost like ten bucks on white pages."

"Don't do that. Finding an address is easy. I'll have it in no time." Patrick turns back to Catie, indicating the disaster zone that is her office, and says, "Anything else, *Queen of Clean?*"

"You've got poop on your shirt."

"What?" Patrick looks down at a dark-brown stain on his crisp-white cuffed shirt. "Ah! We were watching our neighbor's baby. Practice, Avery says." Patrick's wife, Avery, is four months pregnant with their first child. "The kid's an asshole." Patrick grunts.

"I'm sure yours will be perfect," I assure him.

"He'll be an asshole." Patrick takes a tissue from Catie's desk and wipes at the spot. "But he'll be my asshole." Patrick throws the tissue in the overflowing trash can at the side of Catie's white acrylic desk. "And when I want to punish him, I'll let him crawl around in here for a bit."

"Har, har," Catie says. "You'll ask your assistant?"

"I'm on it." He leaves, pulling the stain away from his body.

A few minutes later, the phone rings. Catie dives for it, listens, jots down an address on a scrap of paper, and hands it to me.

"What are you going to say?" Catie asks.

"Give me my fucking money back." I go to stand, but my legs feel like they're filled with concrete as I remember the last time I had a fight concerning money. It's what led to the end of my relationship with my ex, Cole *Motherfucker* Merrick But at the time, I didn't see him as a motherfucker. At the time, I was in love.

"What's the matter?" Catie asks, seeing my hesitation.

"Come with me."

"I can't. Jaclyn asked me to send her some social media

posts. I've already delayed it twice. Aren't you meeting Max for lunch?"

"Not for another hour," I say. "And it's to walk Bailey while he has a meeting with some editor."

"You can't keep being his dog walker," Catie chides, and I know she's right, but that's what happens when you have an all-consuming crush on someone. You jump at any chance to see them. "I like Max, but if he's not interested, put your foot down. Don't let him use you. You deserve to be adored."

"I don't want to talk about it," I say. Sisters have an uncanny way of knowing just where to stick the dagger, even when trying to be helpful. Raising her eyebrows in a way that suggests she's about to take matters into her own hands, Catie presses a number on her cell phone and gives me a mischievous smile. "What are you doing?" I ask.

She turns her back to me, the phone to her ear. "How are you doing? Good, good. No, I haven't burned any kitchens down today. I have a quick favor. Can you meet Natalie a little early to confront a sleazebag that stole some money from her? Right now. Great. Meet her at the corner of Spring and Elizabeth in twenty minutes." She hangs up, a wide grin on her face. It's infuriating. She's getting pleasure out of this. "It's time you use *him* for a change."

"I didn't want him to know about the money."

"Too late." When I don't move, she continues. "Don't keep your boyfriend waiting."

"He's not my boyfriend." Sometimes I feel like I'm twelve years old when I'm around Catie. Sisters are the worst. "And he only said yes because *you* asked him."

"He knows my heart belongs to another."

"Where is Sam?" I ask, not wanting to think about Max and his lack of romantic interest in me.

Frown marks appear across Catie's smooth forehead. "Still in the Alps working on that story about the Aussie snowboarder."

"I thought he was coming back this week." I move to the oval mirror that's hanging on the wall beside her bookcase, treading over boxes and books and discarded shopping bags. My ponytail is crooked and several pieces of blond hair hang loose. I scrape the stray pieces back in their place and tie my thick hair back up.

"The snowboarder keeps winning his comps. It should be over in a week or two." Catie hands me tubes of lipstick and mascara. "Sam promised he'd be back for the Valentine's Day Ball."

"How are things going with you two?" My words are distorted as I spread the lipstick on, but Catie understands me. Sisters always do.

"A lot of start-stops. After the filming, we got kicked out of the townhouse by the cleaning crew before we could...you know. Then he got this assignment, and I've barely seen him."

I don't usually wear makeup; there's not much use when I'm stuck in a kitchen most of the day, but Catie says if I want to be successful, I need to look the part. She's always perfectly put together, not a hair out of place. I'm lucky if I've managed to pull a brush through my locks.

"That was two months ago," I point out.

After four years, Catie finally admitted to her friend and colleague, Sam Harding—the editor of the digital magazine *Limitless*, for the "extreme-sports enthusiast"—that she loves him. He's been in love with Catie for years but didn't admit it to her until the filming, when he pretended to be Catie's husband for the TV special.

"I know. But we've both been busy." Catie dismisses the worried look on my face and hands me a tissue to blot my lips. "You're lucky you have Mom's natural beauty. Now go downstairs. I'll call a car to drive you to Luke's place."

Twenty minutes later, I'm in front of Luke's redbrick apartment building, waiting for Max to join me before I ring the buzzer. The building is next to a bar, which smells of stale beer and late-night regrets. I see the familiar, slender body of a silver greyhound rounding the corner of Spring Street, and I tell myself to keep it cool, but my heart betrays me and leaps into a gallop, knowing who will be holding the leash. When Bailey sees me, his tail wags excitedly, and he bounds forward.

Behind him, Max appears. The grin on his lips lights up his whole face and ignites something warm inside me. God, he's gorgeous. He's all dark haired and hard bodied with sparkling-blue eyes that turn my insides into a hyper carnival ride whenever they look my way. I have to consciously slow my breathing and portray an act of calm.

Bailey jumps up, his paws pressing against my red coat, leaving dirt stains. I don't care. I scratch his head and kiss him behind the ear, his warm, silky fur feeling divine against my cool lips, calming my heartbeat.

"Thanks for coming," I say.

"Of course." Max smiles again, and I look away, worried he'll read the desire that shoots through my body when our eyes meet.

"So what's the story?" Max asks.

I relay the events of the morning, wishing I didn't sound like such a dolt.

"You gave this guy complete access to all your money?"

"He's my business partner," I quickly defend and then add, "and my friend."

"How long have you known him, Bloom?" Max's voice grows stern, and I bite my lip as I go all hot-for-teacher. I become sophomoric around him. It's no wonder he's not interested.

"A year."

"When did you give him access to your money?"

My skin prickles under the interrogation. "A few months ago. He used to be a big shot banker. I've seen where he worked, his office. It was huge. He was obviously making a lot of money. I don't understand why he'd steal from me."

The look Max gives me is incredulous. "There are a lot of reasons. When did you last see him?"

"Not since…since the night of my farewell party." My cheeks burn, thinking of that night. I thought Max and I were starting our happily ever after, but the opposite happened. "We've been mostly communicating through texts and e-mails. I look over all the invoices and then send them to Luke who double-checks them and then pays them. Most of my time is spent at the restaurant site with the architect, designer, or contractor, but Luke doesn't need to be there for any of that."

I quickly push into Luke's building as a woman with a Chihuahua comes out. The miniature dog barks wildly at Bailey, and the owner picks the small dog up and scurries down the street.

"This is where he lives?" Max asks, following me in.

"Yes." I quickly walk down the wide entryway and turn right toward the elevators, a vague recollection of the layout of the building resurfacing in my brain. The first and only time I was here, it was late and dark, and Luke and I had been drinking at a bar around the corner and discussing the restaurant. I walked Luke back, and as I turned to leave, he grabbed me and kissed me. I was taken aback at first, worried how it would affect the business, but his kisses melted in my mouth, and soon we were stumbling through the lobby into the elevator and up to his apartment.

The next morning, we laughed it off, and I left, not thinking much about it. We both agreed it was a mistake, and then I was off to help Catie film the special. When I got back, it was as if the night never happened.

"Are you two together?"

"Why does that matter?" I shoot back and then regret the defensive tone in my voice.

"I want to know what I'm walking into." Max stops me as I arrive at Luke's door. "Is this a lovers' quarrel?"

"No. Nothing like that. He's my business partner. That's it."

"So nothing's happened between you two?"

Instead of answering, I knock on the door and hear shuffling behind it, but no one answers. I knock again. Soft footsteps patter behind the door and stop. I hold my breath, waiting for the doorknob to turn.

"Luke," I call. "I see your feet. Open the door."

Max is raising his foot, as if he's going to kick the door open. I bat it away. "Put your foot down, Bourne."

I raise my hand to knock again when the door opens. A petite girl with dark hair stands before us, decked out in Lululemon: capris, cami, and sweatband.

"Luke isn't here," she says.

"Oh, uh…" I stumble, not expecting to see this little chipmunk in front of me. "Do you know when he'll be back?"

"I have no idea. I barely know him."

Max and I exchange a confused look.

"Then how—"

"I rented it on Airbnb."

Why would Luke rent out his apartment? Unless it's just for the weekend. A lot of people rent out their apartments these days to make a little extra cash when they're traveling, or they just shack up with someone else for the weekend.

"How long are you staying?" Max asks.

"Six months."

"Six months!" I yell.

The girl shuts the door slightly. "Yes. Look, I can't tell you anything else. I don't know the guy. I met him for two seconds when he gave me the keys."

"When was that?" Max asks.

"A month ago."

My mouth hangs open. Where has he been for a whole month?

"He didn't say anything else?" Max asks, giving me a sideways glance in response to my silence.

"No," she snaps. "That's it." And she slams the door.

We're halfway to the elevator when the girl pokes her head out again. "He did say one thing."

"What?" I ask.

"He'd be traveling out of the country and hard to reach." She closes the door before I can ask her another question.

The elevator chimes, and Max and I step in, Bailey sitting next to me, quiet and sullen, as if he knows the seriousness of what's just been revealed. If the girl is right, and Luke has run off to another country and won't be back for six months, something very wrong is going on. You don't leave the country on a whim. And you don't rent out your apartment for six months on the spur of the moment. Luke's been planning this.

This time was going to be different. I was using my head instead of my heart when it came to the restaurant. That's why Luke was perfect. He's a friend and an expert at money management. Everything about Luke screamed money: his job, his apartment, his tailored suits, his investments. How did I get it so wrong?

Luke invested thirty grand in my restaurant. If his goal was to steal from me this whole time, it seems like a high risk for such small amount of money—a small amount in his world of million-dollar deals, but not in my world. Unless he pulled this scheme on a dozen other women across the city at the same time.

Max puts his arm around my shoulders and squeezes me in a sideways hug, speaking the same thought that runs through my head. "I think you've been Madoffed, Bloom."

It would be funny if it weren't true.

Two

My mind is spinning from my devastating change in circumstances. This morning, I woke up excited for the meeting with my contractor, knowing it would bring me one step closer to my dream. Then I was off to continue to help my sister disentangle herself from her little white lies that would disentangle me too and then meeting up with the one person who is on my mind most of the day, every day—Max.

Now, none of that matters until I can find Luke.

"Why would he do it? He doesn't need it. Why invest money in my little business only to steal it back? I know you said that could've been his scam the whole time, but he spent countless hours with me, learning to cook and how to run a kitchen, the ins and outs of the restaurant business, and going over business plans and design plans. Is he a sociopath? I don't think I've ever met one. Would I have even known—"

"Bloom, slow down. Take a breath." I try, but my throat is constricted. Max guides me across Elizabeth Street toward Bowery, hurrying me to the curb as a delivery truck barrels by. "What do you know about this guy?"

"I'm an easy target. I was so worried about screwing up

that I practically jumped at the idea of Luke—a successful businessman and banker—helping me with the finances. I know how to run a restaurant, but I have no idea how to start one from scratch. I tried once. It was a disaster."

I halt at the corner of Prince Street, and cars zip down Bowery. Bailey bounces next me, eager to continue the speed walk. I mindlessly pet his head and stare at a white-brick wall with a crack running up the side. I've always liked white brick. I especially like exposed brick inside an apartment or restaurant. Maybe I could—

"Bloom. Earth to Bloom."

Strong arms grasp my shoulders, and I look up into Max's brilliant-blue eyes. The corners of my lips involuntarily turn up. "Huh?"

"I said, I have that meeting with my friend, the editor from *The Huffington Post*. We're meeting at a café near Tompkins Square Park in five minutes," Max says, while Bailey happily dodges the pedestrians that are wrapped up in coats, scarves, and hats as we hurry over the long crosswalk at Houston Street.

"Okay," I say. I could try to track Luke down, use Find My iPhone or something. I pull out my phone but realize I have no idea how to track someone else's phone with it. Catie would know. I stop, calling her, Bailey crashing into my legs. It goes straight to voice mail, so I send a text instead.

"Bloom!"

"What?"

"Look at me." Max has stopped in front of the massive Whole Foods on the corner, and I remember I need milk. I had to use the carton of soy milk Catie left in my fridge for my cereal this morning. It was tasteless and watery.

"Where are you going? Wait! I can't go in there with Bailey."

I stop. Max has a bewildered look on his face.

"I need milk," I explain.

"You're in shock. You need to stop for a minute."

He takes a few steps into the store, grabs my hand, and leads me back out and across the congested street. Sliding the loop of the leash onto his wrist, he takes hold of my shoulders again and makes me look at him.

"Luke may not be out of the country. He may have said that to cover his ass. There are ways to find him. I can help you." I'm nodding but only half comprehending his words. "But first I have this meeting. Why don't you take Bailey to the dog run in Tompkins Square Park, and I'll come meet you as soon as I'm done. Then we'll figure this out."

"I'm not your dog walker, you know," I snap, Catie's words ringing in my ears.

Max blinks, looking startled. "I know. It's not...I didn't mean that. Bailey can come with me if you don't want—"

"No. No, it's fine. I'm just...upset."

Max cautiously hands me the leash when we reach the south edge of the square. "I really don't think of you as my dog walker." When I don't say anything he continues, "I shouldn't be long. He said he has a story he wants my help with."

When Max leaves, I lead Bailey to the dog run in the park. It stinks of wet dog, urine, and dirt. I let him off his leash and sit, pulling my wool coat closer around my body and covering my nose. It's midafternoon, near four o'clock, but the sun is already setting. It's depressing how early the dark comes during winter in Manhattan. But I don't mind today; it suits my mood.

The cold and dark have kept most other dog owners away, so Bailey and I have the dog run entirely to ourselves. My phone rings, and I release my coat, answering it. It's Catie.

"I called my detective friend, but he said it's illegal and near impossible to track someone's phone if you don't have their account e-mail and password," Catie says when I answer.

The mention of an account shakes me awake. "The bank!"

"What?" Catie asks.

"I need to call my bank." I hang up before she can answer.

It takes a few attempts to locate the right person to talk to and for me to remember all my account information, but I explain my situation and make sure Luke no longer has access to the account. The manager says there's not much they can do about the money that was withdrawn since I gave Luke access to the account.

"One more thing," I say before the bank manager rings off. "When was the last withdrawal?"

"January 6."

"From a branch or ATM?" I ask.

"ATM."

"Can you tell me where it was located?"

"Miami International Airport."

My entire body deflates. An airport. Luke could be anywhere. Even out of the country like the chipmunk said. I swipe through my phone and open both the Facebook and Twitter apps, but Luke hasn't posted anything on either of them for months. This isn't a surprise. He hardly posts on his social media accounts, except to share an interesting news article or podcast here and there.

"Find out anything?" Bailey whizzes past me at the sound of Max's voice as he pushes the metal gate of the dog park open. It's dark now, the dim lights of the lamps above us creating crooked shadows around the dog run. Across the park, the twinkling lights strung among a row of trees flicker on. I stare at them, wishing for the magical feeling that fairy lights usually spark inside me, but it doesn't come. It's been snuffed out by Luke, the bastard.

"His phone is a dead end. And I called my bank. The last ATM withdrawal was at Miami airport." Bailey nudges my hand with his nose, and I automatically oblige, rubbing behind his ears, feeling the taut muscles of his neck. Max nods as if none of this is a surprise. I guess it's not to me either. "How did your meeting go?"

Max's face darkens. "Not good."

"You couldn't help him with his story?"

"I can, but it isn't the kind of story I usually write."

"What do you mean?"

He scoots closer, considering me. "I…it doesn't matter. It's just a sensational story that won't benefit the public in any way. The media will latch on to anything sensational these days. Just look at what happened to me." Max rubs his temple, and I see a small scar there I never noticed before.

"Is that from the guys you chased after in Greece?"

"Yeah. One of them hit me with a metal pipe. The doctor said if it had been any higher, I would be dead."

My heart clinches in my chest at the thought. I want to reach out for his hand, to reassure myself that he's here, that he's alive. "Is that what caused the amnesia?"

While working on a story in Greece last summer, Max witnessed a little girl being snatched from her mother. He jumped on his moped and raced after the van. When the men realized they were being followed, they jumped out and attacked him—Max stabbed two of the men with a knife before the third man wacked him with the pipe—and left Max unconscious in an empty parking lot, the guy probably thinking he was dead. Luckily, the injuries Max inflicted on the kidnappers slowed them down enough for the police to catch them and return the girl to her mother.

A tourist caught the abduction and the start of the chase on their phone, and it went viral. Max became a media sensation immediately. I've watched that video a dozen times, and each time Max shoots by on his moped after that van, my heart stops, and I fall for him a little more. He was so courageous and heroic. There was no hesitation. It's the most selfless act I've ever witnessed.

"The doctor said the amnesia was probably a combination

of the physical trauma with some psychological stuff piled on top of it, since my parents deaths involved a van." Max rushes on before I can ask any questions. I know his parents died in a car accident when he was about thirteen, but I've never heard him talk about it directly. Except on the interview Catie did with him during the special. "It was weird seeing my story all over the news, and at that point I couldn't remember anything about my life."

I suspect his aunt, Gillian Kennedy, the owner of Kennedy Media, also had something to do with him becoming a media sensation. She's the one that cooked up the idea of having a big homecoming special hosted by America's number-one domestic goddess, Catelyn Bloom. Which is how I met him. I was discreetly helping Catie with the cooking segments during the weekend shoot. But Max isn't an idiot. He saw through our charade pretty fast.

"My story isn't any more extraordinary than the hundreds of heroic acts that occur daily, but my story was caught on camera and had a happy ending, so it went viral and touched a lot of people's lives." Max pauses and then rolls his neck and shoulders, as if he's pulling himself out of the past and back into the present. "I've been humbled and amazed by the generosity of other people during it all." Max stands, hooking the leash on Bailey.

"Are you still writing for *Unchartered?*" I ask, referring to the travel magazine he wrote for when he was in Greece. Also part of the Kennedy Media publications.

"I haven't officially quit. I'm not sure if I want to continue my nomadic life as a travel writer. In some ways, it's thrilling, and I love learning about different people and cultures, but as I get older, it's becoming less adventurous and more work. But I've never stayed in one place for longer than a few months since I started working. I'm not sure how I'd adapt to settling down."

"Would you stay in the city?" My voice catches. If he left,

I'd be crushed.

"I don't really have a reason to stay." Max locks eyes with me, and I hurry forward, worried he'll read my heart's desire: *I want to be the reason you stay.*

I dodge the cracks in the sidewalk where roots have pushed the concrete up and apart, echoing the feelings in my heart as his words reverberate inside me.

Max's phone rings, disrupting our conversation, and he answers it.

"Everything okay?" He listens, furrowing his brow. "I'm sorry. He shouldn't have...I understand. Right now? Nothing, just walking Bailey." Max turns slightly, and I kneel down and pet Bailey on his silky back, pretending I'm not dying to know who's on the other end of the line. "Okay. I'll call you later."

He hangs up, and we continue walking in silence, the air thick with what he's not saying. "That was Jess." I'm surprised when he speaks.

"Oh."

Jess is his ex-fiancé who broke up with him right after the filming. They got together under tragic circumstances, and when the dust settled, they both realized they were drawn together out of desperation more than love.

Plus Jess started seeing someone else.

"She wanted—"

"It's okay," I stop him, not wanting to hear about Jess. I shift the subject, in case Max feels a need to continue talking about her. "If Luke did steal my money, can I sue him?"

"Yes. And you should."

"Even though I gave him access to the money?"

"It's called embezzling." Max lowers his chin and raises his eyebrows to press the point.

"Would it be worth it? It could get messy and expensive. And I know how this is going to sound, but...Luke is my friend." I rush on as Max begins to protest. "I get it. He's a scumbag. He stole my money. But we've shared a lot. It's hard to believe the man who sat next to me for hours, listening to my hopes and dreams and excitedly gave me suggestions and helped me begin to realize those dreams, was lying the whole time."

"He's a con artist. It's what they do."

But I slept with him, I want to say. What does that say about me? We spent hours laughing in the kitchen when he tried to flip a fish filet and it flew across the room and when he baked a soufflé that deflated as soon as he took it out of the oven. It's hard to wrap my head around the idea that he was doing all that just to steal thousands of dollars from me.

"Don't worry. I'm going to find him, and I'm going to get my money back," I assure Max. "I'm just not ready to ruin both our lives yet. I want answers first."

My phone beeps as a message from my mom pops onto the screen. It's a picture of tuna canapés she just made. When I spoke to her yesterday, she said she's throwing a dinner party at her villa in Panama, where she and my stepdad stay about three months of the year.

My love of cooking comes from my mom and Mamé—my father's mother. My mom used to run a catering business before my mamé passed away. Their love of cooking is what bonded them together after my father died. Before that, they couldn't stand each other. Cooking was the only thing they could do together that didn't end in a bloodbath of stinging words and blame. It helped them latch on to the one thing that kept the memory of him alive. Each other.

I text her that they look beautiful and suggest using plantain chips instead of tortilla chips. Suddenly, I miss her and her strength. If this had happened to her, she would have called every media outlet by now, and Luke's name would be slandered across all social media accounts.

As Max walks Bailey to the curb to pee, I call Mom on FaceTime Audio, to avoid the expense of calling internationally. Right now, every penny counts.

"Baby." My mother's soothing voice wraps me up like a toddler clutching a lovey. "How are you? I miss you."

My chin quivers, and I bite my lip, regaining my composure before I speak. Telling my mom what has happened will make everything real. I've been moving ahead, like a snowball rolling down a hill and gathering speed, but now that I've stopped, the size of it chills me. This could mean the end of my dream. When I speak, my voice is tinged with pain and anger. "Not good. You remember Luke?"

"Of course. Actually, I—"

"He stole my money."

My mother takes a sharp intake of breath.

"Mom?"

"That little shit. I'm going to kill him." I hear movement on the other end of the line and a door opening. Then there's rustling, like wind.

"What are you doing?" I ask. Knowing my mother, I bet she's driving down to the dock right now to board a flight home to me. "Don't rush home. I'll figure this out."

"He's here."

The words bounce around my head like a Ping-Pong ball, disorienting me. I must have heard her wrong. Did she say—

"Natalie, he's here. I saw him two weeks ago at the marina."

What? Max mouths beside me, watching my face contort. I put the phone on speaker and hold it out.

"I don't understand. What do you mean Luke's there?"

Wind is rushing over the phone on the other end, and my mom's voice is loud, talking over the roar. "He was on that boat in the marina, the one that looks like a pirate ship. It's a restaurant, but it's been vacant for years."

I nod and then say, "Yes," realizing she can't see me.

"He was there, and the restaurant was open. He was running it with some girl. I went to speak to him, but Marty and I were late for our flight to David. When we returned a week later, it was late, and the restaurant was closed." The whooshing on the other end stops. "I assumed you knew he was down here. I thought you gave him the idea. You know how I'm always saying someone would make a killing if they opened a good restaurant down here. With all the expats and retirees bored and ready to spend their money, how can you lose? I'd do it my self but—"

"Mom. Mom!" I cut her off.

"Sorry. I'm here, but I don't see anyone."

"Where?" I ask.

"Overboard, the restaurant." There's shuffling as my mother explores the boat. A minute that feels like ten goes by. "No one's here right now."

"We're coming down there." Max grabs my phone and speaks into it.

"Who is that?"

"It's your daughter's friend, Max."

My mom's voice becomes soft and lulling. Of course, she knows who he is. I mention him every time I speak to her. I can't help it. "Oh, hello, Max. How are you?"

"Mom," I say, grabbing the phone back. Bailey is tugging at Max's hand, and he instructs Bailey to sit, which he does, in the middle of the sidewalk. A man walking by and texting on his phone nearly trips over Bailey and shouts at us to *move your damn dog*, but we're too enthralled in what my mother has revealed. "Go talk to the owner of the boat, and call me back."

"I'm on it!" Mom loves a good fight, especially when one of her daughters has been wronged. If she finds Luke, he's a dead man.

"We'll book a flight, and be there in a day or two, Mrs. Bloom," Max says. Mom goes by Mrs. Donovan now that she's married to Marty, but I don't correct him. It's a trivial point.

"Bollocks!" Mom shouts. "Marty and I are going to Boquete tomorrow." My eyes automatically roll to the sky as they always do when Mom peppers her conversations with British slang. She picked up the habit after she and Marty lived in England for a summer while he taught at Cambridge. Her obsession with British detective shows only adds to the phenomenon. "I'd cancel, but we're going with friends."

"Don't worry," Max says. "I'll be there to take care of Natalie."

I almost tell him I don't need taking care of, my feminist instincts pushing through, but realize this is neither the time nor the place. Traveling across a foreign country is not something I want to do alone.

Mom hangs up, and I stand staring at my phone for a long moment.

"We should look into tickets," Max says as Bailey tugs him forward.

I stop him, the reality of what we're doing sinking in. "Wait. Why are you coming? I mean, I want you to come, but why?"

"Are you kidding, Natalie. This is what I've done for the past decade, chase stories across unknown countries. It's what I love about travel journalism."

My lips turn down into a frown, realizing his decision to come has little to do with me. "If all you want is an adventure, then don't worry about it. I'm perfectly capable of going myself." I jut my chin out, disappointment and anger whirling up inside me like a helicopter taking off.

"I meant you can't fly off to a foreign country, chasing after a man you don't really know, despite what you say, by yourself. What if he's dangerous? This has been my life for the past decade. I can help you."

I bite my lip, giddy from his words, despite my situation. "Okay. Let's go."

Max may be worried about Luke, but I'm not. Luke might

be a swindler, but he's not violent. And I can't shake the feeling there's more to the story than we realize. Max would scoff if I said that out loud, and I don't blame him. I'd probably react the same way if I was looking at this situation from the outside, but Luke and I have shared a lot over the past year. He stood up to my asshole ex-boyfriend when I couldn't, he praises my cooking to anyone who'll listen (almost to my embarrassment), and I've met his family. His family! I had a three-hour dinner with his dad and sister when they were visiting Luke and then spent the next day showing them around the city. Something has to have happened to make him do something so drastic. There's no way he was planning this the whole time.

I could be fooling myself, but I won't know until I find Luke.

Three

It was surprisingly quick and easy to book tickets to Panama City, and two days and one flight later, Max is rolling my beat-up carry-on out of the grungy terminal and onto the curb at the international airport, his small duffel bag slung over his shoulder. He wears dark Ray-Bans, a white T-shirt that fits snug across his chest, and dark jeans. My heart flutters at how effortlessly cool he looks.

"How long until the next flight?" he asks.

We've made it to Panama, but we still need to taxi across town to the domestic airport, fly to Bocas Town, and then hop on a boat to the island where my mom's villa is located. And I'm already exhausted from the stress of the past two days and the flight from New York. But looking at Max, knowing he chose to come all this way to help me, makes it almost worth it.

My mission is to find Luke, but I'm only human. Having Max traveling in such close proximity all morning stirred up my craving for him. So far, the journey doesn't seem to have had the same effect on him. He was immersed in his laptop most of the flight. Still, it felt intimate traveling as a pair.

There were several times it felt like we were a couple: when the flight agent checked us in together, and the TSA agent called us both up to check our passports, and the immigration agent asked where we were staying and finally, when we boarded together, taking our seats, our hips touching the whole time.

Once on the plane, Max kept his head in his computer, raising it only twice to ask me questions about Catie, making me wonder if he'd rather be sitting next to her instead. When he met Catie during the shoot, they had a flirtation, but she is head over panties in love with Sam. Once Max realized that, he graciously pulled out. He says he never really liked her in the first place; it was just a fun distraction. I'd believe him, except he's been focused on her the entire plane ride. Is he having second lustful thoughts about my sister?

Ugh, I can't think about it.

Which means I have to focus on Luke and my disappearing money. I've avoided giving it any real thought, since every time I do, it turns my stomach. Don't get me wrong. I'm pissed, and I'm going to get my money, but worrying about it now isn't productive. I'd rather think about beautiful Max or the book Catie and I are going to start working on or all the delicious recipes I'll be putting together for my menu at the restaurant.

I'm hoping this trip will inspire a couple of recipes for either the book or my menu. Food isn't my main focus here, but a girl's got to eat, and I haven't had a lot of experience traveling to different countries. Some chefs travel all over the world trying different cuisines, but I've never had the opportunity, too busy with school and working my way up the restaurant chain. My first and only other trip to Panama before this one was spent licking my wounds from my last restaurant fail. Food was a reminder of everything I was escaping. Still, I couldn't help notice how fresh the seafood was, and I fell in love with *Ojalda*, the most delicious fried bread I've ever tasted.

The thought of food makes my stomach growl like a bear.

"Hungry?" Max asks, his mouth twitching, holding back a laugh.

"Starving. But we need to get to the domestic airport. Our next flight is in two hours, and it takes forty-five minutes to travel across town," I say, keeping my gaze on the cars passing by the curb and looking for a taxi.

A short man with dark hair and cocoa butter skin approaches. "Taxi?"

"Si," I say. That's about the extent of my Spanish.

The man waves his hand, and a cab zips to the curb. He smoothly places my suitcase in the trunk. Max scoots into the back seat, shoving his duffel bag between us. The gray fabric seats are torn, stained, and bleached from the sun.

"Where to?" the cab driver asks. I slam back into the seat as he speeds out of the terminal.

"Albrook Airport," I answer, grasping the seatbelt, but I can't find the buckle to snap it into. I dig my hand under the seat, feeling only crumbs and dirt. I vaguely remember the same problem the last time I traveled here three years ago. Giving up, I clutch the door, and I'm thankful for the heavy traffic as we reach the main motorway, which keeps our speed slow.

"How are we getting to the island your mom lives on?" Max asks, rolling his window down to get a bit of not-so-fresh air and relief from the humidity.

"When we land in Bocas, we'll walk to the Red Frog office. There'll be a boat waiting for everyone who is going to the resort that was on the flight."

To my left, the Panama Canal cuts into the vast ocean. A dozen freight ships idle in the water, waiting to pass through the busy throughway. Out my window on the right are newly developed skyscrapers soaring above me, generic shops and restaurants underneath them, catering to the tourists and expats that occupy the buildings part of the year.

We make a turn into the guts of the city, and the skyscrapers slip away, replaced by squat, rundown buildings and newer, remodeled side-by-side structures. If we had time, this is where I'd explore the local eateries, not the overly priced and underflavored restaurants where the expats frequent, but the hole-in-the-wall places the locals favor.

Everything in the city has a layer of grit, but it's relaxed, and no one seems to care or notice. Just one of the charms of Panama City, my mom would say sarcastically, but I like it. It's what makes the city unique and not generic, like so many other foreign cities. Or so I've read.

Max is studying the GPS on his phone and looking back and forth from his screen to the streets we're passing.

"What's the matter?" I ask.

Max doesn't get a chance to respond. The cab takes a sharp left into an alley and I'm thrown against the door, and Max is thrown against me. The cab stops suddenly halfway down the narrow alley. Standing outside my window, a tall man with a colorful sleeve tattoo on his right arm startles me. The driver waves to him, and the tattooed man slides into the front passenger seat.

"Get out." Max's voice is low and urgent.

"What?" I look around confused. We're nowhere near the airport.

"Now, Bloom," he growls. His duffel bag is in his hands, and he slides toward me, pushing me against my door.

"What are you doing?" My words falter as he thrusts his body over me, pulling the door handle. Is Max having some sort of PTSD from being in a car? Come to think of it, I've only seen him take a taxi once in New York City.

"Are you okay?" I push him back as his duffel collides with my face. I'm thrown against the glass of the window as he reaches over me for the handle again. Finally, he catches it, and the door flies open, the retched stink of the alley attacking my nose. "Ugh. It stinks."

The driver is yelling in Spanish as Max pushes me harder, and I tumble onto the street, my cross-body tote landing heavily on my stomach, Max tumbling after. My breathing is labored as Max's weight presses down on me. I wiggle, trying to move Max off me while sucking air into my constricted lungs. Finally, Max falls onto the dirty concrete next to me, but before I can regain normal breathing, the tattooed passenger in the front seat opens his door and my eyes follow his broad form *up, up, up* as he towers over us. Max leaps to his feet and yanks the strap of my bag, flinging me down the alley.

"What are you doing?" Now I'm panicked.

The driver has stepped out of the car, and I turn to him as he comes around the car. My shoulders don't have a chance to rise into the shrug I'm trying to give him to say, *Sorry about my friend. I have no idea what the hell has gotten into him. I think he has PTSD*, because Max throws me in front of him, pushing me forward. My feet stumble, but Max catches me by the arm, dragging me down the alley.

"My luggage!" I spin around, knocking Max off balance and run back to the car, clawing at the trunk. The driver screams above me, fury covering his face. Suddenly, the luggage doesn't seem so important.

"Leave it!" Max reaches for my jeans but snatches my underwear instead, giving me a massive wedgie as he yanks me toward him, and we tumble down onto the hot cement, pebbles digging into my elbows. My tote hits the ground with a loud *thunk*, and I pray my laptop that's inside isn't damaged.

Regaining my footing, I stand, pulling my tote back on my shoulder. I'm horrified to see a piece of pink lace from my underwear in Max's hand. My feet gain traction, and I move down the alley as the driver pounds the roof of the car, screaming after us.

"Run!" Max yanks me forward. My heart is speeding as

fast as my feet as we race down the cluttered alleyway, dodging broken chairs, overflowing trash bins, and torn garbage bags, the stink of hot trash circling us. Max whisks me around the corner into a mass of people. We push through them, running down the sidewalk, passing cafés, drugstores, and boutique hotels. My lungs are screaming in pain when Max finally ducks into the lobby of a large casino hotel. The air conditioning envelops me, and I moan in sweet relief, collapsing against a wall. Sweat pours off of me.

"What the hell was that?" I demand, bending over and sucking air into my lungs.

"They were going to rob us." Max throws the scraps of my underwear at me.

"Ew," I say automatically.

"Ew? It's *your* underwear. Is there something I should know? Do you need to...what's it called? Douche?"

"What?!" A burst of laughter pops out of me despite my anger and confusion. "No. This isn't 1980." I pick up the bit of pink lace, and I can feel the rest of my torn underwear inching down my thigh. I quickly fish them out and throw both pieces into a trash can. Great. Now I'm going commando, and it's a hundred degrees outside. I hobble to a chair and take off my Toms, rubbing my left ankle, which I twisted in our escape. "Just because the guy had tattoos doesn't mean he was going to rob us."

"I'm not an idiot. I do my research before I travel anywhere." Max sits next to me, glancing at the sliding doors. "Several people have reported that scam. A cabbie picks up a friend, and they take you to an alley or ATM and rob you."

I shake my head. Max has explored too many sketchy countries as a travel writer. Now he's bringing his paranoid baggage into this one, and making me lose mine. "My luggage was in the trunk."

"You still have your wallet and laptop," he says, referring to the contents of my tote. "You can replace everything else."

"We weren't going to be robbed." I slide my shoe back on and look for Wi-Fi to connect my phone. Once it's connected, I open the Uber app.

"Hey, they have Uber!" Relieved, I show Max, who is walking a little funny. The adrenaline is wearing off, and our injuries are making themselves known. I dab at the bloody scrapes on my elbows with my T-shirt.

"Of course they do."

"You're too jaded," I say, thinking of all my clothes and toiletries left in the trunk. Thank God I didn't pack my chef knives.

"And you're too naïve." Max follows me, watching the Uber car's journey on my phone. "This is a poor country. You have to be careful."

"Did you read about that scam happening to one person on social media, and now you believe it?" I ask, dubiously.

"I do this for a living, Bloom. Trust me."

"You've never been to Panama. The last time I was here, my cab driver had a friend with him for the first half of the ride, then he dropped the friend off on the side of the highway, and five minutes later, the cabbie pulled into a gas station, exchanged money with another guy there, and finally dropped me off at the airport. It's a different culture. They do things differently here."

Max rubs his jaw, shaking his head. "How many countries have you lived in?"

I pinch my lips, knowing where this is going. "One," I reluctantly say.

"How many different countries have you traveled to?"

"Three." I puff my chest out a bit. He thought I was going to say one.

"Outside of North America." He raises his eyebrows, a small smile on his lips.

Damn. He got me. I've only been to Panama and Mexico. And Canada, if you count the north side of Niagara Falls.

"One." My shoulders slump.

"I've lived in six different countries and traveled to dozens. Let's agree I know more about different cultures and people than you do." Max hands me my phone as the Uber driver appears across the street in a shiny white SUV. "We were about to be robbed."

"You're paranoid," I say, but a smile plays on my lips.

"You're gullible," he retorts lightheartedly.

I couldn't exactly argue with that since we've flown across the continent in search of a man who stole my money.

The SUV sits on the far curb, the driver lowering his window looking for us, and I step onto the street to cross. A horn honks, and a car zips around the corner.

"Don't, Natalie!" Max yells, startling me. I scurry back to the curb, even though the car was nowhere close to hitting me. When I look at Max, he's as white as meringue.

His eyes are glazed, and his body is shaking slightly.

"Max, what happened? Are you okay?" I place my hand on his shoulder, but he shakes it off.

"You have to be careful. You never know…" His words trail off, because he's unable or unwilling to finish his statement, and he grabs my hand. "Let's go."

He looks three times in either direction before crossing the street and climbing into the SUV. I confirm our destination with the driver and then sit back on the clean black-leather seats and slip my seat belt on. We sit in silence until Max speaks, his voice soft and low.

"Don't ever step out into traffic like that," he says.

I steal a sideways glance at Max. Color has returned to his face, but his eyes are wide with fear or worry or remembering, and his hands grip the sides of his jeans.

"I looked. The car wasn't going to hit me."

"You never know what could happen." He looks at me, his eyes shiny. "It can happen in an instant. That's how my mom died."

His face falls, and I think he's crying, but his chest rises several times in a controlled motion, and when he looks up, his eyes are clear.

"I thought your parents died in a car accident. In a van." I speak the words calmly, slowly, as if drawing out a scared animal.

"Most people think that, and I let them. It's too exhausting to explain the truth." He pauses, taking another deep, calming breath. "That's how my dad died. A semitruck went around a blind curve and hit the back of his car. He died instantly. My mom wasn't with him. She was driving me home from soccer practice when we passed the accident. I was watching the police officer motion everyone through the traffic light and around the ambulances and police cars when my mom slammed on the brakes. She leapt out of the car. She must have recognized my dad's van. The officer yelled at her to stop, but my mom either didn't hear him or was too focused on my dad's car to realize the officer had motioned a motorcycle through, and it didn't have time to stop. It swerved, but it didn't matter. The bike hit her sideways and she flew in the air before landing in a…a twisted heap. She died on the scene."

My arms feel like magnets tugging toward Max, but his arms are tight against his body, and everything about his body language screams *don't touch*. Max is pragmatic. He's not one to wear his tragedies on his sleeve and probably spends more energy holding his emotions in than he does on letting them out. I want to shake him and tell him it's okay to scream or cry or lose control. But this isn't the time or place, and as we turn into the small domestic airport, Max stops his story.

We pull behind a short line of cars in front of the squat building, and Max practically jumps out of the car, escaping any questions or comfort I may have for him. Inside, we check in, whizz through security, and board the small two-propeller plane. By the time we take our seats, I can tell Max doesn't want to talk about it anymore. But Max rarely mentions his past. It's a miracle he told me that much.

As the plane takes off, the air bumpy in the small vessel, Max grabs my hand suddenly. "Promise me you'll be careful." When I don't speak, too overcome by the intensity in his voice, he asserts, "Promise."

My lips press tightly together, holding back the emotion that threatens to spill out all over us. I nod. He releases my hand and looks out the window.

"How long is the flight?" Max asks, the urgency gone from his voice. I want to draw the moment out, but he's moved on, focused on what lies ahead.

"About an hour. Then we'll take a fifteen-minute boat ride to the resort. But don't be fooled. It's more rustic than resort."

"They don't make water like this in the states, do they?" Max looks down at the crystal-blue waters and coral reefs that are as clear as if we were diving under the water instead of thousands of feet in the air. He leans his head back on the headrest. "Sorry about your luggage."

I shrug, even though the only clothes I have are what I'm wearing, a gray T-shirt and torn blue jeans. Not exactly attire for a tropical island. Oh well. I can borrow something of my mother's. I don't plan on being here that long.

The hour-long flight goes by quickly. I drink a soda, eat some butter cookies, take in the serene blue water around the small lush islands we soar above, and before I know it, we're landing on the short runway and walking down the steps from the plane to the tarmac. Inside the shabby terminal, a plump woman in a white T-shirt and long white skirt sits behind a folding table, and we pay the three-dollar tax to enter the island and then walk out of the tiny airport onto the rundown streets.

"That's the only ATM on the island." I point to the small bank on the corner. "It works, sometimes."

Shack homes line the side streets we walk down, the structures nailed together with random boards and beams. We pass small grocers and the occasional Chinese department store housed in narrow three-story buildings. I take Max through the middle of the island, where there's a cement town square lined with market stalls selling beaded bracelets, leather sandals, and other knickknacks for the backpackers and tourists.

The smell of fried food draws me to the main thoroughfare, which borders the water. The buildings are more colorful and crowded together here, filled with bars, restaurants, grocers, boutique shops, and travel services. An array of clothing hangs outside some of the shops, while others have rows of sunscreen, lotion, and toiletries on display in windows facing the street.

When we reach the Red Frog office, the woman behind the desk informs us that the boat won't leave for thirty minutes. She suggests we buy groceries before we head over, since there are only basics for sale on the island, and even that's not guaranteed to be stocked.

I lead Max to Super Gourmet, the only decent grocery store on the island, according to my mom. If I had time, I'd explore the other grocers and markets and decide for myself, but I trust my mom. She loves cooking as much as I do.

"What do people do if they run out of food when they're on the island?" Max asks as we step inside the small store.

"It's a short boat ride to get back here. Plus there are a few beachside restaurants and food stands on the island. You won't starve," I say, picking up a basket. I walk the short, narrow aisles and pick out fresh mangos, a pineapple, a small island chicken that has been cooked on a rotisserie, freshly baked cinnamon rolls, a fresh loaf of nut bread, plantains, and a few other staples. Max grabs two bottles of wine and a dark chocolate bar made from local cocoa trees.

The cashier places all the items in a cardboard box, and

Max shoves cash into the woman's hand before I can give her my credit card. I thank Max, feeling slightly guilty that he paid, since I'm the reason he's on this crazy trip, but he brushes off my promise to pay him back. As we walk down the busy main street, passing pedestrians dressed in bathing suits, cover-ups, and sundresses, I stop at a donut shop I recall my stepfather raving about and then at the seafood market. Two filets of mahimahi and a bag of sorted donuts are now added to the box of goodies.

"We're not going to have time to eat all this food," Max says, peeking into the heavy box.

"I'll leave the rest for my mom and Marty."

We enter the Red Frog offices again, and I connect to their Wi-Fi while we wait for the boat to arrive that will take us across to Isla Bastimentos.

My phone pings with several new messages. One is from my mother. *Sorry we can't be there to meet you, honey. There's not much in the fridge, but I'm sure you won't be able to resist the markets when you arrive. We'll try to get back in a couple of days. Ask for Enrique when you get to the welcome center. He has the keys to our villa.*

A moment later, another message pings.

We've left you our golf cart xo Mom

Except for a couple of trucks used by the workers, the only mode of transportation on the island is by foot or by golf cart.

"Thank you again for paying for these." I indicate the box of groceries I place at my feet as we board the long water taxi and sit on one of the six rows of narrow bench seats. When the taxi is half full, the captain shoots out of the dock, and we race across the shallow, crystal-blue-green water to the island. The salty air licks my face, and I point out the few landmarks I remember—Hospital Point, Cosmic Crab, Coral Cay—but when we arrive at the dinky dock of the welcome center, my knees bounce as adrenaline and nerves course through my body.

I've never been good at standing up for myself. When it comes to others—my sister, my employees, my friends—I'll put up a fight, but when it comes to my own life, I struggle. Growing up, I was always protecting and fighting for my sister. I haven't had much practice fighting for myself. And the last time I tried, it cost me a restaurant and a relationship.

"Did your mom go back down to the restaurant yesterday?" Max asks as the boat is gently maneuvered next to the dock.

"She talked to Chip, the manager of the marina, and he said he didn't know what was going on with the restaurant." I slide the groceries onto the small dock and step out of the boat.

"He runs the marina; how could he not know?" Max hands me his duffel and picks up the heavy box.

"Mom says it's typical down here. No one ever knows what's going on. I remember the other villa owners always complaining about the poorly run management on the island."

Under the thatched roof of the open-air welcome center, Enrique is waiting for us with a kid-like smile spread across his face. I remember him from last time. He always has a smile on his face, which lifts my spirits. Enrique hands me the keys to the villa and then instructs me how to use the beige golf cart parked in the circular drive. When he's done, Max and I slide in, and I drive the hundred yards over to the marina next door.

"You ready for this?" Max asks as I climb out.

"If he's here. Yep."

Passing through the tall marina gates, we stop in front of the large vessel with the word *Overboard* written across the side of the ship in tall white letters. Max fingers a small sign strung across the steps leading onto the boat that says *Closed on Mondays*. It's Monday. We step on board and look around, but it's a ghost ship. No one is here.

Suddenly, the day weighs heavy on me, like a bag of rocks sitting on my shoulders, pushing me down. We've been traveling since five this morning.

"Chin up, Bloom." Max rubs my shoulder encouragingly, and the gesture lightens the load slightly. "The marina office is up ahead." Max walks with purpose as I try to keep up. "Let's talk to the manager and see if he's found out any more information. You said it's a small island."

It's a tiny island. If Luke is staying here, we're bound to bump into him. But he could be staying on one of the surrounding islands.

Max halts, putting his finger to his lips in the universal sign to be quiet. I soften my steps and look where he's pointing. A small fur ball is sleeping in a palm tree. Max slides his phone out and puts a lens attachment on it, creeping up to the creature.

"A sloth," I whisper.

Max is concentrating on taking the picture and doesn't speak. He's been a travel journalist for so long, he can't help it.

"He's so cute." I step closer. The sloth makes a sudden movement and swings off the tree and onto my back. "Ah!" I'm screaming and batting at the thing as its claws dig into my shirt and shoulder. "Get him off!" My foot catches the edge of the dock, and I fall into the mangroves, branches cutting into my side. "Ah!"

The creature hops off and bounds past Max, who stands above me on the dock, the setting sun darkening his face.

"They're meant to be slow. They're meant to sleep and eat all day. Whoever heard of a sloth attacking someone? Who?!" My breathing is rapid and my heart pounding. Max reaches down and pulls me from the mangroves, the branches scratching at me more. I brush off the dirt and leaves and walk toward the office, my steps shaky. "I was attacked by the laziest creature in the jungle." I continue my protests. The nerve.

"It wasn't a sloth." Max stops. He gently rakes his hand through my hair, and I close my eyes, enjoying the unexpected touch. He releases my hair; a clump of dirt, fur, and leaves is held between his fingers.

"It was a monkey." He drops the mess of dirt and leaves on the ground.

Oh.

I hurry to the office and avoid looking at him so he doesn't see my embarrassment. Duh. Of course it was a monkey. I wouldn't feel so stupid, but since I like Max, everything I do I examine under a microscope. Even in the middle of a crisis—like traveling across the continent to find the jerk that stole my money—my head and heart are still focused on Max. I really need to let this stupid crush go. But it's hard with him so near, and traveling with someone is so intimate.

Inside the small office, a man sits behind one of the two desks, looking at a computer screen.

"Hola," I say, even though his skin's too light for him to be a Panamanian, and almost everybody in this part of Panama speaks English.

"Hi," he answers.

"I'm Natalie Bloom. Cora Donovan's daughter."

"Oh, right. She said you were coming down today. I'm Chip." He stands, shaking my hand. "Did you get in okay?"

"Great. It was—"

"Do you know where Luke is?" Max butts in. "Luke Hawker. Natalie's mom said he's running that restaurant on the boat in the marina, Overboard."

"He was. But I talked to the owner of the boat this morning. He said Luke skipped town a week ago," Chip says.

"What?! Where did he go?" I ask. I shouldn't be surprised by this new information, but I am. If Luke isn't here, he could be anywhere, even back in New York.

Chip comes around his desk and leans against the edge. "I don't know. We'd like to find him too. Ray said Luke skipped out of town, and he still owes rent on the restaurant, and some of the Chinese vendors say he owes them money too."

This isn't promising. In fact, it's sounding like a pattern.

"Did he run off with a lot of money?" I ask, trying to understand.

Chip laughs. "I doubt it. It's hard to make money down here. If I had to guess, he ran off because he lost a lot of money and didn't want to lose more."

"Do you know where he was staying?" Max asks. We turn at the sound of a wheelbarrow passing over the gravel drive outside the office. An older couple is hauling groceries from the marina and loading them into their golf cart. It reminds me of the fresh-off-the-boat mahimahi I bought earlier that's sitting in our golf cart, roasting in the afternoon sun. For some reason my anger grows, thinking of one more thing that might be ruined because of Luke.

"He was shacking up with some girl in one of the Palmar jungle lodges."

"Is she still here?" I ask. "What's her name?"

"Sonja, I think. But she skipped town with Luke." Chip presses up from the desk and crosses back behind it. "She was teaching yoga on the beach before she hooked up with him, and then she began helping him run the restaurant." He taps rapidly on his computer. "He was only here a month, but he racked up quite a bill. A lot of people would like to know where he is. If you find him, let me know."

I thank him for the information, and we step out of the office into a blanket of humidity. The sun is setting, and I want to check out Palmar, the beach Luke was staying at, before the no-see-ums and mosquitoes begin to attack.

The golf cart jostles us down the rocky trail, which is in desperate need of a new layer of gravel, as we follow signs to

Palmar. The last time I was here, it was a bustling coved beach with a jungle lodge, tent city, open-air restaurant and bar, and a couple other beachside shack eateries. Travelers could sway in a hammock, practice yoga on the beach, learn to surf, snorkel, and other typical beach activities—if you're here on vacation and not chasing after a thief.

My whole body feels like a bobblehead as we bump along the unkempt roads. Blessedly, the setting sun is tucked behind the canopy of trees in the surrounding jungle, but the humidity still sticks to me like the stink on the monkey that attacked me. We park the cart next to a sandy path and climb out, avoiding the three-foot mound of dirt—which is actually an enormous ant hill—and zigzag our way past the tent village and up the steps of the beach bar and restaurant. It should be bustling with the early dinner crowd, but the dark wood tables are empty, and there's no one behind the bar.

The sound of a loud motor barreling up from the beach draws my attention. A red ATV slams to a stop at the bottom of the stairs and a towering, broad-shouldered man with a shiny scalp and a deep scowl jumps off, bounding up the steps.

"You friends with Luke?"

"Huh?" I ask, my neck straining to look up at the man. Max steps in front of me, creating a wall between me and Man Giant.

"You friends with Luke?"

By the man's tone, I'm guessing he is *not* friends with Luke. How many people has Luke pissed off on this island?

"Uh, no. I mean, we know him, but we're not friends." The last word is bitter on my tongue.

"Why? How do you know him?" Max asks, pushing his shoulders back and standing taller, though he is still dwarfed by the other man.

"He owes me money." Man Giant steps closer to Max, and I automatically step back, but Max doesn't falter, his feet planted. Then it dawns on me who this man could be.

"Are you Ray?" I ask, hoping Luke doesn't owe anyone else here money.

"Yeah. Why?"

"He owes us money too," Max says instead of answering him.

Ray takes Max in, considering him. "You're just saying that to conciliate me." I want to applaud this large man on his word usage. I was expecting more grunting, less vocabulary. "Chip said he's your friend. He's gone. He owes me money. Now it's your problem."

Ray reaches out for Max, and in a swift movement, Max shoots his right leg out, causing Ray to fall to the ground and let out a loud *oomph*. Max yanks Ray's arm, flipping him on his stomach, and twists it behind his back as Max presses his knee into the guy's neck. It all happens in one fluid movement. I'd read that Max had martial arts training, and it's impressive to see it in action. He's like a real live action hero.

"I told you he's not our friend, and we won't be bullied into giving you money we don't owe you." Ray is squirming, sand clinging to the bare skin on his cheeks, neck, and arms, but the movement seems to hurt Ray more than help him, and he stops. Desire unexpectedly coils around my insides as I watch Max, perched on top of the giant, powerful and in control. "I'm going to release you, but if you come at me again, it won't be your neck my knee digs into." Max looks at the guy's crotch so he understands.

Ray struggles against Max one more time, but he groans in pain and acquiesces. Max gingerly releases Ray and takes several measured steps backward, keeping a keen eye on the man. Ray stands, brushing the sand from the front of his board shorts and Billabong-emblazoned singlet, and then glowers at Max, obviously not used to being dominated.

"How much does Luke owe you?" Max asks, crossing his arms and leaning against the thin railing surrounding the restaurant. His stance is calm, but the balls of his feet dig into the sand, ready to pounce again if he has to.

"Five grand. I don't know how much he owes the vendors, but they've been raging for the past week since he left." Ray spits sand into the low brush beside him.

I have a feeling my mother discovering Luke the other week had something to do with his quick exit. He wouldn't have expected to see her down here yet. After I spoke to my mom, I racked my brain for an explanation as to why he came here of all places, and I landed on a conversation we had a couple of months ago at Chez Bella. At the time it didn't seem significant but now it does. Mom came up for an unexpected visit in the city and tagged along to one of my casual cooking lessons with Luke. That night, I was teaching him how to make basic sauces.

He'd just ruined a béchamel sauce—he forgot to sift the flour, causing it to turn lumpy—and I was locating more butter when my mom said I should come down to Red Frog and run a restaurant. She was regaling us with tales of all the rich expats and how they are ready and willing to spend their money, but there aren't any good restaurants at her resort. It's mainly huts on the beach that sell food, and the few sit-down restaurants are constantly changing hands. If someone opened up something with quality food during high season—when all the expats are there—they'd make a killing.

I didn't think much about the conversation at the time, having no desire to move down here, but that might have been what sparked the idea of an untapped gold mine for Luke.

"Do you know where he went?" I ask. My hand whacks my calf as I feel the sting of a mosquito bite.

"If I did, I wouldn't be talking to you," Ray says, stomping back to his ATV.

"Is this open?" I eye the empty restaurant.

"Pretty much everything on the island is closed on

Mondays. You'll have to come back tomorrow if you want to talk to someone." He revs the engine. "But I've already asked. No one knows where Luke went."

After Ray speeds off, sand spraying us from the large tires, the anxiety that's been twisting around my gut during the encounter releases, along with the last bit of energy from my body. I sink into a hard wooden chair, feeling like a balloon that has been deflated. Part of me still wanted to believe that Luke, who's meant to be my friend and who I *slept* with—oh God, does that make me a prostitute?—wouldn't con me. But if Luke really has run off again, owing money to even more people, then it's true.

When Ray is out of sight, Max shoots me a sharp look that emanates the same thought I have, *Who the hell did I get mixed up with?*

Four

We drive in silence up the bumpy road until we reach the only paved area of the island, where my mother's villa is located. How am I going to find Luke now that he's run away? Again. The only clue we have is the girl he was with, Sonja. I've checked Luke's social media accounts every day, and he still hasn't posted anything. If I can find out more about this girl Sonja, she could lead us to him.

We pull onto the driveway, chugging up the steep hill, and I look out beyond the thick jungle brush, palm trees, and the half-moon shimmering on the ocean, and I yearn to feel the tranquility of the scene wash over me, but it doesn't.

We park under the portico, lush island vegetation surrounding us. I glance down at the plunge pool beside the villa and long for a dip, but I'm about to pass out from hunger. Inside, Max drops his bag on the cool marble tiles and walks down the three steps from the open foyer into the main living area, setting the box of groceries on the speckled-granite countertop of the open kitchen. It's not a chef's kitchen, but it has a four-range stainless steel gas stove. Most villas have a run-of-the-mill knife set, but my mother brought down her set of Wüsthof knives and a few Shuns for good measure. Bless her.

I quickly prep and grill the fish—a bit of salt and pepper is all it needs—and chop a simple mango and pineapple salsa to go with it. Our bodies and minds are too tired to do much else than eat. I devour the meal, the buttery flavor of the fish exploding my taste buds. I forgot how heavenly fresh fish tastes. You can eat good fish in New York, but it will never taste this fresh, like it was plucked from the ocean and put on your plate.

"I'm about to collapse. Let's sleep and then go back down to Palmar tomorrow and talk to someone," I say, dropping my empty plate into the sink.

Max nods in agreement; his eyes look as heavy as mine feel.

The villa has two guest rooms and one master bedroom. My mom and Marty are staying in the master, and I show Max the smaller room with the queen-size bed. I take the larger room with the twin beds since it's the room I usually sleep in. Catie always insists on the queen bed, but I don't mind. All the mattresses are new and firm, and the quilts are thick and cozy. Plus, I have a bathroom attached to my room.

With my clothes still on, I plunge into the pillow, and I'm asleep almost instantly.

**

When I wake in the morning, I'm swimming in sweat. The air conditioning unit on the wall in my room broke, and I woke halfway through the night, the sheets slick with perspiration. I had to sleep with the ceiling fan on and the windows open, but it's so humid outside, it didn't do much good.

The banging of cupboards pulls me from the sticky covers, and I pad toward the noise, spotting Max in the kitchen. I blink at the vision before me. Max is shirtless—his chest firm, his abs washboard. I gawk at his taut muscles and then look up at his bright-blue eyes and shake my head. It's too early to start fantasizing.

"We forgot to buy coffee," he says.

"Tea?" I ask.

"None." He looks at me and sucks on his lips, holding back a laugh. I know my hair looks like I stuck my finger in a socket, but I'm too exhausted to care.

"You look cute, all sleepy and mussed."

"Thanks, I think." I smile, and he looks like he wants to say more, but then he breaks contact, and the moment is lost. "Let's go down to Palmar and kill two birds with one coconut." Max squishes his face in confusion. "Get some breakfast and ask about Luke," I explain, covering my mouth with the back of my hand as I stifle a yawn. "But first I'm washing this layer of salt and sweat off my body."

After the shower, I manipulate my wet hair into a loose braid and put on an old bathing suit of Catie's that I find— since my clean undergarments are in my long-gone luggage— and a pink-and-white paisley beach wrap from my mother's closet. It was the only thing I could find that didn't swallow me and look like a muumuu.

Not bad. With the sunglasses covering the dark circles under my eyes, I actually look like a girl on vacation, even if I don't feel like one. This isn't a vacation, I remind myself— this is a mission

"Ready," I announce. Max is reclining on one of the overstuffed lounge chairs on the expansive front patio, overlooking the panoramic view of the green-blue ocean. When we climb into the cart, this time I drive. My back aches from bouncing around the island last night, and I feel the bumps less when I'm behind the wheel, able to maneuver the vehicle myself. The stress of this situation is hard enough on my body and mind. I don't want any more bruises.

"How do you want to handle this?" Max asks.

"Ask if anyone knows Sonja," I say, skidding to a stop

next to the path by the anthill, the wheels kicking up wet mud from the rain overnight.

"People get suspicious when you ask questions like that straight out." Max climbs off, his feet sinking into the mud. I leap over the puddle and somehow land gracefully.

"So how do we get info?"

"Follow my lead." Max walks ahead, and I do just that. We arrive at the restaurant, and Max skips up the few steps that lead into the open-air structure. The tin roof and dark wood floors and tables make it feel more like dusk than dawn. A pair of flip-flops is cast aside at the top of the steps, and I kick my tan Toms next to them—since my own flip-flops are, you know, in my lost luggage.

We're alone except for the young man behind the bar, who looks like a surfer—and probably is, paying for room and board by working here since there's a very relaxed work exchange on the island—rubs his eyes and stares, waiting for us to speak.

"Coffee," Max says, taking in our surroundings.

There's a small bookcase to the right of the bar with grimy books and magazines, their pages warped and stained. Board and card games are strewn over the shelves, their containers torn and most certainly missing pieces. The bar has four backless barstools, bamboo siding, and a row of liquor bottles that have probably never been wiped down. There would be about a dozen health code violations if this were New York, but I remind myself that we're in another country, and this is part of the charm. A beachside bar, open to the elements, is never going to be pristine.

There are a half dozen dark wood tables and matching chairs and a U-shaped bench with cushions strewn across it. I cringe, doubting they've ever been washed. And yet, there's charm to the place. It's cozy and laid-back and what you'd want and expect if you were on vacation on a mostly undeveloped island.

"Brewing," Surfer Dude answers to Max's request for coffee.

"Food?" I ask, putting my hands on the bar and regretting it as soon as I feel the tacky surface.

"Not until lunch."

My head falls to the sticky bar. I don't even care. I'm tempted to lick it, just for a bit of sustenance.

"I can make something." I lift my head. It's not an offer I'd usually make, but my stomach is about to flip inside out and start eating me.

Surfer Dude eyes me.

"She's an amazing chef," Max says. "Seriously, she's going to be famous one day." He gives me a wide smile, and I'm so flattered that all I can do is blush. It's the best compliment I've ever received.

"Where's your kitchen?" I ask, buoyed by Max's confidence in me.

Surfer Dude shrugs and points to a small area behind a wooden partition at the end of the bar. My face is already squinting in anticipation of the grime I expect to find, but it is surprisingly clean. Cluttered and a mess, but clean. After I wash my hands, I open the refrigerator and pull out milk, goat cheese, onion, and a plate of cooked salmon. I smell the fish, and the fresh, salty aroma tickles my nose. The eggs are in the cupboard next to the small stove. I pull down two small pans and begin heating them on low and then crack the eggs into a bowl. The gorgeous orange color of the yolk sends tingles down my back. Fresh, organic eggs from wild chickens, I'm guessing. I whip the eggs and pour them into the pans. I sprinkle the ingredients on top of the bubbling eggs and, holding each pan in a hand, flick them with my wrists as the cooked eggs flip over, creating two perfect omelets. I smile at my concoction.

I plate them, adding a bit of sliced red pepper on the side for color—the presentation of a meal is almost as important as how the meal tastes—and bring them back to the bar with two cups of fresh orange juice from a jug in the fridge.

"A woman after my own heart," Max says, taking a big bite and smiling as he swallows. He has no idea how right he is. Inwardly, I beam as I watch him devour my creation. I taste it and close my eyes, enjoying the sharp, salty taste of the salmon against the mild, creamy flavor of the eggs and cheese.

"Damn, those look good." Surfer Dude smacks his lips, his long blond locks swinging in front of his face. "Can you make me one?"

I'm about to say yes, but Max speaks first. "We had a question about the yoga," Max points to the chalkboard giving details about the surf conditions and lessons, massages, and yoga classes. "Then Natalie can whip you up whatever you want."

Disappointment and hunger cross Surfer Dude's face, but he complies. "Whatever, mate."

"Is Sonja still teaching yoga down here?" Max asks, sitting back on his stool. "We hear she's the best."

"Just missed her. She left last week."

"Where to?"

He shrugs.

"Damn." Max looks genuinely disappointed. "My girlfriend is kind of a yoga nut and heard Sonja was something of a guru. We traveled hundreds of miles just to meet her."

Did he just call me his girlfriend?

Surfer Dude buys the story, or doesn't care if it's true or not, and says, "Wow. I took one of her classes. I didn't realize she was a guru."

"You have no idea where she may have gone? Or when she'll be back?" Max takes the last bite of his omelet and looks imploringly at Surfer Dude, who rests his arms on top of the bar.

"No. But she has a blog or Instagram account or something." He looks at me and smiles, and I sit up a little straighter, anticipating the information that will lead us to Luke. "But I'm sure you know that."

"Of course!" I bite my lip, wondering how I can get him to divulge the name on her accounts. "But, uh, I lost my phone, and all my accounts had the passwords automatically saved, and when I tried to log into my Instagram account, it blocked me. You don't happen to remember her handle? I'm such a space cadet."

His eyes take me in, and I wonder if he's caught us out. But then he brushes his hand through his blond hair and says, "It was something like Sonja sunshine yoga or sunrise or sundazed."

"Right. Right. That sounds familiar." I stand, taking both plates. "How about that omelet."

Standing on the beach, away from Surfer Dude's curious eyes—I doubt they'd be prying, since he's devouring the omelet I just made him, but Max is overly cautious—Max searches online using Sonja's possible handles. He hooked his phone up with an international data plan before we left, which I could've done too, but since all my money was stolen, I opted out of the expensive convenience. Luckily, my mom gifted me miles last year, which is how I flew down here without going into further debt.

"Found her."

I grab his shoulder, looking at the screen. Finally. Now let's hope there are some useful posts. Max scrolls through the photos on an account called SonjaSundaze. Almost every picture is of a petite brunette in some yoga position with the sun behind her, making all her photos a silhouette. Not one photo shows a clear view of her face. Just her lithe body in Gumby poses.

"How do we know that's even her?" I shove the phone back at Max.

"Look at the background in the last dozen photos."

I do. She's on coved beaches with palm trees and hammocks surrounding her or balancing in an impressive pose on the front of a boat or wooden dock. "That looks like every tropical beach around here."

"No. Look." Max is pointing to a painted sign in the background of one photo. It's partially blocked by her arms, but I can make out the word *Momma's* written in red letters.

Before the word *so* can escape my lips, Max turns my head to a small beachside eatery with lounge chairs and low tables under a wood awning. The sign above it reads Nachyo Momma's.

"It's definitely her," he says.

"Has she posted anything lately?"

We scroll to her last entry, and she's doing a headstand on top of a tin roof overlooking a small waterway. There are signs and boats in the background, but it's blurry, and I can't make out any of the words. The caption reads *Yoga wherever you can get it #hotsticks #yogalife #lovepeaceharmony.*

"Do those hashtags mean anything to you?" Max asks.

"I think they're pretty straightforward. I assume hot sticks is referring to her legs."

Max lifts his T-shirt and wipes the sweat from his brow, exposing his taut abs. Damn. "It could be any beach along this coast. Hell, they could be in Miami or the Keys."

He's right. Every beach here looks the same as the next tropical beach.

"Let's head back to the villa. It'll be easier to do more digging on my computer," I say.

Once we're back, I turn the AC unit up to high in the living room while I search. Max takes a dip in the pool to cool off, and I promise him I'll come get him if I find out anything. I'd like to have a moment to relax, but I need to locate Sonja. If she's a yoga instructor, she'd want her students and followers to know where she's teaching, especially if she hops around from resort to resort, but my extensive search online only leads to her twitter page, which has the same exact posts as her Instagram account.

"Any luck?" Heat from the midday sun radiates off Max as he enters. Water drips from his hair down his broad shoulders and cascades over the taut muscles of his chest and torso and onto the floor, leaving a puddle. I strain to keep my eyes above his neck. He leans over me to glance at the screen. His breath is minty from the gum he chews, and my mouth waters as I imagine pressing my lips to his and tasting the warm freshness against my lips.

My insides clinch. *Never gonna happen.*

During the filming, I thought there was a spark between us, but afterward, his only interest in me seems to be as a dog walker for Bailey. The greyhound was sort of a consolation prize from the crazy weekend shoot—a replacement for his family dog that passed away. In my deluded mind, when Max asked for help with Bailey, I thought we'd be doing the walks together, like co-parenting, but the first time I went to meet Max, he threw the leash at me and ran off to a meeting.

And I, the pathetic loser that I am, kept coming back, believing that the walks would turn into something bigger. I'm embarrassed to think of how many fantasies I had while listening to Sara Bareilles on the subway on my way to meet Max. At first, I thought he kept me at arm's length because he'd just broken up with his fiancé. And in my fantasies— that I hoped had a kernel of truth—I believed he was using Bailey as an excuse to see me without making any commitments until he was ready.

Max had been through so much when I met him—with the hospitalization, amnesia, breakup, and media circus that was around him at the time, I doubted he wanted one more complication. I didn't want to be something else he had to worry about. So when he needed me for Bailey, I was there.

Now I see that the walks were just walks. Men aren't

complicated. Especially Max. If he wanted me, he would have made it clear by now. Oh, wait. He did make it clear when he ran away from me the one and only time I tried to kiss him. *Stupid. Stupid. Stupid.*

I really need to move on.

"I've reached a dead end," I answer, keeping my eyes locked on the computer screen. If I turn my head, his lips would be inches from mine. My heart sinks at the thought, already knowing he'd turn his head away if I tried. *Enough.* "I've followed her, so if she adds any more photos, I'll be alerted."

"I don't think there's anything else we can do right now." Max steps away, and my body relaxes. "I'm going to take a water taxi into town and do some exploring." I wait, expecting him to invite me, but instead he says, "Tonight there's a bonfire on Red Frog Beach. You should check it out."

"Aren't you going?"

"I'll meet you if I get back in time."

A notification chimes on my computer. It's a reminder that Max's birthday is in two days.

"Hey! Your birthday's coming up."

"I know." His deep voice lowers in contempt.

"We should celebrate. I make a mean chocolate cake."

"No, thanks."

"Come on." I walk toward him. If I can't win him over with my charming personality, maybe I can with my to-die-for dessert. Mamé was an amazing baker and taught me how to make many delicious French delicacies. "You have to have cake on your birthday, or I can make macaroons, chocolate mousse, pral—"

"I said no. Thank you, but no." He shuts the front door, accentuating his words.

Not much rattles Max. This is the first sign I've seen that some pain and anger may be bubbling under the surface.

After losing his parents, celebrating his birthday may not be a magical time of the year for him. Even though I lost my dad to pancreatic cancer, Mom and Mamé made sure my sister and I still had full, happy childhoods. The first few years were difficult because both Mom and Mamé were raw and depressed from their mutual loss. They were just going through the motions of living, but I always made sure Catie, who was only nine at the time, never felt the emptiness, and that filled me with joy too.

So, yeah, I don't feel lonely on my birthday. I usually feel like a kid again. But Max is different. He was an only child and lost everything when he lost them. He was shuffled around relatives' homes until he finally moved to India when he was eighteen to teach English as a second language and to pursue writing.

With Max gone, this is the first quiet moment I've had in the past few days, and I feel antsy, my mind racing with the realization that I may never see that money again. Needing a distraction, I scour through my mother's closet for something to wear besides this beach wrap. At home in the States, my mother dons colorful shorts and patterned shirts most days, but on the island, she embraces the laid-back beach culture and dresses like a middle-aged hippie—or what her version of a hippie would be. Her closet is an array of long, colorful skirts, tank tops in every color of the rainbow, and maxi dresses with bright, tropical patterns adorning them. Her jewelry consists of chunky, fake gemstone necklaces, bangles, and long, dangly earrings.

My suitcase was filled with jean shorts and T-shirts and one black dress. When I wear jewelry, it's a simple necklace or small studs in my earlobes. There's not much room for self-expression while working in a kitchen, except through my food.

I pick out a short cotton dress with large red hibiscuses circling the hem. It'll be appropriate for a bonfire on the beach. For now, I'll lie by the pool, gathering my thoughts and strength, and try to resist the urge to update my Instagram every five minutes.

I rest the dress on the bed to change into it later this afternoon, peel my sweaty cover-up off, and gasp when I look in the mirror. The black bottoms of the swimsuit I'm wearing are practically dental floss up my backside. How did I not feel that? I'm nearly blinded by the mass of pale hind staring back at me. Catie has a strict workout regime, which keeps her trim and toned, and she's never been shy about her body. Luckily, the amount of back-and-forth I do running around the city dealing with Catie, my new restaurant, and Chez Bella is enough to keep the extra pounds off, but I work with food. I'm never going to be a twig.

Confident no one will see me by the pool, I scurry out and sit on one of the lounge chairs. I close my eyes, trying to enjoy a moment of peace, but I jump when my phone buzzes. I snatch it, hoping it's a notification from Sonja's Instagram account. But it's not. It's an e-mail from Williams-Sonoma announcing a *1-DAY ONLY SALE!* Until their next one. Probably tomorrow. I lay my head back and try to enjoy the slight breeze and the sounds of birds chirping in the foliage around me.

"You don't seem too stressed about getting your money back."

I jump at the deep voice growling above me. I look up and see Ray towering over me, blocking my sun. The chirping stops.

"I'm working on it." I lie back down, hoping he takes the hint and leaves.

"Your boyfriend left you alone up here?"

My chest clenches; his tone is dripping with smarmy innuendo. "He's in the shower. He'll be done any minute." I sit up.

"I just saw him leave the dock in a water taxi."

63

Busted.

Ray sits on the lounge chair next to mine.

"After Luke took all my money from the cash register and left me indebted to all those nasty Chinese vendors, I was really pissed off. But then you show up." Ray smiles, and I cringe. His teeth are covered in yellow plaque. "I figure you can work off his debt."

I leap up as he leans forward.

"Stay away from me, pervert."

His eyes widen at my implication. "Whoa. I didn't mean it like that. I don't treat women like that. Ever."

He sounds so offended, I'm tempted to believe him, but I keep my distance.

"I meant that you're a chef, right? Word is, you make a mean omelet." He licks his lips, and it makes me want to toss up the aforementioned omelet. "You can make things right with me by working in my kitchen until I can pay off those damned Chinese."

He stands, and I involuntarily cower, his towering presence making me realize I'm totally screwed if he decides he's not such a gentleman after all.

I'm about to agree—just to get him to leave—when the sound of a golf cart chugging up the drive makes us both turn. My breath, which was hitched in my throat, seeps out when I see Max behind the wheel. Before the cart is halfway up the driveway, he jumps out.

"What the hell are you doing here? What's he saying to you, Natalie?"

"Threatening me." Which is kind of true. Max leaps at Ray, and he bounds away—surprisingly lithe for such a big man—jumping over the short wall between the pool and plant beds next to the driveway.

"Just offering her a job. I heard she's a great cook. But, hey, if you don't want to share—"

He doesn't get a chance to finish. Max darts at him, and

Ray runs down the driveway, laughing. "Make some sweet love," Ray sings up to us. "And relax. You're in paradise."

"I thought you were in town—" I start to say, standing.

"What the hell are you wearing? Cover up," Max interrupts.

My mouth drops as he throws my towel at me, shaking his head at my display of skin. Geez, is my backside that grotesque to him?

"What if I hadn't come back, and you're prancing around in front of that guy in almost nothing." Max looks genuinely upset by this notion.

"I wasn't prancing." I cross my arms. "And I was handling the situation."

We stare at each other.

"Fine." Max breaks the connection. "Anyway, the boat broke down and they had to tow us back here. I'll leave you to it, Miss Independent." Max stomps inside, leaving me feeling small and confused. I hear the shower running when I go inside and slip my mother's dress on. I stand in front of the bathroom door, listening to the shower run, thinking of the water running down his body. So close, yet so far away. I shake myself, trying to discharge the feelings that erupt inside me. I step back and yell at Max through the bathroom door that I'm going down to the beach.

"I think I'll stay here and do some research," he yells back.

I'm disappointed he's not joining me, but I can't let him get me down. I have enough real problems doing that.

It's midday, but the festivities at Red Frog Beach are already underway. Punta Lava, the only restaurant on the beach, is to my right as I walk down the short hill. Inside are several couples and families enjoying a late lunch and colorful cocktails. A couple of workers in red polo shirts are placing logs in the middle of the fire pit, readying it for the bonfire later tonight. Past the restaurant is a narrow path leading up a rocky cliff. The path leads to a large platform overlooking the headland. To my left, there's a bar set up at the edge of the jungle along the small coved beach. On the beach, lounge chairs are filled with revelers drinking and basking in the sun. A few people have left their chairs and are dancing to the pop music someone is playing on portable speakers, and the water is dotted with body surfers riding the rough waves.

"Wanna drink, Chef?" Surfer Dude is next to me with a coconut in his hand. A straw pokes out of the top, pineapple and mango garnish beside it. "What is it?"

"An eggnog colada."

Interesting. "Why eggnog? Christmas was ages ago." I take a sip. Mmmm...delicious. In three gulps, it's gone.

"They over ordered. Need to use up the inventory. Another?"

Three coconuts later, life is good. Very good. Surfer Dude has secured us two lounge chairs under a tiki umbrella, and we cook s'mores over the raging bonfire—chocolate and marshmallow covering our mouths and fingers, which we wash off with a swim in the ocean, and then we're back on our chairs.

When the sun sets, the bonfire grows bigger, the drinks get stronger, and my inhibitions dissolve. I don't even care that my ass is hanging out for the world to see. Surfer Dude—he told me his name but that was two coconuts ago, and I've forgotten—seems to appreciate it. He lightly slaps it every time I stand up, and I giggle like a schoolgirl. I don't care that it jiggles a little.

We walk over to the black lava rocks on the far side of the beach and stumble over their uneven surface, looking out into the ocean raging around us. I'm unsteady and slip several times, cutting my hands on the sharp rocks. The waves pound the edges, spraying salt on us and calling my name.

No, they're literally calling my name.

"Bloom."

I close my eyes and smile. Wow, I never knew they could

do that.

"Bloom!"

Those waves sure sound angry.

"Natalie, get the hell off there before you kill yourself!"

Okay, that was definitely not the waves. I turn around and can just make out Max marching toward me; a stern look curtains his face.

"Maxie!" I step to him but fall, my knee bashing the side of a sharp rock. He throws me over his shoulder, my backside in the air for all to see. Do I care? Hell no. When we're on the soft sand, Max drops me. Blood is running down my knee.

"What the hell has gotten into you?" His face is furious.

"Chill, dude." I laugh, sounding like Surfer Dude. Where is Surfer Dude? I spin around looking for him.

"He's throwing up by that palm tree." Max points.

Gross.

"Lighten up, Max." I run into the surf, kicking water toward him.

"Knock it off, Bloom." His hand grasps my wrist, but his eyes register worry. "You could have gotten hurt up there."

I move my foot across the water again, aiming for Max when I hit something solid but spongy. "Ah!" I yelp, pain shooting up my foot. I fall into the shallow surf, and Max loses his grip on my wrist.

"What's wrong? What happened?" Max scoops me up and lays me on the sand. His hands run over my body, inspecting me. I let out a soft moan. My body is conflicted. My foot throbs in pain, but everywhere his hands touch sends delicious heat pulsing through my body.

But the slight stinging in my foot grows to an intense burning, and I reach down, moaning in pain. "It hurts. Max, it really hurts."

"It's a jellyfish. One of the blue ones. I don't think it's deadly, but—"

"Deadly!" I yell, releasing my foot.

"It's not. It's not. It's just gonna hurt for a bit."

I fall back, writhing in the sand as my foot explodes in pain. It feels like it's on fire. "Make it stop!"

Max takes the coconut from my last drink, emptying the contents on the sand, and runs over the small bridge toward the bonfire. A minute later he comes back, a yellowish liquid sloshing back and forth inside.

Oh my God, did he just urinate in that coconut?

"Get that away from me!" I yell, sliding back on the sand. I've heard of surfers resorting to urine for jellyfish stings. When they're desperate. I'm not that desperate. Max takes a step closer, and I shoot to my feet. Big mistake. Pain blasts up my leg. I fall to the ground, tears streaming down my face as the pain takes over. "Okay. Okay. Do it."

I turn away and hold my nose as the warm liquid is poured over my foot. Relief is almost instantaneous. Funnily, it doesn't smell that bad. Actually, it reminds me of a salad.

"What have you been eating?" I ask, lying back on the sand, my body melting into the release of pain.

"I don't know. Fish."

"You're urine smells like…like apples," I say, recognizing the smell.

Max screws his face into a question mark. "My urine?" Then he crumples into a laugh. "You think I peed in that coconut? And you let me pour it on you?!"

I let out a huff. "It's…it's not urine?"

"It was vinegar. Apple vinegar. It's all they had at the restaurant." Max has fallen to his knees, laughter rippling through his body. "I can't believe…you thought…I…"

I sit up, fuming at my own stupidity. *Surfers swear by urine as a way to treat jellyfish stings*, I want to yell. But he wouldn't hear me or care at this point.

"Are you done?" I ask when he stops laughing and catches his breath.

"I think so." He wipes at his eyes and scoots next to me, inspecting my ankle. "It'll probably swell and be red for a few days, but you should be okay." He pulls me into a sideways hug. "You're too much, Bloom."

I look up, and his face is inches from mine, his blue eyes sparkling down at me. They really are gorgeous. My eyes drop to his lips, and warmth spreads down my spine and into my thighs. I close my eyes and lean forward, my lips touching his, and heat explodes inside me as his lips press firmly against mine.

Desire weaves from my mouth down through my thighs and into my toes as his lips massage mine, soft and warm and wanting. The sting in my foot and the joyful screaming around the bonfire all disappear into the kiss.

I blink my eyes open. The roar of an ATV as it bounces down the gravel road draws Max's eyes away from mine. I close my eyes and press forward again, yearning for more.

"Jess?"

"Natalie," I correct.

"Jessica."

"No, Natalie."

I tilt my head toward his, but instead of soft lips, I fall into empty space. I open my eyes and see Max several feet away, walking quickly over the short bridge. I stumble after him and then stop as everything comes into focus. It's dark, but the firelight illuminates her black hair and porcelain skin.

Climbing off of the ATV is Jessica Crossman. Max's ex-fiancé.

Five

It's like déjà vu, except on a tropical beach instead of a bedroom in Brooklyn, where Jessica Crossman last made a surprise appearance. Max never mentioned he had a fiancé until she showed up unexpectedly at the end of the shoot.

To break up with him.

So why is she here now? She's supposed to be in Vail with her new boyfriend, a soldier from her army unit. Yep. Jess is a soldier. A hot female soldier. Very rare. Except in movies. Or standing in front of me.

Max and Jess met when he was covering a story on her unit in Afghanistan several years ago, and they got engaged after a near-death experience from a suicide-bomb attack. But when I spoke to Jess about it when I met her in November, she said they both agreed they'd rushed into the engagement in the aftermath of the attack.

Are they having regrets now? My shoulders slump, and the coconut libations turn sour in my stomach. My mind is still sloshed from the multitude of drinks I've consumed, and I straighten, limping over to them. For a moment, I think I'm mistaken. The last and only time I've met Jess, her hair was unkempt and shaggy, her face devoid of makeup, and she wore a pilling gray sweater.

The girl Max talks to now wears tiny jean shorts, accentuating her lean legs, and a white tank top that presses against her taut abs, and her hair is cut in a fashionable long bob that touches her shoulders. But then I see her unique eyes—wide but pinched at the corners—and I know it's Jess.

A new-and-improved Jess.

She'd been traveling for seventy hours, after living in Afghanistan for years, when I met her, but even then, it didn't hide her stunning features. Her lips are pink and plump, and her mother is half Chinese, giving Jess her unmistakable, exotic features. Multiethnic, I think, is the term these days. Gorgeous, I say.

Dammit.

"I rushed into it," I hear Jess saying as I come upon them.

"Hi," I interrupt, brushing back the wild blond strands that stick to my face.

"Oh, hi, Natalie." Jess rakes her eyes over my body, taking in my sandy, disheveled state. "Sorry to crash. I had to get away, and when Max said he was on a tropical island, I wanted nothing more than to escape the zero-degree weather in Vail and play on a beach."

There are millions of beaches. Why'd she have to choose this one?

"Where are you staying?" I ask.

"I'm not sure. I kinda decided to come last minute."

The fire pops at our feet, and I take a step back.

"Why doesn't she stay with us," Max says, looking at me. "Would your mom mind?"

It's almost unperceivable, but at the word *us*, Jess flinches.

"I don't know." The balloon of elation that floated inside me during our kiss bursts, leaving discarded scraps of gloom in its place.

Max widens his eyes at me, urging me to say yes.

"It's my mom's place. I have to ask her."

Jess's face drops. "It's okay. I should've given you some warning." But her eyes search Max's face, silently extricating some ex-fiancé sympathy.

"Your room has twin beds, Nat. I doubt your mom would mind." Max grabs my hand, and it makes me falter. I can still feel his lips on mine. "And your mom's not even there right now."

If I say no again, I'll be the bad guy, and they'll be the poor, injured parties. This sucks. Can't we go back to kissing on the beach?

"Okay. But I need to let my mom know before she gets back."

"Great." Max takes the duffel bag Jess is carrying and escorts her to our golf cart. He turns the key and puts it in drive and then looks at me as if it's an afterthought. "Aren't you coming?"

"I'll walk up in a minute."

Without a backward glance, he drives away over the gravel hill, leaving me alone next to the raging flames of the bonfire.

***

Jess is annoyingly perky the next morning. I wake up and find her grinding coffee beans (where did she find those?) and making eggs and toast. Death Cab for Cutie is blaring from my laptop on the counter, and she's bouncing around as she prepares the food. I want to close all the curtains and put my head under a pillow, but I'm dying to know what's going on with Max and her. Does he want her back? Are they already back together?

I passed out when I returned last night, and I don't remember if she was in her bed or not. It's perfectly made this morning, which means she's a neat freak—don't soldiers have to make their beds with army corners or something?— or she didn't sleep in the bed at all.

My stomach turns at the latter thought.

"Coffee?" she chirps, pouring a cup.

"Black."

I drink it in one gulp. Jess laughs and refills it. I hate that she looks so fresh and cheerful this morning, and she smells lovely, of vanilla-coconut soap. I look and smell like the bottom of a trash heap.

"Where's Max?" I ask.

"I heard him walking around before dawn. Last night, he said he wanted to go into town today."

My ears perk at the word *heard*. That means she most likely didn't sleep in his bed. *Ugh! Stop it.* Stop obsessing. I know we kissed last night, but I was very drunk, and it's all hazy. For all I know, I threw myself at him, and he was too polite to stop me. Until she showed up.

My phone pings, and I pull it off the charger, looking at the message. My breath catches. It's a notification from my Instagram account. SonjaSundaze has posted a new photo. When the picture appears, I yelp and knock the stool I sit on over.

"What is it? What happened? Is Max okay?" Jess is around the counter, looking over my shoulder.

"How can this Sonja girl be so stupid? She ran off with a thief and just posted their location," I say, more to myself, but Jess looks at me for an explanation. "I just figured out where my lying, cheating business partner is."

"Max told me about that." Jess scoops the eggs onto two plates and spreads butter over the four pieces of toast. She walks around the counter and sits on the empty stool next to me, placing the plates in front of us. "Where?"

The photo is a shot of Sonja lying on a beach, her hands over her face, blocking out the sun and obscuring her features again. I can make out a frown on her lips. The caption reads, *Another day in Mercury Retro. Bad luck keeps coming. Will it ever end?*

Jess laughs. "That's not a location. She means Mercury

retrograde." As Jess takes in my confused expression, she explains, "It's an astrology thing. Bad stuff happens when the planet looks like it's moving backward. If you believe in that stuff."

My shoulders slump. Back to square one. I take a bite of the eggs—too salty and overcooked. Jess is scrolling through the photos of Sonja's account on my phone and stops at the picture Sonja posted two days ago.

"Have you looked up Hot Sticks? She used the hashtag under this photo."

I put my fork down, taking the phone. "I thought she meant her hot legs or something."

"I think it's a famous beachside hot dog stand in Costa Rica."

Immediately, I Google it, and a location in Costa Rica pops up. Jess is right! It's a hot dog stand that some famous chef set up a few years ago. How did I not know this?

"I have to go there. Now." I shovel the rest of the eggs down and call the help desk for information on how to get to Costa Rica from here.

Puerto Viejo, the town this Hot Sticks place is located— only four hours away!—can be reached by bus from Bocas, the man on the phone tells me. But the next shuttle bus doesn't leave until tomorrow. I want to go today, but the shuttle is the only reasonable way to get there. I hang up after asking the guy to hold two seats on the bus for tomorrow.

"I found Sonja!" I say as soon as Max walks through the door an hour later, relaxed and gorgeous. The sun suits him. His skin is already turning a nice shade of copper. My skin is a nice shade of puce.

"Where?"

I stand from the couch where I've been sitting, watching the door, waiting for his return. Jess grew bored about thirty minutes ago and is sunning herself by the pool.

I show him the Instagram photo and hashtag.

"Jess recognized the name," I admit, not wanting to give her credit. "It's some famous hot dog stand Sonja tagged."

"When do you leave?"

My stomach drops. Doesn't he mean *we?*

"The next bus leaves tomorrow morning from Bocas." I keep my voice neutral as I say, "I booked two seats on it."

"What about Jess?" Max asks.

"I doubt she'll want to come. She said she came here to relax." But I think she wants more than that.

"I'll talk to her. She wasn't feeling too well after all her traveling."

My stomach drops farther as anger rises up my spine. *Who cares if she's not feeling up to traveling,* I want to yell. This has nothing to do with her, but I'm starting to suspect that Max may care a lot about what Jess wants.

"Listen." He slides his palms over the granite countertop, moving closer to me. "About last night. When we—"

"Don't worry about it," I cut in. I'll die in a heap of embarrassment if he tells me the kiss was a mistake or apologizes. I can't bear to hear it. "It was nothing. I was wasted. Obviously." I indicate the small cuts on my hands and knee. And my red, throbbing ankle from the jellyfish sting. Battle wounds from the night before.

He blinks a few times and then says, "Oh, I thought…it felt…uh, like you…"

Like I'm in love with you? Yep, I am. But I'm not about to admit it to him. I'm not crazy.

"Like I would have kissed whoever was in front of me," I finish. "I drank way too much last night." I laugh and quickly move on to another subject. A subject that matters more to me right now. "You're still coming tomorrow, right? It's why we traveled all this way."

"Going where?" Jess walks in from the pool, her body strong and toned in her little red bikini, her olive skin already darkened to a lovely shade of caramel.

If I were in the army instead of behind a stove all day, I could look like that. Maybe. At least working on my feet and living in New York, I'm not a complete heifer. I'm slim enough, but I've never had muscles like hers. I'm not sure those muscles exist in my body. I've never seen any of them.

"To Playa Viejo."

"You're going too, Max?" Jess skips down the few steps from the foyer into the main living area. "I thought we were gonna stay here for a few days."

"That was before Natalie found Luke's location." Max turns around and leans against the counter.

"Possible location," Jess corrects, patting her limbs dry with the towel she carried in. "They could have moved on by now. And I'm so tired from all the traveling yesterday. Let's stay here for a couple days before we run off again."

We. I knew it. They're definitely back together.

"Jess, you can stay here while Max and I go. I don't expect we'll be gone more than a day or two. I'm sure my mom won't care." My mom will care, but when I tell her it's all in the name of love, she'll be fine with it.

"I don't want to stay here by myself." Jess places her hand on Max's arm and strokes his skin with her thumb. Every stroke is a kick in my gut. Kick. Kick. Kick. *Vomit.* "Come on. Just for a few days." He stares at her, and I can see him weakening. "Then we can go on your little chase. Like we did in Turkey that time."

What about me?! I want to shout. *You're supposed to be here for me!*

He lowers his head and takes hold of Jess's hand, and I feel like I've been pushed off a cliff. My stomach leaps into my throat as my breath constricts. I find it hard to think, let alone make a rational decision, as anger boils inside me.

I'll be fine, I think, breathing in the thought. I don't need him. I can go to Costa Rica on my own. But even as I think it, fear circles my insides like vultures ready to eat my rotting confidence. I've never traveled by myself.

"I'll let my mom know you'll both be staying," I say as Max opens his mouth to speak. I grab the phone and laptop and hobble out to the wide patio at the front of the villa.

The sound of heavy footsteps follows me as Max walks outside, his arms folded over his chest. "Stay here for a few days, and go to Costa Rica later. You shouldn't travel by yourself."

Warm, salty airy rushes over my skin, making my hair dance, but it does nothing to shift my bitter mood. "You're right. I shouldn't be traveling alone." The sting has the effect I hope. Max shifts; discomfort and maybe regret cross his face, and I hurry on, not wanting to hear his excuses. "Luke could leave Playa Viejo any minute, and I don't want to play cloak-and-dagger across Costa Rica."

Actually, I do. With you. With only you.

"It's not safe," Max insists, sitting down on the plush lounge chair across from me, his eyebrows raised to accentuate his point.

He's right. It's not safe, and I'm too chickenshit to do it by myself. If Max isn't coming, I realize I won't follow Luke any farther than this. The bag of stones that had been on my shoulders since we arrived grows heavier. I'll fight for my money and kick Luke in the balls to get it, but not at the expense of my own safety. And if Max is saying it's not safe, then it's not. He has much more experience traveling than I do.

I'll book a flight home instead and start over. Well, not over over. Catie and I do have the book. If she ever follows up with the publisher. And I can talk to someone about suing Luke. He has to come back to the States at some point. But even as I think it, I know the battle wouldn't be worth the monetary and emotional cost.

"Max." Jess comes outside still in her bikini. *Okay, I get it! You're perfect.* "Let her go if she wants to. We can meet up in a day or two."

The pause Max takes as he considers this makes me solidify my decision to forgo any further chase. I don't want to be his second choice.

"No," Max speaks, his voice resolute. "You can't go by yourself. And Playa Viejo isn't that far. When does the bus leave?"

Nah, nah, nah-nah-nah, I want to sing and stick out my tongue at Jess.

"Tomorrow morning." I sit up straighter, feeling lighter.

"That still gives you today to relax before we're off." Max pushes off the chair and stands across from Jess, stroking her arms with his hands. I turn my head, not wanting to see the affectionate touch. "And you don't have to come if you want more time to relax here."

Jess's sour face reflects how I felt moments ago. "Max, you know how carsick I get, and boats aren't any better. I've been feeling gross all day after all my traveling. I can't jump on a bus tomorrow. And after what happened in Afghanistan…"

Max looks between us and settles on Jess. He breathes out heavily. "I know. I know," he soothes, a whimpering breath escaping Jess's lips. Max looks at me, his face sullen. "I'm sorry, Natalie. Jess does get sick if she's on the move too much, and it can trigger some tough memories." He takes my hand, which I want to snatch away. "Wait a day or two until Jess feels better, and we can all go."

"No. You two lovebirds can relax and have a holiday here while I go find Luke," I snap, cringing inwardly at the bitter tone in my voice.

Jess's little act—yes, I think it's an act—turns the elation I felt a moment ago into an angry coil that twists around my insides, hardening my heart. I look down at my laptop and hear the patter of Jess's feet as she walks back inside. Max stands over me, making my anger hug me tighter. His presence is like a wave of energy pressing against me, making it impossible to focus on anything except him. I'm staring at my computer screen, but all my attention is on him and what's just occurred.

"If this is because of last night—" Max finally says.

"It's not!" I shout at him. "Geez, I know you're cute, but not every girl wants you." I shoot my eyes at him, and he takes a step backward. "You came down here to help me. If you don't want to do that anymore, fine. But don't make this into something it's not."

"I didn't mean…I'm sorry if you're upset."

I look at him, and the pity in his eyes fuels my anger. "If I'm upset, it's because you came here to help me find Luke, and now you're abandoning me. It's shitty and selfish."

"Okay, fine. I'll come." His face screws up with anxiety, and I can tell he's trying to figure out how to juggle Jess and me.

"Forget it. I don't want you to come just because you feel bad for poor little Bloom. I'm not saying these things to change your mind. I'm not manipulative." I make a point to look toward the open doors where Jess went inside the villa. "I want you to know how spineless I think it is that you're suddenly staying behind at this five-star tropical resort because boats and cars make your girlfriend's tummy hurt. She doesn't need to come. She can stay here and relax, like she keeps moaning about. But I'm going to get on that bus and travel through a foreign country. By myself." Which I'm not, since I'm not suicidal, but he doesn't need to know that. "I thought we were friends. I would *never* do this to a friend."

I take a deep breath, calming my racing heart.

"Are you done?" Max asks, crossing his arms.

"That's so condescending. Don't ask me if I'm done. If you have something to say, then say it."

Anger shadows his features. "I am your friend. It's just…it's complicated."

"No, it's not. You made a promise, and then you broke it." I slam my laptop shut and stand. "There's nothing complicated about that."

I quickly walk off the porch and down the road until I reach Punta Lava, my injured foot throbbing from the effort and sweat soaking my dress. I sit at the bar and snap my computer open, the fight still heavy in me, suffocating my thoughts. My heart hurts, and I'm jealous, but I meant what I said. A real friend would never do this.

I swiftly book my return ticket home, which is easy to change since it's on points. By the time Max realizes I'm gone, it'll be too late for apologies. I may have no money, apartment, job, or love life, but at least I'll have my dignity intact.

Six

Rain pummels me as I carry my tote into the truck that's taking me down to the dock at the welcome center. After I booked my flight yesterday morning, I stayed away from the villa all day and didn't return until late last night. I crawled into bed and woke up early, quietly making my exit. After the fight with Max, I worried my resolve would falter if I saw him again.

Enrique—still all smiles—helps me into the cab. It's early, the dawn barely breaking between the palm and eucalyptus trees, and Max and Jess are sleeping. She slept in my room last night, so maybe they aren't exactly back together, but there's no doubt she wants to be. Why else would she have flown all this way? It's not an easy trek to get down here—a plane, a taxi, another plane, and a water taxi. It wasn't just to escape her last relationship. It's to be with Max.

And Max made his choice clear yesterday.

The wind and rain pummel the welcome center when we arrive, reflecting my own mood. The storm has knocked over half the chairs and tables under the thatched roof. I slide out of the cab of the truck and directly into a puddle, mud splashing up the legs of my jeans. Rain comes at me sideways, and I run to the middle of the welcome center, which doesn't give much shelter. I huddle next to two other couples as we wait for the boat captain to arrive.

A young Panamanian worker comes out from the enclosed office behind the welcome desk. "All flights have been cancelled out of Bocas this morning."

There are several voices of protest, which echo the protests inside my head. I just want to get out of here and go home. Manuel, the worker, explains that the weather is too dangerous for the small planes to fly in right now. If it clears up, we can take the afternoon flight. Which means I'll miss my flight home from Panama City.

We all cram into his office and make alternate arrangements using his antiquated computer. Once I've rebooked my ticket for tomorrow morning, the rain has begun to let up, but the wind howls like two wolves fighting to the death. I'm starving and grateful when Manuel hands us all clear bags, each filled with a granola bar, yogurt, and an apple.

As I take a bite into the red apple skin, juice dripping down my chin, a golf cart skids to a stop under the awning of the welcome center. Max jumps out of the passenger seat, his hair and clothes soaked through.

"You can't leave," he says in lieu of a greeting. I stare at him midchew. "It's…it's too dangerous to travel today."

"I'm not a child. I can take care of myself," I shoot back, a reminder to myself more than Max. I don't want him to change my mind. "I can't leave today anyway. The flight's been cancelled."

"Flight?"

Oh, crap.

"I mean bus." I discreetly fold my new flight schedule and tuck my hand behind my back, but Max snatches the paper and quickly scans it.

"This is a flight back to New York." Max slicks his wet hair back from his forehead, frustration covering his face. "Fuck, Natalie. What's going on? Why are you running home?"

"It's none of your business what I do from here, Max. You've made your choice." I don't mean to make it sound like I'm the outcast woman in a bad Lifetime movie, but the pain I'm feeling from his betrayal is bubbling close to the surface.

"Dammit, Natalie. It's more complicated than that. I...Jess has been through a lot. And we never really resolved...everything. And...and..." Max falters.

"And...and...what? Because it doesn't look complex to me. I get it. You two were engaged under intense circumstances, and you broke up suddenly. But all that stuff you two haven't dealt with would've been there when we got back. It's not urgent. The only thing urgent in this situation is finding Luke." I shake my head, tired and frustrated by what feels like me trying to convince Max to be on my side. I hate that. I will not plead for him to pick me. "But that doesn't matter. Your life has nothing to do with me."

Hurt curtains Max's face. "That's not true. You're a part of my life. I love hanging out with you. You're always so positive and a bright light on my gloomy life. Since I got back, I haven't had much direction, which isn't like me. I was eighteen when I started my career and I've been moving forward at full throttle. To be flailing in the wind like this is unsettling. But it's been refreshing watching you so determinedly go after your dream. I don't want to see you lose that."

"Then help me find Luke," I say, emboldened by his unexpected words. They wash over me like a waterfall of encouragement, and suddenly I don't want to just walk away.

At his hesitation, I snatch the paper back and jut my chin out. "Forget it."

"You can still go after Luke."

"I told you yesterday, I'm not traveling across a foreign country by myself. I'm not like you. Or Jess. I haven't traveled to distant places or been in a warzone. It was fine when you were coming along. But, like you said, it's not safe. Especially for an inexperienced traveler. I grew up in the suburbs of Boston and then moved to Manhattan, which is a jungle, but a jungle I know how to traverse."

Max lowers his intense cerulean eyes to mine. "I'm sorry about yesterday, but you don't have to go alone. Wait until tomorrow. Just one more day. You can't let that asshole get away with what he did. Confront him. Even if he refuses to give the money back, he can't stay down here forever. He has to come back to the States at some point. And when he does, you can sue him. Come on."

I bite my lip, his words penetrating my resistance. I want nothing more than to confront Luke and get my money back, and since I have to wait until tomorrow anyway, I might as well get back on track and go after Luke. With Max by my side. If Jess doesn't get her claws into him again.

"Okay," I say, and the smile that spreads across Max's face puts a sunny light on this rain-soaked day.

When we get back to the villa, the sun is peeking through the separating storm clouds, mimicking the feeling in my heart. Despite everything, Max racing to the dock and fighting for me to stay has lifted my spirits. But I'm not letting him off the hook yet. I want him to squirm a little more and prove I can trust him again.

"I've booked us on the zip line canopy tour," Jess is saying as we step inside the foyer. "We need to be down at the—oh, Natalie. I thought you left."

"Change of plans," I say, and the crestfallen expression at my return—which she quickly adjusts to a smile—makes me continue, "I'd love to do the zip line. I'll call down and add myself to the reservation."

Her smile tightens. "Great."

I'm terrified of heights, but if I'm going to be stuck with these two, I'm not sitting around here and sulking all day.

***

An hour later, I'm being flung through the air from tree to tree, held up only by a rope diaper sixty feet from the ground. The trees rush under my feet, and I clamp my lips shut, holding back the urge to upchuck. When I did the zip line a few years ago, it was brand new, and the workers were still cautious with all the different contraptions and obstacles. Now, I realize, as I'm slung toward the next obstacle, the workers may be a bit overconfident in the safety of the course. And a little bored after so many years of running the adventure tour.

All the ropes, logs, wires, and platforms are slick from the recent rain, and my feet barely get a grip on the log bridge I'm now walking across, high in the treetops. My hands are strangling the rope above my head, and my whole body is shaking from the terror of slipping. Jess zoomed through the course and is already done. Max hung behind waiting for me. I wish he hadn't. My fear is palpable, and I don't want him to feel it.

I exhale, and my feet find solid ground on the next platform. Thank God. Only one more obstacle. But when I see the long zip line I'm meant to tackle next—flying across the treetops and then down to the jungle floor—I sink onto the wood platform and cross my legs. I'm exhausted. My blood's been pumping like a freight train through my body for the last hour.

"Come on, Bloom. You're almost done." Max nudges my shoulder, and I grip the trunk of the tree that the platform is built around.

"My nerves need a break," I say.

Max sits down next to me, and for a moment, we sit in silence; the only sounds are dripping water from the earlier

85

rain and the next zip line victim screaming in the jungle somewhere behind us.

"Are you still mad at me?" Max asks.

"Dammit, Max." The anger that rushes up surprises me. "I'm not mad at you. I'm disappointed and hurt. I learned a long time ago to only keep people who really care about me in my life, and I'm not sure you do."

"I care about you, Bloom."

"Stop calling me Bloom. My name's Natalie."

"Sorry. Natalie." Max and I sit in tense silence, the yelps from the other zip line victims growing closer. "How's Catie? Living life as an honest woman?"

"Mostly," I say, glad for the change of topic. "She's not lying to her boss anymore, but her public still doesn't know the truth. It'll be a little while until she can move her image away from being America's top domestic guru to America's top designer. That's her hope at least. And maybe I'll slide into the slot of America's top gourmet chef, once we get the next book written."

"How did the charade start?"

He's purposely distracting me, but it's working. My heart rate is slowing down. I tell him the story of how Catie's little blog, with only three readers to start—Mom, Mamé, and me—grew slowly, building a modest following, until one of her blog posts was picked up by *The Huffington Post*, which propelled her into the public eye. She was soon hired at *Simply Chic*, which launched her into stardom, and she became America's favorite housewife and homemaker. With the help of my recipes and meal-planning tips, of course.

"When did you get involved?"

"At the beginning. Catie wanted some original recipes for her blog, and I provided them. It wasn't a big deal until she was hired at the magazine."

"How did she keep it a secret from everyone?"

"It wasn't hard. Not at first. The difficult part was when

she started making guest appearances on *Wake Up, America!*
Before that, we convinced ourselves that we weren't actually
lying. Catie posted recipes for her blog and the magazine, but
she never actually said she could cook them herself. TV is
different. We had to make her look like the pro everyone
believed she was."

"And the husband?"

"Her reader's assumed she was married, and she never
denied it, even starting a column called *Husband Emergency.*"

Max raises his eyebrows at me, not buying the it-was-all-
so-innocent act. "Who else knows about the charade Catie
and you perpetrated?"

"Perpetrated is a bit strong. Patrick, Sam, you, Mom,
Gillian, your uncle Charles and…uh, Jess. I think that's it.
The crew from your homecoming special may be suspicious,
but I don't think they care enough to give it much thought."

"Anyone else?" Max asks.

"Not that I know of. Catie's good at keeping secrets, and I
have no reason to tell anyone."

"Does Luke know?"

"I don't think so. I never told him."

Max looks over the canopy of trees, thinking. "Any of
those people ever threaten to expose Catie?"

"No. Never. Why?"

"Just wondering." Max leaps to his feet. "No time like the
present."

Julio, our guide, who has been waiting patiently at the edge
of the platform, hooks my carabineer to the zip line wire, and
before I can protest, I'm flying through the air, screaming
and, surprisingly, laughing. Adrenaline shoots through me,
making me buzz from the natural high. Trees and forest fly
past me, and I bounce back and forth at the end of the wire
until I come to a stop a few inches from the jungle floor. This
isn't so bad.

Later, after we've showered and changed, we take a water

taxi to my favorite restaurant, Cosmic Crab, on Carenero Island. The seafood is amazing, often brought in fresh from the local fisherman as you order, and the drinks are legendary. The last time I was here, I ordered a Sex in the Mud. It came with a banana sticking out of the frothy drink, which the owner poured chocolate sauce over, as if, you know, the banana just had sex in the mud. It was divine. And strong.

We are seated at a table on the deck of the restaurant that juts out over the clear water, sea life swimming all around us. Before we even sit down, two stingrays swim under the platform, and a school of blue-and-yellow fish follows close behind them. Without looking at the menu, I order a Sex in the Mud. Jess orders a Hot and Dirty Martini, and Max orders a beer.

Jane, the owner, brings our drinks over and hands me the menu, and I remind her of who I am. My mother and Marty are good friends with Jane and her husband and frequent the restaurant weekly.

"Oh, honey, you have to see the crab and lobster we caught today," Jane says as she pours the chocolate sauce over the banana.

Sipping the delicious concoction, I follow Jane to the kitchen where the biggest crab and lobster I've ever seen stare back at me from the counter. The lobster is the size of a large cat and must weigh over twenty pounds. Both creatures are still alive and wriggling.

"How are you going to prepare the lobster?" I ask, almost tasting the chewy, buttery flavor in my mouth.

"I was going to make a stew."

The cool drink in my hand almost slips. "Don't you dare."

Jane laughs. "Your mom said you were a brilliant chef. How would you like it prepared?"

"A classic lobster boil with lemon and garlic butter melted on the side. I want to taste the ocean in my mouth when I bite into the meat."

As the lobster is being prepared in the kitchen, I order another round of drinks as I pass the bar on the way back to the table. The bartender, a short Panamanian man in a blue Cosmic Crab T-shirt and khaki shorts, brings the squeeze bottle of chocolate sauce with him and looks like he's performing surgery as he drowns the banana in dark chocolate sauce. As he walks away, my eyes catch Jess's, and she has the same look of amusement on her face as I do, and we burst out laughing.

"I've never seen someone take their job so seriously." I chortle; the banana is unrecognizable. I'm trying to figure out how to eat the banana, and then I shrug and slip my mouth over it and bite off the tip, chocolate sauce dripping down my chin and onto the table. Jess and I collapse in laughter again, and chocolate sauce flies across the table from my mouth, landing on Max's arm. Jess and I almost topple off the table as a new ripple of laughter hits us.

"Disgusting," Max says, wiping the sauce from his arm, but he's smiling.

"Wanna taste?" I ask, sweeping my tongue over the chocolate sauce on my chin.

"I'll pass." But his gaze stays on my lips as I slide the sauce back into my mouth with my finger. A feeling of warm familiarity vibrates between us. For a moment, I think there's something more—desire maybe—but then he looks away, and it's gone.

I don't want to be having this much fun with Jess, but it's exhausting hating someone. I don't even hate her. I just hate what she's doing. But having a nemesis is hard, and I decide to take a break for one night and pretend we're just a couple of girls having a night out. I'm sure she'll give me a reason to dislike her again soon. Until then, I want to have fun.

"Your feast is ready!" Jane announces as she slides a large platter with the steaming lobster onto the table. The tail and claws are cracked open, the meat resting on top of the large beast.

My taste buds spark to life, and I cut the tail into three pieces, dividing it between us. We don't speak until the entire heavenly meal is consumed and happily in our bellies. The corn sits untouched. I don't want anything to ruin the bliss of my palate.

Except the Sex in the Mud. I'm on my third one. "What happened with your boyfriend?" I ask Jess, feeling bold.

"Natalie," Max protests, but he looks at Jess, expectantly. I have a feeling she hasn't talked to him about it either.

"It's okay," Jess says as a small boat filled with a group of divers looking red and peaked from a day out in the salty water and sun glides by the restaurant. "Carter—that's his name—is a nice guy, but he's not that bright, which I discovered in Vail." Jess scoots her chair toward mine, conspiratorially, and whispers, "Our relationship was mainly physical." She sits back, opening the conversation back up, but it's obvious Max heard her last statement, and it's obvious she intended him to. "My mom would have been thrilled if it had worked out. His parents are Chinese."

All I really know about Jess is what she told me when she crashed the filming of the homecoming special and bits and pieces I've picked up from Max over the past two months. I know her mom is Chinese, but her dad isn't, which caused tension with her mom's family, and Jess grew up in San Francisco and at some point joined the army.

"Does your mom want you to marry someone who's Chinese, even though she didn't?" I push my drink away, the rushing water under us making me dizzy.

"She felt guilty about it, and her parents almost disowned her. My grandmother loves me, but she's very cold to my father. She'll only speak Chinese around him, even though she speaks English." A look of annoyance and possibly hurt passes over her face. "My mom thinks if I marry a Chinese guy, her mother will forgive her."

"She must have been upset when you and Max were engaged."

Jess drags the last piece of lobster through the butter drippings on her plate and pops it in her mouth. Once she swallows, she says, "Yeah. But I don't live my life by what other people think. Even my mom."

"You grew up in San Francisco?"

"Yep." Jess licks her fingers and sits back, looking across the water at the colorful buildings dotting the edge of Bocas Town.

"Her mom met her dad when she was arrested protesting the Vietnam War at Berkeley. He was one of the arresting officers," Max inserts, placing his hand on Jess's shoulder briefly. "It's a great story. He fought in the Vietnam War but was injured. Nothing major. Something with his knee. He came back to the States, joined the police force, and then met her mom. He had to arrest her, but by the time they arrived at the station, he was in love." Max's eyes soften as he gets lost in the story. I don't know if it's because of the beer or if Max is really a romantic at heart.

"Your father's the reason you became a soldier?" I ask as Jane clears our plates.

"Yes. And I loved serving my country, but I'm done. I don't want my whole life to be defined by my service." Jess glances at Max, who's calmly drinking his beer and watching Jess as she speaks. "Carter grew up an army brat, living on army bases all over the world. I'd never spent any time with him outside of our unit—except one quick trip to Italy when we were on leave—but it became clear when we were in Vail that he's a career soldier. And that's just not me. This was my last tour. I don't want to go back. Too much loss. You go in one person and come out another."

"Who did you go in as?" I don't want to be interested in Jess's story, but she's had a life so different from mine. I grew up in the quiet suburbs outside of Boston. There wasn't much diversity or culture unless we traveled into the city, which was rare. Jess has led a rich life filled with a variety of experiences and was surrounded by Chinese-American culture. Max's eyes brighten as she speaks, and my heart sinks as I see us compared in his eyes. My life is so boring next to Jess's.

"I thought I was tough shit when I enlisted, but I quickly learned I knew nothing about what it takes to be a soldier. My dad tried to warn me, but I didn't listen. After a year of getting my ass kicked, I toughened up and became as strong, if not stronger, than many of the men in my unit. It's a man's world in the army. And I'm sick of it. Don't get me wrong. I love my guys, but it's time to get back to the real world." Her eyes flutter toward Max, and the corner of his mouth hooks up into a smile.

They broke up, I remind myself. But breakups never end with a clean break. It's more of a tear up. And sometimes a couple will tear for a long time before they break apart.

That's what happened with my first love, Cole. We tried to break up for six months before we finally broke. And it wasn't because I wanted to. He was married. And I was a fool.

"What are you going to do if you're not a soldier?" I ask Jess, not wanting to think about Cole and the messy demise of our relationship.

"I'm not sure, but Max wants to write a book about his time in Afghanistan, and I'd love to help with that."

Max snaps to attention. "I'm not writing about that."

"But it's your dream. It's what you've always talked about, hon."

Max doesn't balk at the term of endearment. I take a long sip from my drink.

"I want to write a novel inspired by my time there, not a biography. It's different. I've had several publishers approach me about writing a memoir. Readers want to hear the 'untold story of Max Euston's life.' That's how the publisher put it. I doubt anyone would take me seriously as a novelist."

"You won't know unless you try," I say, sounding like a bad meme. But I mean it.

Max shrugs.

"So you're moving to New York?" I ask Jess.

"Not sure," she looks at Max. "Maybe. I could be Max's manager."

Max laughs. He thinks she's joking, but I can tell by the pain that flashes in her eyes that she's not.

"Have you ever managed anything?" I don't mean for it to, but it comes across as a challenge.

"Yes." Her voice prickles. "I was the signal officer for my unit." Jess scrapes her chair back against the wood platform. "Where's the bathroom?"

"I'll show you," Max offers, escorting Jess around the bar and behind the restaurant.

"Dessert?" Jane asks, sliding a menu into my hands. I glance over the delicacies, curious about what her menu offers. The Careening Cay Lime Pie looks delicious, but the chocolate cake suddenly reminds me it's Max's birthday today. He's made no mention of it and neither has Jess, but you have to have cake on your birthday.

"One piece of the chocolate cake with a candle. It's Max's birthday."

When Jane comes back with the cake, the candle isn't lit. "I thought you'd want to wait until Max came back. He walked to the garden with your friend to see the kinkajou."

"You still have the kinkajou?" I stand up, feeling giddy. It's the most adorable, furry creature I've ever seen. It looks like a cross between a monkey and a baby bear, and I fell in love with Jane's the last time I was here. If I could, I'd keep one as a pet. Paris Hilton used to have one…which makes it less appealing.

I meander over the sandy path through the maze of low

foliage in the garden behind the restaurant, the perfume of the night jasmine tickling my nose. There's a little playground a few feet off the path, and I step toward it, remembering that the kinkajou cage is nearby. As my eyes adjust, I see movement in front of me, but it's dark, and I can't make out the forms.

A soft breeze blows the branches of the trees, and the moon pokes through the leaves, illuminating the swing set in front of me. In a perfect spotlight, Max and Jess come into view, swinging slowly knee to knee.

And mouth to mouth.

Seven

M ax received his birthday present in the package of one Jessica Crossman last night. Any delusion that they were not getting back together quickly evaporated when I saw them kissing on the swing set. During my quick exit, I tripped over several plants, but Max and Jess were too into their face sucking to notice me.

My heart hangs heavy in my chest as I lie in bed this morning, trying not to think about their nocturnal activities. Thankfully, any noises made by the two rekindling lovebirds didn't make it across the hall to my room. The pillow over my head the entire night might've helped.

I don't want to get up. I don't want to go with them to Costa Rica. I want to go by myself. I want to get my money back, open my restaurant, and forget all about Max and stupid Jessica Crossman.

The thought of the postcoital grins on their faces makes my stomach seize. To avoid seeing them, I quietly get dressed in one of my mom's maxi dresses—which looks like a muumuu on me of course—and walk down to Punta Lava for breakfast.

It's a gorgeous day. The sun rises in front of the row of villas leading down to the beach and would brighten most people's mornings, but it only sends my mood plummeting down to the depths of the ocean. My feet drag me to the top of the hill. Right before the turn to Red Frog Beach, I stop to take a breath. Below me, the half moon beach and bent palm trees next to the crystal-blue waters clear my head slightly.

At the restaurant, I pour a steaming cup of coffee and sit at one of the small tables overlooking the ocean; the sound of waves whooshing over the sand washes away a little more of the bitter layer that hangs tight to my skin like the salt in the air.

"Nat, baby?"

The familiar voice makes me feel like I'm ten years old again, in that great way that burning leaves remind me of the Halloween of my youth or the smell of pine reminds me of Christmas mornings.

"Momma." I stand and give her a tight hug. Tears fill my eyes. I quickly blink them away until my eyes are nearly dry. "You're back."

"Why are you wearing that? It looks awful."

I laugh, taking no offense to Mom's candor. "I lost my luggage."

"Marty, get me some tea and an omelet with cheese and ham."

I wave and smile to my stepdad, who always looks the part of an islander with his khaki shorts and floral button-down tops. Even when we're on the mainland. I like my stepdad, but he married my mom after I graduated high school and had moved out of the house, so we have a mutual respect for each other, but we're not particularly close. I love him because he makes my mom happy. And he loves me because I'm the daughter of the woman he loves.

"Did you find that scumbag?" Marty asks, putting down two plates filled with food from the buffet.

"He ran off last week, but I think we located him again."

"We?" Mom asks, raising her right eyebrow, reminding me of Catie, who perfected that expression in her teens.

"Max." I scoop eggs into my mouth. "And Jess."

"His ex-fiancé?!" Her face looks rightfully disgusted. "What is she doing here?"

I lower my chin and raise my eyebrows, as if to say, *I'll give you one guess.*

"Bitch."

"Mom!"

Man, I love my mom.

"I'm sorry, but no woman should chase after a man. Especially when my daughter is in love with him."

"Thanks, Mom." I sit back in my chair, the warm breeze petting my cheek. "But it doesn't matter. They're back together."

"Bit—"

"Cora." Marty shakes his head.

Mom looks annoyed but doesn't finish her statement. "What are you going to do about Luke?"

I go refill my plate, and then I launch into my plans. I know my mother would jump at the chance to go with me, not afraid of adventure, but Marty would hate it. It's hard enough getting him on the three planes and one boat it takes for them to get here.

"I don't like it one bit. That Jess needs to bugger off and leave you two alone." I laugh inwardly at her word usage. I'll know she's really upset when her sentences start lilting up at the end, making them sound like a question, as the English do but without the full-on accent, a la Madonna, circa 2000.

My phone chimes, reminding me that the boat to Bocas Town leaves in one hour. Having Mom by my side when I enter the villa gives me strength and comfort. If I could, I'd fold her up and pack her in my bag.

"We have to leave in fifteen minutes if we're going to

catch the boat to town," I say when I see Jess in the kitchen, still in her sweat shorts and tank top, hair tousled.

"We're not going," Jess says, shoveling a spoonful of Raisin Bran into her mouth. Max walks in, his hair wet from a recent shower. Mom comes in just behind him, and her face darkens when she sees Jess in her kitchen looking smug and cozy.

My insides churn with annoyance at Jess's nonchalance. I turn to Max. "You aren't going?"

"Oh, uh, I wanted to talk to you about that. Jess still isn't feeling good."

I turn around, not wanting Max to witness my chin quiver as disappointment and hurt rush through me. I busy myself by closing the cereal box and putting it in the cupboard.

"You're Max?" Mom walks toward him, Marty close behind her, dropping their two small bags in the entryway. I can see Marty wants to reach out and stop Mom from continuing, but by now, he knows better.

"Yes, ma'am." Max smiles, and I hate how good it makes him look. "It's nice to meet—"

"What do you think you're doing?" Mom places her hands on her hips and looks pointedly at him. Max glances around the kitchen, looking for some infraction he's not aware of. "You're letting my daughter travel by herself across a third world country because your ex-fiancé has a tummy ache?"

Jess stops midchew, her eyes growing wide.

"You made a promise. If she—" Mom shoots a razor-sharp glare at Jess—"isn't up for traveling, she is welcome to stay here for a few days with us. I raised two daughters and know how to take care of a sick child."

I'm biting down on both my lips holding back the smile that is threatening to explode onto my face.

When Max recovers from Mom's unexpected scolding, he takes a quick glance at Jess and then says, "Well, Jess gets sick when she travels, boats and buses and cars, and—"

"You're a soldier, aren't you?" Mom challenges, directing her question at Jess.

Jess stands a little straighter. "Yes."

"And you can't handle one little bus ride up the coast of Costa Rica? Where were you stationed?"

Something triggers in Jess's face, and suddenly, she stands tall, pushing her shoulders back. "Afghanistan."

"If you can handle being jostled around in one of those hummties"—I think Mom means Hummers—"in the middle of a sweltering desert, you need to grow—"

"Mom, stop. It's okay." I finally step in.

"It just doesn't make any sense to me," Mom says, throwing her hands up. "And you should stick to your promises." The last part is directed at Max. "Like I said, you're welcome to stay here if you're not feeling well, but it makes no sense for Max to stay behind. We have every comfort of home. Where Natalie is off to is quite literally a jungle and no place for a girl to travel alone." Not waiting for an answer, Mom spins on her heels and marches into her bedroom.

Marty gives a not-so-apologetic smile, probably a witness to these kinds out outbursts from my mom daily, and follows after her, taking their bags. I can tell Max and Jess want to chat after being pummeled by Mom, so I exit to get my few things together. A few moments later, Max knocks on my door and walks in.

"We're coming with you."

"Oh, her tummy ache is suddenly gone?" Gathering strength from my mother, I let the words fly out of my mouth. He flinches, as if I've physically assaulted him, but then his jaw tightens, and his eyes darken at the implication. "Come if you want. I don't care," I rush on. My feelings are mixed about his change of mind. I'll be traveling with two people who clearly do not want to go with me but have basically been bullied into it by my mother. The bit of regret that rises into my throat, causing me to falter for a moment as I look at Max, quickly turns to anger. I bite my lower lip, hard, resolving to focus on the money and finding Luke. I will not let Max or Jess deter me again. I came here for a reason, and I'm going to finish it.

"There's some Dramamine under the bathroom sink if Jess needs it," I can't help saying as Max walks out of the room.

She's obviously lying or exaggerating to get out of the trip, either because she really doesn't want to go or she feels that I'm a threat. Ha! She need not worry. Max made it very clear last night who he wants. And I won't steal a man who belongs to someone else. I did it once before, and it ended badly. Very badly.

There's nothing sexy about being a mistress or trying to take another woman's man. It's messy and painful and self-destructive and ruins everyone's lives that are involved. At the beginning, it's thrilling, but it always ends in disaster and heartbreak. At least, it did for me, and I've never met anyone where it was a happily ever after. Even if the mistress wins, so to speak, the guilt is carried long after the affair is legitimized.

I certainly never intended on being the other woman. Most women probably don't plan on it. But Cole Merrick was a hotshot chef and instructor at my culinary school in Manhattan, and I wanted him from the moment he pulled his knife out and demonstrated his skills on a large piece of top round. He walked in with an air of confidence and a conviction for food that mirrored my own passion. I was in awe of him. In New York City, top chefs are celebrities, and he was riding high on the success of his first eatery, Market Bazaar, which opened to rave reviews and a waitlist a month long.

Cooking was my life, but I didn't realize I had a real gift for it until I met Cole. He was impressed by my ingenuity and asked for my opinion on recipes he was experimenting with for a sister restaurant he was opening, Café Bazaar. At first, it was purely a mentor-protégé relationship. He was living my dream, and he was kind enough to take me into his restaurant and teach me how to run a business and kitchen efficiently.

I was intoxicated by his success and his godlike prominence in the world of New York society. One night, as he was showing me how to make a dry rub, we were overcome with desire, and he took me on the counter, right next to the raw meat. I was picking paprika out of my hair for a week. In hindsight, I would have chosen a more sanitary place to consummate our relationship, but you can't talk sense into passion.

I'd never felt so taken apart and put back together by a man. We couldn't stay away from each other. It was magnetic. We were so consumed that his restaurant began to suffer. He was spreading himself too thin, with his restaurant, trying to open the second location, teaching, and having an affair with me. And our desire for each other was never sated. We were blinded by lust, and in the end, it was our downfall.

But I won't let love (or the lack of it) tear my life apart again. This time I know better.

That's what I'm thinking when we reach the dock at the end of the welcome center twenty minutes later, waiting for the shuttle boat to arrive to take us to Bocas Town. Jess has a scowl on her face, and Max looks miserable. God, this is going to be awful.

"Holy shit."

I spin my head and see Max pointing into the water. The entire surface is bobbing with a swarm of small, round jellyfish. My foot throbs at the sight of them. They don't look like the one that stung me on the beach the other night; their bodies are rounder, and they're transparent instead of blue, but they still look ominous.

The shuttle boat cruises next to the floating dock we stand on, and it sways under my feet. The captain takes our few bags and puts them into the boat, and I climb in. A group of teenagers runs down the dock, causing it to rock fiercely. Max grabs on to the side of the boat, finding balance. Behind the boat, there's a splash and, a moment later, high-pitched screaming.

As he spins around, Max's eyes widen, and he flattens himself at the edge of the dock, reaching into the water. Leaping over the seats, I look over the edge of the back of the boat. Jess is in the water, her arms flailing, and she's screaming as jellyfish surround her. "Ah! Help!"

In one swift movement, Max grabs Jess by the arms and pulls her onto the dock. The teenagers have halted and are staring at the scene.

"Ugh." Jess is moaning. "They stung me! They stung me!" She keeps repeating it. The boat captain is yelling at us, shaking his head and pointing at Jess, saying something in Spanish I don't understand. The teenagers are snickering and clamor into the boat next to me. Still yelling, the captain throws our bags back onto the dock, and I leap out after them as he starts the motor and shoots away.

My insides are in knots as Jess writhes on her back in misery. Scooping her up, Max carries her back to the welcome center, and I traipse behind. I know I should feel sorry for her, but instead I'm annoyed. And suspicious. It seems very convenient that she happened to fall into that water. Is she so desperate to get out of the trip that she'd purposely fall into a sea of jellyfish?

When we go back to the villa, Mom and Marty are gone. They said this morning they were going for a walk to Polo Beach on the north side of the island. Max finds vinegar for the stings and soaks rags, but Jess insists on putting it on herself, locking herself in the bathroom.

"What's going on?" I ask as Max enters the kitchen, the bitter smell of vinegar making me blink.

"What do you mean?" He spins the cap back on the bottle

and places it on the kitchen counter.

"You don't really think that was an accident, do you? Jess has been trying to keep us from going to Costa Rica since she got here."

Max works his jaw, his eyes narrowing. "What are you saying?"

"She purposely fell into that water."

"Jess is twisting around in pain in there, and you think she did this to herself. Why?"

I can't say because she's jealous. Or she thinks I'm a threat. It'll sound petty, and I'm afraid he'll see the truth behind it.

"It doesn't matter. I'm getting on that bus today," I say instead. "If you're not coming, I'll go alone. It's only a four-hour bus ride filled with backpackers. I'll find a friendly looking couple and ask them if I can tag along until we get into Costa Rica. It's the backpacker way, right?"

Jess calls out before Max responds, and I grab my bag and stomp to the door.

"Natalie, wait." Max follows me.

As I reach for the handle, it swings open, causing me to jump back. Mom stares back at me. "What are you doing here?" she asks, looking around suspiciously.

"Jess *accidently* fell into the water when we were boarding the boat." I shoot my eyes at Max, daring him to disagree.

"Is she okay?"

"Just sore from all the stings," I say as Marty closes the door and the wave of humidity with it.

"Stings?" Marty's face curtains with confusion.

"From all those jellyfish," Max explains. "The water was swarming with them."

Mom's lips purse. "Where is she now?"

"Resting in her room."

Marching to the door, Mom swings it open. Jess lies on her side with the covers pulled to her chin, flipping through a travel magazine. I chase after Mom.

"Hey!" I hear Jess yell as Mom pulls the magazine from her hands.

"Get out of this bed right now." Mom grips the sheet and rips it off Jess's body, letting it float to the floor. Jess scoots up against the headboard; she's wearing only a tank top and bikini underwear.

"Get out of here!" Jess yells. "Max!"

"What the hell are you doing?" Max shoves past us, taking in the scene. "That's enough, Mrs. Bloom—"

"Donovan," Mom corrects but doesn't move.

"Mrs. Donovan, please, step back." Max has tightened his hands into fists, and I doubt he'd hit my mother, but it's obvious he's serious about protecting Jess.

"That's very noble to try to defend your girlfriend or fiancé or whatever she is," Mom says, her voice calm. "But I think it's you who needs protecting. From your own stupidity."

Oh, no. This is going too far. Even I'd have hit Mom by now.

"Jess is in serious pain," Max says, stepping between the bed and us.

"Really? How interesting since those jellyfish don't have tentacles."

I stare blankly back at Mom, but suddenly, my middle school science class comes back to me. "If they don't have tentacles, they can't sting," I say.

Mom smiles triumphantly. "Which means she's lying."

Eight

Half a day later, which really feels more like a week, we stand inside the small immigration office in Guabito, the last town in Panama before the Costa Rican border. The bus ride was beautiful as we rode over the mountainous and seaside terrain, but the tension was as tangible as the steamy air inside the bus. I had nothing to do with what happened with the jellyfish, but Jess sure is acting like I'm part of some evil plan against her.

"How are you feeling?" I ask Jess as we move forward in the immigration line, waiting for the next officer at the border crossing out of Panama.

"Fine." Her eyes register distrust when she looks at me, but I'm the one who should be wary. She lied. Not that she's admitted it. After Mom called her out, Jess insisted she was stung and in a lot of pain. Max defended Jess but backed off when my mother tried to drag him down to the marina so he could stick his hand in the water to prove to him that they are not harmful. I don't think he wanted to know. I can tell part of him still wants to believe that Jess wasn't flat-out lying.

After the fiasco, Mom said Jess was no longer welcome to

stay and basically told me I'd be sleeping on the patio if I didn't get my butt back down to the dock and on the bus to Costa Rica. I was glad to be on my way, but Jess and Max came with me, begrudgingly, when they had no other choice.

"¡Que pase el siguiente!" the scary-looking immigration officer, a woman with frizzy hair and dark circles under her eyes, yells, and I jump. My hand squeezes my passport in my sweaty fingers as I approach and hand it to her.

My bladder is suddenly full, and I'm in the middle of the pee-pee dance when the woman grunts and hands me my passport back, motioning me to go through. Not waiting for Max and Jess, I rush into the bathroom—too disgusting to even talk about—do my business, and rush back outside, where Jess and Max are waiting in front of the old railway bridge we need to cross into Costa Rica.

Jess hurries ahead, seemingly unworried about the sad state of the crumbling bridge. The water flows a sickening distance below, and I keep my eyes pointed ahead, my stomach in my throat and my toes tingling as I try not to think about what would happen if one of the rickety boards broke under my weight.

I take a breath of courage as my foot gingerly hovers over the rotting-wood slats. It creeks as I grasp the metal sides of the bridge and slowly make my way across.

"Stay toward the edge, and hold on to the side, and you'll be fine." Max comes up beside me, his hand sliding under my arm. I didn't realize I was shaking until he touched me. "Step where I step."

"Why are you here?" I ask, cautiously following his path. If I talk about something else, I won't think about the fifty-foot drop below us.

"To help you."

A laugh escapes my lips, loud and clipped. "You wouldn't even be here if my mom hadn't kicked you out."

A man runs past us; his backpack that's loosely hung over

his shoulder swings out and hits me. I fall on the old tracks and yelp, my sweaty hands grasping the hot metal rails. My hands burn, but I don't let go. Max is beside me, helping me stand.

"Asshole!" he yells after the guy and then, "I came for you. I don't want you traveling alone. Despite what you may think, I *am* your friend."

His words loosen my resolve to hate him. A little. "Sonja posted another picture on Instagram," I blurt out. She posted it before we left Bocas Town, but I didn't tell Max because I was hurt, and my trust in him was broken. "It's a shot of her doing a backbend in front of a lodge called El Pájaro. I looked it up. It's in Playa Viejo."

I keep this image in my head as I continue to cross the bridge. When I finally get to the other side, I want to kiss the metal edges of the bridge in gratitude but stop myself. I don't want to end up in some jungle hospital with a tetanus shot that probably won't work and my obituary in a local paper no one will see: *Death by rusty bridge. She was a nice girl but not very bright.*

As Max and I enter the Costa Rican immigration office, I hear raised voices. Jess is yelling at the immigration officer, an old, weathered man who looks like he'd rather be enjoying his afternoon cerveza than having some American woman yell at him. When she's done with her tirade, he simply shakes his head and points his finger toward the door.

Red faced, Jess huffs out the side door of the building. We hurry after her. "What happened?" I ask, pushing the door open.

"They won't let me in." Jess plops down on the hot cement sidewalk.

"Why not?" Max asks.

"They need my proof of exit," she says, pulling out a bottle of water and drinking it. "Like a plane or bus ticket."

"You can go online and buy a ticket for the return bus to

Bocas. It'll take five minutes," I suggest.

Jess places the cool bottle to the back of her neck. "You can't buy a bus ticket online. Only in person," Jess says. "I already asked."

I sit down next to her, my Toms kicking up dirt and rocks as I stretch my legs out. It's so hot, the broken asphalt almost crackles. "What about your return flight home?"

"I haven't booked my flight yet. And they want to see a bank statement. No one said anything about that." Jess exhales and opens a ziplock bag of all her valuables from her duffel, but there's nothing that suddenly appears to prove she isn't planning to pitch a tent and sell gonja for the next three months.

"Do you have any documents on your phone?" Max pulls the bottom of his shirt up, wiping the sweat from his brow. His brown, taut abs are inches from my face, and my hand tingles, wanting to reach up and feel them under my fingers.

Stop! I am not into him.

"Not on this relic." Jess indicates her flip phone.

"Use mine," Max says.

Several minutes later, Jess pulls up her bank account on Max's phone. "Even if I show them this, I still don't have proof of exit." Jess pushes off the sidewalk and paces in front of the building, dodging other travelers coming in and out of the doors.

"Buy your return ticket now," I say, indicating Max's phone.

"I'm not going to buy a plane ticket just so I can get into Costa Rica. I don't know when or where I'm flying home from." She leans against the wall, dust and dirt sticking to her arms, but she doesn't wipe it off.

My stomach is growling, and the heat is beginning to suffocate me. "Why don't you walk back over the bridge, and see if the bus is there, and buy your return ticket," I suggest.

Jess looks at Max and then shrugs. "Fine."

Not wanting to risk my life again, I stay behind as Max and Jess head back in search of the bus. There's a small stand selling coconuts and fish tacos, and I chance food poisoning and order both, ready to pass out from heat and hunger.

I find a tree to stand under to escape the hot sun and bite into the soft skin of the tacos. The fish is fresh but bland. But I'm not eating it for the enjoyment of the dish. Sometimes food is just a necessity.

It's another thirty minutes until I see Jess and Max crossing back over the bridge, Jess's face covered in a scowl.

"The bus was gone," Max explains as they approach.

"Just use Max's phone to book a plane ticket," I say, frustrated. The heat is covering me like an angry woman, and I want to get to Playa Viejo before Sonja leaves again.

Jess scoffs. "I'm not paying for a flight I may not take."

"I think Orbitz or one of those travel sites has a no-fee, twenty-four-hour cancellation policy." I fan my face with the flimsy napkin in my hand.

"I doubt it."

"Oh my God!" I explode. "How the hell did you survive in the army? Stop making excuses, and find a solution. You're a grown woman. Act like it!" Both Max and Jess stare back at me in stunned silence. Several people milling around, waiting to board the next bus up the coast, look over at the commotion. I adjust my canvas bag on my shoulder. "Look, the shuttle to Manzanillo is arriving soon. Just meet me there."

I've already made it to Costa Rica. The rest should be easy. Confront Luke, get my money back, and go home.

"Natalie, wait." Max takes two steps toward me, and I pause, waiting for him to grow a pair. "We'll sort this out soon and take a later bus. Okay?"

"For a soldier, Jess sure needs a lot of looking after," I spit out, still angry.

"Hey!" she yells, hearing me. I've never fought a woman,

but the adrenaline rushing through me after my outburst makes me feel invincible. My feet are tingling, ready to bounce up and down like a fighter in the ring.

"Relax. Both of you." Max reaches out to me, and I step back, not wanting his touch right now. "We'll figure it out and meet you there. I promise."

"Fine." *Fine!*

A boiling hour later, the bus arrives in the small fishing town of Manzanillo in Playa Viejo. My anger is palpable as I walk the couple of miles to El Pájaro, the jungle house that Sonja took the picture in front of. I see a man standing on the deck of the open-air lodge, a bundle of linens under his arm and a beer in his hand. At first, I think it's Luke, but as I approach, I see the man is taller and slimmer. His sun-painted hair hangs shaggy against his tan skin.

"Hi." I look up at him from the bottom step that leads up to the deck. Two ceramic iguanas overwhelm what should be the banisters of the steps. "Is this El Pájaro?"

"Sure is," he says in a thick accent I can't quite place. Maybe Australian? He puts down the linens and rests against the face of one of the iguanas. "Did you make a booking? I haven't checked the online reservations this morning."

"Actually, I'm looking for someone who may be staying here or nearby." I pull up the picture of Sonja—or what you can see of Sonja on her Instagram—and then swipe to a picture of Luke I saved on my phone. "Their names are Luke and Sonja," I say in case the names jog his memory.

"Sure. They were staying here." A surge of adrenaline rushes through me. "But they left this morning." And it rushes back out.

"Do you know where they went?"

"They were going for a hike at the wildlife refuge. I...I'm not sure where they were going after that."

"Where's the refuge?" I'm already backing up, ready to turn and run to find them.

"About a mile that way." He points north, the word *that* sounding more like *thit*.

"Where are you from?" I ask.

"South Africa."

"Oh, right. Well, nice to meet you, and thanks," I yell over my shoulder.

"Wait." The man puts the beer and linens down. "The refuge is a big place. Are you familiar with it?"

"No." I stop.

"They were going to hike out to one of the caves, I think. It can be a little treacherous. You shouldn't go out there on your own." He looks back at the lodge, considering, before he continues. "I can show you."

"Uh…" I hesitate, not sure I want to hike out to some unknown cave by the ocean with a stranger. He seems harmless but so did Ted Bundy.

He reaches into the pocket of his swim trunks and hands me his phone. "Here. Ring my mum."

"What?"

"Ring her. She'll tell you I'm a nice, normal bloke."

I cock my head but take the phone and search until I find the entry labeled *Mum*. A couple moments later, a woman answers, her voice thick with sleep.

"'Ello?"

"Oh, uh, hi. This is…uh, my name's Natalie. I just met your son. And well, I just want to make sure he's not some serial killer." I laugh self consciously. What mother would ever admit her son is a serial killer.

There's stirring on the other end and some movement before I hear an answer. "Serial what? Is this a joke? Is Leo there?"

"Not a joke," I say, clearing my throat. "I guess he thought if I talked to you, I'd feel safer going on a wild-goose chase with him."

"What? You're chasing geese?"

"No, no. I... never mind. Go back to sleep."

I hang up, but before I hand the phone back, I send Max a text (he made me memorize his number in case I lost my phone) explaining that I'm going to the refuge with Leo, who runs the lodge. I tell him that if I don't text him in two hours, he should call the police. I highly doubt any of this is necessary, but no one ever thinks something bad is going to happen to them until it does. And I'm too trusting. So I've been told.

"Okay, Leo, let's go."

His eyebrows furrow. "How did you..."

"Your *Mum* said it."

"Oh, right. Let's get cracking before it gets too late."

My body is dripping with sweat when we arrive at a sign announcing the entrance to the refuge. It lists several activities that can be done in the wildlife park—hiking, bird watching, snorkeling, turtle watching. We continue down the hard-packed sand trail, passing impressive rainbow eucalyptuses and several varieties of palm trees I can't name. I screech when Leo points out an orb spider, with its long, pointy legs and colorful striped body.

A couple of native children run past us as we walk across a coved beach, the turquoise water caressing the white sand. They wave at Leo and yell, "*El médico!*" before disappearing into the thick jungle brush.

"What are they saying?" I ask as Leo slices through thick underbrush with his machete. If I hadn't known how common it is to carry a machete here, I would've run the moment I saw Leo take one with us. But Marty always brings a machete on his hikes through the dense jungle in Panama. A lot of the locals have them for this reason.

"Doctor." The machete swishes through the air, slicing thick palm leaves in half that block our path.

"Wouldn't it be easier to go that way?" I ask, indicating the well-traversed path we've just ventured off.

"Not if we want to get there and back before the sun sets."

"Do you mind if I borrow your phone again?" I ask, a little hesitant to follow him, but those kids knew who he was, and I did speak to his mom.

He hands me the phone, and I send another text to Max telling him exactly where I am in the refuge and that I'm still okay, but send out a search party if he doesn't hear from me soon.

Whoosh! The machete whizzes through the overgrowth as another orb spider crawls hurriedly up his web. I move closer to Leo and hand him the phone. "Why do they call you doctor?" I ask.

"Because I am one." I pause, not expecting this. He smiles at my reaction, the skin around his eyes crinkling. "Most people have that reaction. I'm a surgeon, but I don't like to be stuck in stuffy hospitals, so I work with Doctors Without Borders when I have the chance."

"Is that what you're doing here?"

Before he can answer, a dark-skinned woman wearing a loose black skirt to her calves and a ratty T-shirt runs up to us from the path. "Doctor! Doctor!" Her accent is thick, the word unfamiliar in her mouth. "¡Socorro!"

She grabs his arm, running and speaking rapidly in Spanish. I tumble after them. A half mile later, I'm out of breath as we come upon the opening of a cave, water rushing in and out of the mouth. A small boy is sitting on a wet rock, blood dripping down from his ankle and tears pouring over his cheeks. Leo speaks gently to the boy and lifts his ankle, inspecting the wound. Taking his shirt, Leo wipes around the cut. The boy cries louder, squeezing his eyes shut. Standing, Leo speaks to the woman, and she nods several times. Then he makes a call on his phone and lifts the boy into his arms, walking past me.

"Is he okay?" I ask, running to catch up.

"He'll need sutures, but he'll be fine." We walk to a more open path, and I hear the rumbling of a motor as a boat pulls up to the beach. Leo motions for me to wade out to the boat as the mother climbs in with Leo and her son. We zip south until we're at the beach by the lodge again. Leo gingerly carries the boy to one of the beds on the first floor of the jungle lodge and pulls out a red bag with medical supplies. When he pulls a needle from the bag, I walk outside, my stomach too weak to watch.

An hour later, the sun is setting, and the boy and his mother have gone. It was a quick procedure; two stitches and a lollipop and the boy was all smiles once it was over.

"Sorry about that." Leo collapses into the chair next to me at the beachside bar near the lodge. "I'm knackered."

"So you're the village Superman, huh?" I offer Leo a sip of the beer I'm drinking. He takes it. It was exciting watching Leo take care of that boy, but as the adrenaline seeps from my body, so does the realization that I may have lost Luke and my money. Again. Again, again, again.

"It's not as hard as it looks."

"Whatever you say." I sit back, the half-moon shining light on the gentle waves rolling in. Suddenly, Leo smacks my arm.

"What was that for?"

"Mosquito."

"Oh." I lay my head back, trying to enjoy this quiet moment, but my brain keeps circling around what I'm going to do now that Luke and Sonja have slipped through my fingers again. At least I know they're still traveling together.

"How about a surf?" Seeing my hesitation, he continues, "I mean body surf."

"No, thanks. My friend should be arriving soon."

"Max?" Leo asks.

I shoot up, alert. "How did you know his name?"

"He texted you on my phone. He said he's on the bus on his way here."

114

"Oh." Lying on my back, I close my eyes as the warm breeze cools my skin. Leo's arm brushes mine, and I don't move it away. The hike and drama of the day exhaust me, and I drift into a fantasy of living here and setting up a beachfront food stand and living a simple but lovely life. It would solve a lot of my problems.

A shadow crosses over my face.

"Natalie?"

I tense at the familiar voice. Max.

"Oh, hi." My calm exterior contrasts the restlessness I feel inside from his arrival. How can one man unhinge me with the sound of his voice? It's so freakin' annoying. "This is Leo. He runs the lodge Luke was staying in."

"Is he still here?"

I sit up, Leo's arm sliding away from mine. "He checked out this morning."

"Have you done anything more to find him?" Max's voice is tense.

"Yes. We hiked for miles through the refuge, but he wasn't there." I sit back, exhaling loudly.

"So that's it?"

"What else can I do? This is the last destination Sonja posted."

His breathing grows heavy above me. "Fine. Jess and I will go into town and look. In case he's still here."

"Knock yourself out." There's an edge to my voice, which I can't seem to keep out.

"Where are you staying tonight?" Max asks. "Should we look for a place in town?"

Far away from you, I want to say.

Leo shifts in his chair. "You all can stay at the lodge. It's not booked until next week."

What? No, no, no. I want to get away from Max and Jess.

"I'll give you the friends-and-family discount." Leo is still talking, and I want to punch him in the shoulder and tell him to shut it.

"Perfect. Thanks," Max says and walks toward the lodge where Jess has been hanging back.

I follow Leo as he gives us a quick tour of the two-story dwelling. It's a simple structure, mostly open to the jungle, with three bedrooms upstairs and an open living space and kitchen downstairs, which is surrounded by a wrap-around deck with hammocks and rocking chairs. It feels more like a large tree house than a lodge. I place my bag in one of the upstairs bedrooms and notice Jess and Max have claimed separate rooms across the hall. I don't ask why.

Heavy footsteps draw my attention to the doorway of my room, where Max appears. "Are you with that guy?"

"Leo? I just met him."

"Exactly." Max's eyes widen as if he's made his point.

"Ever heard of a holiday fling?" I say, not that I plan on having a fling with Leo, but Max's big brother act is too little, too late. He's made it clear he doesn't want a fling or anything else with me. He has no right to be jealous.

"You just met him."

I raise my eyebrows, as if to say, *What's your point?*

"Haven't you learned anything after what happened with Luke?"

"Luke wasn't a stranger. And I wasn't romantically involved with him. Not really." Except for that one night.

"What do you mean, not really?"

Why is Max latching on to that. It's not even relevant.

"We hooked up once."

Max's features darken, and he crosses his arms over his chest. "You had sex with Luke?"

"It was no big deal."

"When?"

"A few weeks before my farewell party at Chez Bella. In fact, my party was going to be the first time I saw him after it happened, but he never showed up." I pull the mosquito net that hangs from the ceiling in front of me, fiddling with the mesh fabric as I remember the end of that night.

"I showed up that night." His voice drops.

"I know." Oh, do I know.

The night of my farewell shindig, Max arrived after all the partygoers had departed. It was late; the only people left in the restaurant were a few busboys and Jacque, my sous chef, who was busy in the kitchen, prepping for the next day. I was turning out the lights and finishing the last of many glasses of champagne. When Max stepped through the door, I thought this was finally it. Our love story was going to begin.

I put the French jazz music back on the speakers, and we danced in front of the bar to Nina Simone, and I looked into his cobalt eyes, and he smiled down into mine, and as the song ended, I leaned in, but he ran out, leaving me stumbling for his lips and an explanation.

I hate remembering that night. There I was, my lips hanging in the air but no one on the other end to receive them. And now it's happened again. I drunkenly threw myself at him the other night, and he rushed into his ex's arms.

Ugh. Ugh. Ugh. It's just so embarrassing.

"Is that what this is about?" His voice has dropped an octave, and he's stepped fully into my room. "You like him."

"What? No way. This is about a man who stole my money. And my dream. God, do you really think I'm that pathetic. To run after a man who stole from me, because you think I like him?" I shove the netting aside and swing my feet to the floor. "You don't know me at all."

I stomp past him and down the stairs to the main floor until I reach the kitchen. Max hasn't followed me to tell me all the wonderful ways he does know me. Sam did that for Catie when she gave him the same challenge. He sprinkled her with every way he knew and loved her, and at that moment, she said she knew he loved her.

I throw open the fridge and look at the meager contents.

It's about as empty as I feel.

***

"Luke isn't staying at any of the hotels in town," Max announces when he and Jess return from their walk into town. "But I may have stumbled onto a story."

Max drops the bag of food in his hands on the counter and starts unloading the contents: fresh tuna filets, lettuce, tomato, carrots, avocado, a variety of fruit, and rum.

"I can make tuna steaks and a grilled-pineapple-and-avocado salad," I announce, placing the filets on a cutting board and wiping away the few ants that are crawling around the counters. I'm learning to coexist with Mother Nature on these travels. It's impossible to avoid her.

Leo offers to start the grill on the deck at the edge of the kitchen to cook the tuna once I prepare them. The windows and screens are open to the jungle, and the cicadas and night insects grow louder as they announce their presence to the awakening night.

"What's the story?" I ask Max, sliding the avocado onto another cutting board. I sink a knife into the soft skin and slide it around the fruit and pull it apart, and then I whack the knife into the large seed and twist it out.

"Have you heard about that guy, Thomas Carmel?" Pulling open his laptop, Max sits on a stool at the counter. "He's been all over the media. He disappeared while traveling through Costa Rica and was found a week later severely dehydrated in the middle of the jungle."

"Sure. He's been on all the morning talk shows. His wife's pregnant, right?" I ask as I cut the avocado into large slices and scoop the meat out.

"It turns out it all happened about an hour north of here."

"Hasn't the story been told?" I ask as I quickly slice the tomato—bright red and dripping with juice—and then stand over the trash can, peeling the carrots.

"Maybe not the real story. One of the hotel owners we

118

met today while looking for Luke said Thomas was staying at his hotel the day before it happened. And he suspects Thomas planned it all."

"Why?" I wash and shred the lettuce and put it into a wooden bowl I find on a low shelf and dump the tomato and carrots on top. I sprinkle it with salt and pepper and set it aside.

"The owner suspects Thomas was dealing drugs and staged the kidnapping and disappearance for money."

"I still don't understand how setting up your own kidnapping gets you money," Jess says, walking into the kitchen and dabbing the sweat from her face with a hand towel. She's been outside practicing some type of kung fu–yoga–tai chi thingy.

"I'm not sure either, but I want to find out. This could be a big story if it turns out to be true. A GoFundMe account was set up for Thomas and has raised forty-three hundred dollars already." Max turns his computer for us to see.

"There's your answer. Look how much money he made on his kidnapping already," I say, pointing at the screen with my knife.

"Maybe." Max doesn't sound convinced. "The owner gave me the name of a guy I should talk to near the town where Thomas was taken. I'm going up there tomorrow to look into it."

Jess looks over my shoulder at all the ingredients spread out on the counter. "Need any help?"

I'm startled by the offer. Since the jellyfish incident, she's been quiet, keeping clear of me. I don't know if she's mad or embarrassed. Probably a little of both.

I look around the counter and point at the most difficult task. "You can cut the skin off the pineapple and slice it into rounds." I roll the spikey fruit across the wood countertop to Jess. She brings it over to the dining table along with a large knife, then hacks the top and bottom off and looks at it, perplexed.

"Use the knife to slice the skin off." I take the pineapple in my hand to demonstrate. Grasping the top, I slice the outside from top to bottom and then do it again a couple inches apart and pull off that portion of the prickly skin. "Do that until all the skin is off and then cut it into rings. Then"— I look around for something small and round and find a metal shot glass, handing it to Jess—"use this to cut out the core in the middle of each ring."

"I've taken suicide bombers down with one finger; you'd think I could slice a pineapple," Jess says, swiftly sliding the knife down again and again, cutting off all the skin before slicing it into rings.

"Military?" Leo asks as he walks in from the deck, taking the lightly seasoned tuna from me.

"Army." Jess nods. "Eight years."

"Retired?"

"Sort of," Jess says, slamming the shot glass into the middle of each ring, removing the core. "My shoulder was injured, and it has limited range of motion now. I've been given the option to ETS."

"What does that mean?" I ask.

"I can be honorably discharged."

"My brother, Craig, was a contract worker in Iraq," Leo says. "His plane was shot down over Baghdad in '09."

My hand pauses over the bowl of marinade I've been whisking. "I'm so sorry."

"Shit happens." He shrugs, obviously not wanting to talk about it. "It really messed my parents up. I couldn't handle being around their grief. Mine was hard enough to deal with. That's why I started working for Doctors Without Borders and then came here. There's not much that gets me down in paradise. Craig would have loved it." He shakes his head as if to shake the emotions creeping up on him away. "What brought you guys down here from…"

"New York," I answer. "Luke, the guy I'm looking for is, er...was my business partner for a restaurant I'm opening, and he...well, he stole all my money."

"And he came here?" Leo asks, sliding the tuna steaks into the bowl of chile-lemon marinade I whisked together. "How did you find him?"

"Because he's an idiot," Max says, moving his laptop to the kitchen table, away from the mess of the preparations. Max continues, explaining to Leo that Luke came down to Panama thinking he'd make a quick buck running a restaurant in an expat resort.

"Why did he think that? The restaurant business is hardly lucrative down here." Leo walks outside through the open partition with the steaks.

"My mom, who has no idea about running a business in Panama, gave Luke the idea," I say, raising my voice for Leo to hear. "When she visited me in the city a few months ago, she went on and on about how these million-dollar-yacht owners at the marina and the expats are all desperate for a good restaurant down here. I think Luke pictured an undiscovered French Riviera or something."

"Hardly," Leo yells from the grill.

"Then when Luke realized my mother was at the resort already—she usually doesn't come down until later in the season—he ran out on the restaurant and a lot of bills." I walk out to the grill and look over the tunas. The raw meat is pink, shiny and translucent, which signifies it's Grade #1, the highest grade tuna. If he cooks it too much, he'll ruin it. They only need to be seared.

"I bet he did," Leo scoffs. "It's high season. If he didn't make any money now, he never will. This is the time of year when the retirees come down to lie in the sun and spend their money and complain about the conveniences they left behind." The grill sizzles as Leo flips the tuna; the black lines on the flesh look perfect. And the meat inside is still pink and beautifully raw. "It's an interesting mix of backpackers, surfers, tourists, and rich expats traveling through this part of the world. And the occasional millionaire on a yacht."

"Do you know a guy named Cliff Upton? He owns a couple of cabins here." Max looks up from his computer, where he's been typing rapidly.

"Sure."

"Is he the guy you talked to today?" I ask, taking the tongs from Leo and pulling the tuna off the grill and onto a serving platter, the smell of singed meat filling the air.

"Is he trustworthy?" Max asks.

Leo walks back into the kitchen and pulls out four plates and silverware, setting them on the table along with a pitcher of water. "As far as I know. He's lived here off and on for three decades. Why?"

"Max is looking into a story on Thomas Carmel, the guy that was—"

"I know who he is," Leo says, squeezing three cut limes into a pitcher, pouring in rum and sugar and muddling it together.

"You know him?" Max sits up taller, his eyes two round saucers.

"By reputation mostly. I met him once." Leo takes a tray of ice cubes and dumps it into the pitcher along with a half can of soda water. "He scammed his way through all of Costa Rica. I'm not surprised those guys kidnapped him. Though I doubt it was for money."

"Why not?" Max is completely focused on Leo.

"He didn't have any. And he screwed over a lot of bad people. Plus, he was into drugs."

"Did he sell them? Use them?"

"From what I hear, both." Leo pours the cocktail he's made into four plastic tumblers and hands them around. I take a long sip, the cool, crisp liquid fizzy on my tongue. I set the resting steaks on the table and quickly grill the sliced pineapple.

Max is in full reporter mode, but Leo doesn't seem to mind. He obviously didn't like this Thomas Carmel guy, and his information, if accurate, fuels Max's theory that Thomas Carmel's kidnapping wasn't as innocent as the media (and the Good Samaritans donating money) have been led to believe. Either way, it would be a great scoop if he can prove it.

"What drugs was he into?" Max asks, ignoring his drink.

"Weed mostly. Sometimes coke."

Max continues his interrogation as I pour the dressing on the salad and bring it to the table along with the grilled pineapple and avocado. I sprinkle the side dish with salt and pepper and top it off with a bit of olive oil and lime juice.

"Where did he get the drugs?" Max asks, typing into his computer.

Leo shrugs, looking unconcerned by the peppering of questions. "I don't know, mate. Cliff would know more. He deals a bit on the side. Nothing crazy. Like I said, I only met Tommy once. But the community is small here, and a guy like him doesn't go unnoticed."

I place the steaks and salad on the table, and we gather around it like vultures. The smell of the freshly grilled tuna brings out the hunger lingering inside all of us after a long day, and we momentarily forget about Thomas Carmel and Max's story.

An hour and a full stomach later, I swing lazily in one of the hammocks on the deck, leaving the game of Cards Against Humanity we were playing inside. My head is spinning from the pitcher of caipirinhas we consumed.

Footsteps announce the arrival of Leo. He slides a black notebook onto my lap and flips it open to a page in the middle of the book. Then he sits across from me on the deck railing, watching as I read.

My feet stop the hammock, and I sit up. The notebook is filled with a mix of handwritten messages scrawled across the pages. I realize it's a guestbook—past visitors documenting their stay at the lodge, stating where they're from and where they're going.

Does he want me to fill it out?

"I didn't know they wrote in there, or I would've shown it to you when you first arrived," Leo says.

My eyes track the entries until I reach the last one. Two sentences stare back at me in delicate blue penmanship.

"But they did fill it out," he says.

My ears ring as I realize what I'm reading. The location of where Luke and Sonja have traveled to next.

Limón.

"It's ten miles north," Leo says. "Luke seemed so nice and normal." Leo peeks at the page I'm reading. "They both did. I guess you never really know."

No, you don't.

Nine

The next morning, we wake up early, and Leo drives Max, Jess, and me up the coast in a borrowed pickup that looks and feels like it should be in a truck cemetery. As we race across the bumpy, unpaved roads, I strangle the side of my seat. We miss cyclists—the most popular mode of transportation besides feet—by inches, and cars swerve out of our way at the last second. I've seen my life flash before my eyes on several occasions. It's not a pretty image, which is why I'm making this heart-pounding trip. To get my life back.

A mile out of Playa Viejo, we drop Max off to follow up with Cliff Upton. He's determined to find out more about Thomas Carmel. Jess stayed with us because Max wants to interview Cliff on his own. And it'll only be a few hours. I'm a little wary of Max meeting this guy alone and confronting him about drugs, but Max has been in more dangerous situations than this. Small-time drug dealers in Costa Rica can't be too scary after facing suicide bombers and enemy soldiers in Afghanistan.

When we arrive in Puerto Limón, the lush and busy port town of Limón, we park in front of a row of colorfully painted shops and bars on the main street, store signs jutting out from second-story hangings, announcing their brands like many Western cities. We pass a small street festival; Afro-Caribbean music is being played on steel drums; and the savory smell of baked rice and coconut fills the air. Everyone is dressed in a rainbow of colors and dancing to the music as if they were in a nightclub and not on a hot street in the late-morning sun.

"What's that amazing smell?" I ask, tempted to stop and try the local dishes being spooned out from under tents and tables set up outside the colorful shops.

"Rica and beans. Limón's version of rice and beans."

Unable to help myself, I hand a dollar to one of the vendors and take the proffered bowl of food. Leo leads us across the road and onto a sandy path, passing coconut palms on the way to the beach, and I scoop the hot rice and beans into my mouth. It explodes with fresh coconut, cilantro, peppers, red beans, and a touch of cinnamon. It's divine.

"My friend runs the tent lodge," Leo says. "She'll know if anyone new has arrived in town."

I finish the last bite, wishing there were more, and toss the paper bowl into a trash can. My maxi dress skids across puddles, and I stop and tie up the side of it to avoid the dirty water from the rains early this morning. The dress is the same one I wore yesterday. The material is starting to smell of stale sea air. And my up-the-bum bathing suit is starting to chaff.

When we arrive, we see that the tent city is a small village of a dozen tents, but I use the word *tent* loosely. They are closer to yurts. The triangle structures are tall and wide, with thick hardwood floors and sturdy twin beds and dressers carved out of thick logs. It's basically a hotel room with canvas instead of wood and plaster for walls. I'd hardly call it roughing it. Except you have to walk outside to use the bathroom.

"Hola." Leo smiles, stepping into one of the tents. A

young woman about my age straightens from making the beds as Leo kisses her on the cheek. She brushes her long, dark hair behind her brown shoulders and speaks rapidly in Spanish. Leo laughs and responds. He turns and puts his hand out toward Jess and me, and I give a small wave.

"Si, si." The woman points down the beach and speaks again in Spanish, seeming to give Leo some directions.

"Gracias." Leo kisses her cheek again and walks out of the tent.

"He's here."

I draw a quick intake of breath. *He's here!* I suck down several deep breaths, my throat beginning to constrict. My heart is galloping, and my knees weaken. Could it really be this easy?

"He's selling fish tacos at that stand down the beach."

I've traveled halfway across the continent and through two countries, and he's just hanging out. Selling fish on the beach?

"That was fast," Jess says, echoing my own thoughts. He's only been here a day, and he's already set up a food stand on the beach.

I step forward, jiggling my hands to shake out the nerves, but Jess stops me. "Wait. He doesn't know me. Let me go talk to him, see what story he's telling."

Jess has already stripped off her tank top, exposing her fit body in her red bikini. She pulls the sunglasses from my face—a pair of black Dolce & Gabbanas nipped from Catie's fashion editor—and trades me her green sports sunglasses.

"I'll be right back." She saunters off, and Leo stares after her, ogling her backside. I slap him on the arm.

"Ag, she's got a good body."

Men.

"So do you," he says, still watching Jess. "Under that sack."

"Hey! I lost my luggage."

"What's the deal with Max and her?" Leo asks as we wait.

"Are they together?"

I look at him, but I can't tell if he's asking because he likes Jess or just making conversation. "They use to be engaged, but then they broke up. And now…I have no idea."

We stop the conversation as Jess walks back with a sly smile on her face. "He said he was some hotshot chef from LA who's come down here to look into opening a restaurant"—Jess pauses for emphasis—"because his business partner ran off with all his money."

My stomach drops. "What?!"

Jess and Leo exchange a look that says they're not surprised.

I lurch forward. "That little liar!"

Leo grabs my arm, but I wriggle out, running down the beach. Nearing Luke, I yell his name. His eyes grow wide, and he swivels his head back and forth down the beach.

"Don't you dare run!" I yell.

His deer-in-headlights eyes quickly fade once he sees no way out, and he plasters a sparkling smile on his face. "Natalie, babe. I can't believe you came all this way to see me."

"Drop the bullshit. You stole my money and ran off." I'm in his face, staring up into his cocky smirk. He's tall, and it makes my neck hurt. "But, like the idiot you are, you ran right to where my mother lives."

"Hey, it wasn't like that. I did this for us."

"Ha! I'm not as naïve as I was a month ago." I shove him, but his rock-hard chest doesn't budge. "I want my money back."

"I'm getting it back. And then some." He takes my hands, which look dwarfed in his large palms, and holds them.

"Don't con me." I pull away, and he puts his hands up in retreat. "I know you skipped out on all those vendors and that restaurant owner in Red Frog. You're a thief and a liar."

"I'm not. I swear." He drops his smile. "Seriously, Nat.

Let me explain."

I purse my lips and raise my eyebrows to say, *Dazzle me with your explanation.*

"That contractor guy was ripping us off. He kept coming back with more and more problems and more and more bills." Luke notices Jess and Leo standing several feet away, watching us. "You know them?"

"Yeah. They're here to make sure you don't do anything stupid, like run off again. Or hurt me."

"Nat, I would never hurt you." Luke's face falls, and he looks injured.

"You were saying…"

"Right. The contractor was scamming us, and you were all caught up in helping your sister and then helping that guy Max, and I tried to tell you my plan to come here, but you…you never had time to listen."

"What the hell are you talking about? We texted or called a dozen times a day about the business."

"Yeah, but I needed to talk to you about this in person, and you were never available."

I cross my arms over my chest, exhausted by his flimsy explanation. "I'm here now. Talk."

"When your mom visited a couple of months ago and told us that anyone could make a killing if they opened a restaurant at the marina in Red Frog, I knew that was how we could double our money for our investment. We could work three months down here when all the yachts and expats came down, and then you could make your dream restaurant without any restrictions."

"Mom was just talking. She doesn't know anything. She just wants a decent restaurant on the island. But the reason restaurants are always closing and changing hands is because they *don't* make money. It's not like doing business in the States. The Panamanians strike all the time; it's almost impossible to do any kind of business down here. Especially since you have to hire Panamanians to work for you. And their work ethic is, let's say, a little bit more relaxed. It's a completely different culture here." I throw my hands up in the air, fed up.

"I know all that now. But I didn't then."

"Until you lost all my money."

He has the good sense to look sheepish.

"You did?! You lost it all?"

"Well, it's not my fault. I trusted someone I shouldn't have." A young couple, shimmering from a recent swim in the ocean, walks up and orders two tacos and cervezas and hands Luke cash, which I swipe from his hand. "Come on. Don't be like that. I still had a lot of our, er, your money, but this girl stole it."

"Who? Sonja?"

Luke's light eyes widen in surprise. "Yeah. How'd you know?"

"You guys didn't keep a low profile," I say. He looks lost for an explanation. "Besides, I don't believe it."

"She did. I swear."

"I don't believe any of it," I clarify. A local boy, about eight years old, approaches Luke with a bucket in his hand, selling fresh *pan bon*. I shake my head, and he walks over to Jess and Leo, who buy three round loaves from him.

"I did come down here to make money," he assures me. Out of the corner of my eye, I see Leo take a few steps closer, but I put my hand out low, stopping him and Jess. I want them to stay out of it for right now. They stop, standing back but listening.

"Oh, I believe that, but you weren't planning on coming back and surprising me with all the fresh cash." My mind is spinning. "Were you scamming me the whole time?"

"I wasn't scamming you. I swear. And I didn't run off on those vendors in Red Frog. They were ripping me off. Ask anyone in Bocas. They'll tell you what crooks those Chinese vendors are."

That part I believe. Luke would have realized pretty fast that business isn't as straightforward or honest down here. I've heard many tales since my mother moved down to Panama.

"And then Sonja ran off with the remaining money last night."

"That's convenient," Leo says, walking closer and coming into the conversation.

"Where is she?" I ask, crossing my arms.

"I don't know. She took the money in the middle of the night while I was sleeping. She could be anywhere."

"Let's see about that." I take Leo's phone and pull up Sonja's Instagram account. I'm surprised to see she posted a photo two hours ago. I checked it this morning, and there was nothing new. In the photo, she's walking across a slackline, the ocean and a tin-roof structure out of focus in the background. There's a sign next to the slackline that reads *Don't relax, get slacked.*

"I know where that is. Parismina," Leo says, looking at the phone. "It's a beach about eighty kilometers north of here."

"Then we're going there and talking to Sonja," I say. "And you're coming with us," I tell Luke.

Jess looks at me like I have two heads. "You don't believe him, do you? He's sending you on a wild-goose chase."

"What choice do I have?" I counter. "I have to get my money back."

"Where's your bag?" Jess asks Luke, moving around the stand.

"What?" he asks.

"Your bag? Your stuff? Where is it?"

"None of your business."

Luke is a big guy, tall, broad, and built, but it only takes Jess one swipe of her leg and a knock to his cheek with her elbow to bring him to his knees. Jess squats in front of him.

"Geez, if you wanted it that bad, why didn't you say?" Luke smiles, despite being taken down by this small woman. He's amused. "My stuff's over there." Luke motions toward a large cooler under a mangrove. Jess flips the lid, and inside is a blue backpack and a black shoulder bag. Her hands dig through the bags, swift and efficient.

"Nothing," Jess says, tossing them aside. "But I doubt that girl stole any money. He probably lost it all, and now he's selling fish tacos under a hut on the beach. He's still conning you."

"No, I'm not. Come on, Natalie," Luke implores, his eyes holding mine. "You know me. If I was going to run off with your money, why didn't I do that right away? Why would I wait six months? I *gave* you money for your restaurant. A lot of it."

It does seem odd, but that could have been his scam the whole time.

"I'm going to that beach where Sonja took the picture. You're coming with me." I direct my comment at Luke. "You two can do whatever you want," I say.

"Max isn't going to like this," Jess says.

"I don't care what he likes," I snap.

"Max is here?" Luke looks over my shoulder, searching the beach.

"Yes. He's meeting us later, and I'm not leaving your side until he gets here." I wave my hand at his food stand. "Shut this down. We're leaving here as soon as Max arrives."

***

"So this is the infamous Luke." Max drops his duffel inside the large, shared tent we've been waiting in to escape the hot sun. "We've come a long way looking for you."

Luke looks up from the book he's been reading for the past hour, Michael Lewis's *Liar's Poker*, nonplussed. Appropriate reading.

"What's he doing here?" Luke asks.

"He's researching a story—" I start to tell him.

But Max interrupts me. "None of your business."

Max shoots me a look, but I ignore it, asking, "Did you get the info you needed?"

"I'll talk to you about it later." Max looks around the canvas walls and heavy wood flooring and takes in the luggage on various beds. "Are we staying the night?" Max asks.

"No. We've been waiting for you. Sonja posted again. She's about an hour north of here. Leo's going to drive us there."

"Why? You already found Luke."

"Apparently, she stole the rest of the money Luke stole from me," I explain.

"I didn't steal it." Luke puts the book down on the bed he's sitting on. "I was trying to make more money. For you."

Max pulls a face that suggests he thinks Luke is full of shit. "What lies has he been telling you?"

I explain Luke's not-so-brilliant plan to come down here and double our money. As I explain it, I still find it hard to believe, but at the same time, it doesn't make sense that Luke would invest all that money just to run off with it six months later. It's not like we'd opened the restaurant and made a ton of money, and he'd stolen the profits. There was less money in the bank account than there was when he invested in the business originally. Still, it seems like such a naïve strategy to come all the way down to a foreign country to try to make a quick buck. Especially when Luke's job was to take other people's money, assess the market, and then invest it. If he wanted to gamble with my money, why not go to what he knows? He was very successful at his job, and by the time he was thirty, he'd made enough money to retire early and invest in passion projects, like mine.

At least, that's what he told me.

"Can I borrow your phone?" I ask Max.

Max hands it over without question. I quickly log on to my e-mail account and shoot Catie a message asking if she can look into Luke's background. They have fact-checkers and pseudo-investigators at the magazine. Catie should be able to find something useful. It's what I should have done months ago, before I went into business with him. But I didn't feel I needed to. We were friends by then.

Handing the phone back to Max, I can see a look of distrust on his face as he watches Luke. "So this girl conveniently ran off with the rest of the money. How much was left?"

Luke swings his legs off the bed and stands, his head brushing the top of the tent. He's several inches taller than Max and much broader, but Max doesn't move back. "Enough. I made sure not to put all the money into the fated marina restaurant, even if the Chinese vendors ripped me off."

"It seems everyone's ripping you off." Max looks unimpressed.

"Let me deal with this," I say. But Max keeps his eyes locked on Luke, not acknowledging my plea.

"What's Sonja gonna say when we find her?" Max asks, taking a step closer.

"I doubt she'll admit to stealing. But you can try your interrogation techniques on her. She might be more susceptible than me." Luke smirks, sitting back on the bed and picking up his book.

"This isn't an interrogation," Max says. "I'm protecting my friend from assholes like you."

In a swift move, Luke takes two steps toward Max, his hands twisting into fists. I rush between them; the rising testosterone in the small space and the heat from our bodies create a sauna around us. "Leave it alone." Max doesn't move. I look pointedly at him. "This isn't your fight."

Max exhales and steps back. When Luke's fists relax, Max

exits the tent, and I follow.

"How did it go with Cliff Upton?" I ask when we stop on the sandy path.

Keeping his eyes on the door flaps of the tent, Max answers, "He had a lot of interesting things to say about Tommy." Max lowers his voice as a young man walks by carrying a surfboard, his hair slick from the seawater. "Thomas Carmel really was kidnapped, but Cliff thinks he set the whole thing up. He put me in contact with one of the guys who was in on the kidnapping. I'm going talk to him tomorrow."

"You're meeting with one of the kidnappers?!"

"Cliff called him. I already spoke to him briefly on the phone."

"Is he a drug dealer?"

Instead of answering, Max looks down the path where Leo and Jess are approaching.

"You guys ready to go?" Leo asks.

"Sure. I'll get Luke," I say.

Max grabs my arm. "I'll get Luke. We'll meet you at the truck."

"I can get him," I say, taking a step toward the tent. "Luke is harmless."

"That's what worries me," Max says.

"What?"

"That you believe that."

A half hour later, my butt is aching from being tossed around the back of the pickup. Max wanted to sit in the back of the truck with Luke, but I insisted. The thin blankets between me and the metal truck bed aren't doing much to soften the blows every time we hit a bump. And there are many. Even at the slow pace we're driving.

"Want an energy bar?" Luke asks, reaching into his backpack. He pulls out a Clif Bar and throws it to me. I tear the wrapper off, taking three quick bites. Flipping the top off the small cooler next to him, he pulls out an Imperial. He lifts his hand to throw it, but I lean forward and take it from him instead, not wanting a beer shower when I open it. As I grab it from his hand, his fingers wrap around my forearm gently. "Nat, I didn't steal your money. I wouldn't do that to you. I…couldn't."

A bump sends me backward, falling on my side. I roll to sitting and hold the sweaty beer can in my hands until we stop at the next intersection. "I want to believe you. Except you did steal my money." I pop the beer open and take a sip. The crisp liquid sates my hunger more than the energy bar did. "What aren't you telling me?"

"I told you everything."

"Why don't you want us to find Sonja?" I ask.

"Are Max and you an *us* now?" Luke asks, popping another beer from the cooler and taking a long gulp.

"I mean *us* in the general sense."

"You didn't answer my question." Luke sits up straighter, adjusting the bright-orange blanket behind him.

"I'm not with Max." I take another gulp of beer, pushing down the bubble of emotion that is creeping into my throat. "Why do you care?"

"I want to know what my captors motivations are?"

"We're not your captors." I laugh. Luke is a big guy and could overpower me and jump out of the back of this truck if he wanted. He knows this. "I've always liked you, Luke. I thought we were friends. Good friends."

"We are." Luke grabs the side of the truck as we take a sharp turn. Once the truck straightens, Luke leans forward. Suddenly, I feel that he's about to make a confession. "Sonja didn't steal the money. Well, she did, but I had a feeling she was going to. She really needs it."

It takes me a moment to process this. I open my mouth to press him further, but I can tell he wants to talk, so I look at him and wait.

"Her sister, Mira, is sick. Really sick. She has breast cancer. Sonja came here because she couldn't handle watching Mira dying, but she feels guilty now for abandoning her sister. Sonja showed me her sister's blog, and it tore me up. Mira's an elementary school teacher and a single mother. Her daughter was two when she was diagnosed last year. Mira's raised a good amount of money, but the chemo treatments are really expensive, and she can't work. So when Sonja took the money last night, I knew why. After reading her sister's latest post, Sonja cried all night and was gone in the morning, along with the money. How could I go after her?"

Geez, way to make a girl feel guilty. How can I ask for the money back from a dying woman? I mean, I know it's my money, but the woman has cancer. And a small child. If Luke is to be trusted.

"Show me the blog," I say.

"You don't believe me?"

I put my hand out for his phone, but he says his phone doesn't have data. Mine doesn't either. I knock on the window that separates the cab from the cargo bed. Max slides it open.

"You okay?"

"Yep," I say over the wind. "Can I borrow your phone?"

He hands it through the small partition. I close the window and hand the phone to Luke.

"Pull up her blog," I say.

He types in the address and hands the phone back to me. I wonder if the page will ever load or if this is another lie, when suddenly a woman with a scarf around her head appears on the screen. There are several blog entries underneath the page's title, *Mira's Rotten Melons.*

I scroll through the first two posts, which describe her battle with stage-two breast cancer and the effect on her life and her daughter. Then I tap on the "About" section and wait another minute for it to load. When it finally does, I discover she is an elementary school teacher and a single mother, and she briefly mentions her parents and her sister, Sonja.

So Luke is telling the truth, and I can't go after Sonja for the money. He's right. Her sister is dying. I know what people will do when someone they love is dying.

The truck stops suddenly, and I fly forward, landing on top of Luke. I look up, and his face is close to mine, and I see something soft and wanting flicker in his eyes. Before I can question it, a shadow blocks the searing sun above us.

"That's cozy."

Startled, I pull back. Jess has stepped out of the cab and is leaning over the back of the truck, looking at us. Max and Leo slide out behind her.

"Are we here?" I ask, climbing off Luke.

"Not yet." Leo reaches his arms above his head in a stretch. "I need to get some gas and make a couple of calls. We're about twenty miles away."

"Okay." I hand Max his phone back. "Luke just showed me Sonja's sister's blog. She has cancer." Jess tucks in next to Max, reading as he scrolls through the blog. "It's why Sonja took the money. To help with her sister's medical treatments."

"That doesn't make it okay to steal your money," Jess scoffs, looking up from the phone. "A lot of people are sick. A lot of people have problems and tragic stories. Look at Max. It doesn't mean it's okay to go around stealing money."

"I know." My cheeks burn at her condescending tone. "But…but how can I ask for it back now? The sister has a small child. She's dying."

"Oh my God. Max, please talk some sense into her." Jess puts up her hands, done with me. It's easy for her to judge. She's not emotionally involved. And if she could take money back from someone who's that sick, then she's a heartless bitch.

"Even if this story is true," Max says, pocketing his phone, "Jess is right. You can't just walk away. And it doesn't make what he"—Max looks pointedly at Luke—"did okay."

"It's not as black and white as that," I say.

"Are you fucking kidding me?" Jess snorts. "He stole your money before he ever met this girl and found out her sad story. I can't…this is too stupid. You're so gullible." Jess turns on her heels and marches to the sidewalk, ordering a bottle of water from a street vendor. Leo gives me a sympathetic smile and follows Jess, obviously not wanting to get any more involved in my crazy mess. I don't blame him.

But why is Jess so pissed off? I know she's not saying these things because she cares.

"Jess is right; you're being naïve." Max slams the tailgate down, and I carefully slide across the uneven surface, and he helps me down, the heat from his scolding rushing over me. "Don't let him wiggle his way out of his scheming."

"I'm not. I never said Luke's off the hook. You're not, Luke—" I shoot a look over my shoulder at Luke, who is sitting with his knees up in the truck bed. He opens his mouth to speak, but I turn back to Max—"the story about Sonja's sister may be true, but until I speak to Sonja, I won't fully believe she ran off with the money." For all I know, Luke spent it all and is using Sonja as a scapegoat.

A look of disbelief passes over Luke's face and then anger. He thought I'd buy this story and walk away, I realize, which makes me even more determined to find Sonja.

Then I'll know once and for all how big of a con man Luke really is.

Ten

"I've got to get back to Playa Viejo." Leo leans against the hood of his truck, slurping from the straw sticking out of a raw coconut he bought. "My friend Manny called. Some new backpackers arrived and want to stay at the lodge tonight."

"Oh." I look around at the one-street town.

"Don't worry. I'm not leaving you stranded. I spoke to the guy at the liquor store, and he said a small shuttle bus is leaving for Parismina soon." Leo points to a squat, yellow building with the word *vinatería* painted in red across the front.

Leo climbs into the front seat, tossing the coconut into a nearby dumpster. I lean over the open window. "Do you mind if I check my Instagram one more time before we continue this chase. I don't want to arrive to find out she's already gone."

"Sure." Leo slides his phone to me.

I quickly look at my Instagram, which shows me the same pictures on Sonja's account. I study her photos again, trying to get a view of her face, but it's still blocked in every photo.

All I can see is her petite, svelte frame and dark hair spilling over her shoulders.

"Nothing new." I hand the phone back.

"Shoot me a line when you guys are coming back through," he says.

"Thank you so much for everything, Leo," I say, standing on my tiptoes and hugging him through the open window. "You've been a lifesaver."

"For you, anything." He smiles and kisses my cheek. "Do me a favor though."

"Anything," I say, resting back on my heels.

"Don't be so ready to trust that guy," Leo says, watching Luke, who is walking toward us. "In my line of business, both as a doctor and the owner of a lodge, I meet a lot of people. And you'd be amazed how the most seemingly honest and trust-worthy people are the biggest thieves, liars, and cons."

I nod, taking in his words.

"Just promise me you won't be so quick to believe everything he says without proof."

"I promise."

I step back and watch Leo drive away until the gray truck is out of sight.

"Where is he going?" Luke asks, handing me a bottle of water.

"Back to the lodge. Some guests just arrived. We can take a shuttle to the next town." We walk to a cracked bench next to the liquor store and sit. "Why doesn't Sonja have any photos of her face online?"

Luke slides his feet out of his Reef flip-flops, stretching his legs. "She had an issue with a stalker a few years ago. It shook her up so much that she'd stay offline completely, except she can't. Not with her yoga business. She needs an online presence, but she doesn't want her face out there."

"Do you have any photos of her on your phone?" I ask.

Luke lifts his phone, an ancient Nokia. "I've been using

this down here. No picture function." Mom has a similar phone she uses for local calls when she's in Panama too.

Max and Jess return from a visit to the bathroom in the small gas station, and I explain our new situation to them just as the shuttle bus pulls to the curb. It's really a large van with a sliding door and three rows of seats.

"How far is this town?" Jess asks, avoiding a piece of sidewalk that juts straight up from the curb by the van.

"About thirty minutes," Max says, adjusting his duffel bag on his shoulder. "We're going straight to the beach where the picture was taken to locate Sonja. Then, Jess you stay with Luke and Natalie while I go further west and interview the guy for my story."

"I don't need Jess to babysit me," I shoot at Max. "I can handle Luke."

Max and Jess both give me incredulous looks. They don't trust me, or more accurately, my judgment. But what have I done except trust a man I've known for a year? Everything he ever did—up until he ran off with my money—was kind and generous. Even now, he was quick to confess about Sonja and why she took the money, which, if you're going to steal money, is a pretty damn good reason.

"Max, be careful when you meet up with that guy." Jess puts her hand on his arm, and watching their intimacy physically makes me burn inside. It's going to be a while until my feelings for him are completely gone. "Let me come with you."

Swiping her hand off his arm—don't read too much into that!—he says, "I'll be fine. I already talked to him. He's excited to tell his side of the story."

"How can you know it will be the truth?" I ask as the driver steps out of the van and slides the side door open.

"The same as with all my stories—find confirmation. Or give all the details and let the readers decide the truth."

"I have to pee," Luke announces.

"I'll go with him," Max says.

Luke rolls his eyes but doesn't protest as they walk around the corner to the gas station. When they return, we all pile into the van. I squeeze past the first two rows of seats and slide over the cracked leather on the back bench seat, Luke sliding in beside me. The leather is hot through the thin material of my maxi dress. Jess and Max sit in the middle row, beside a guy with no shirt and a man bun atop his head. The bus is stuffy, a potpourri of mildew, sweat, and BO surrounding me.

"How much money was left when Sonja ran off?" I ask Luke over the dull hum of the motor as we sit, idling.

The water bottle he holds pauses halfway to his mouth. "I...I'm not sure."

I sit up straighter. "What do you mean? You worked in banking. You would have known the amount down to the penny."

"I..."—he drops his head—"we'd had a big day that day, and I didn't have a chance to count the money before she ran off."

"You had a big day selling tacos?"

"Uh, yeah."

Max jumps in. "You traveled from Manzanillo to Limón and then conveniently found that taco stand, got all the ingredients stocked and had a big day selling"—Max pauses for emphasis—"fish tacos?"

"And beer."

"No way." Max laughs, but there is no humor in his voice. "What were you really selling?"

Luke works his jaw, rubbing his three-day stubble. "Tacos. And beer."

"How much money did these amazing tacos and beers make you?" Max asks again.

Two scraggly-looking young men hoist their backpacks into the van and climb into the front row of seats, the smell of sweat and weed wafting in with them.

"Shit," Luke exclaims, frantically patting his pockets. Then he shoves his hands in the different compartments of his backpack.

"What?" I ask.

"I left my phone in the bathroom." Luke's eyes widen out the window at the realization as the driver climbs into the front seat of the van.

"Quick. Go get it," I say.

Luke leaps off the shuttle toward the gas station.

"Where the hell is he going?" Jess stands, hunching over as she looks out the door toward Luke's retreating back.

"He forgot his phone in the bathroom."

The driver says something in Spanish and the door begins to automatically slide shut. "Wait!" I yell. "My friend forgot his phone. He'll be right back."

"Where's his bag?" Max leans over the seats to the empty space next to me. The bag is gone.

"I'll get him." Jess sighs, as if to accent my naïveté. Jess says something to the driver in Spanish before she throws the door open and runs down the sidewalk, disappearing around the corner. The three other passengers watch the action unfold, mildly interested. Costa Rica seems to have the same anything-goes, just-sit-back-and-relax culture as Panama. But after five minutes pass, which feels like two hours, Jess has yet to reappear, and I stare out the window, willing them to materialize. This is so not good.

Suddenly, the van lurches forward.

"Wait!" Max and I both yell, but the driver ignores us, the shuttle moaning like an old man as it pulls away from the curb. I push the window open beside me and see Jess emerge, running after the accelerating vehicle. Max is leaning over the seat, yelling at the driver, but he doesn't stop or slow down. Jess is rapidly growing smaller.

Realizing the bus driver has no intention of stopping, I

grab Jess's bag and toss it out the open window. Her duffel lies on the broken asphalt, and she reaches it just as the shuttle turns the corner, disappearing.

Max leans forward, yelling at the driver, but the van pushes forward, a small grin on the driver's face. Is he a sadist?

"Tell him to stop!" I yell at Max, who's in a heated back-and-forth with the driver. "Stop. Let us off!"

Max falls into the seat next to me. "I said that. In Spanish and English. He said he's late and won't get paid if he doesn't make it to the next town by noon."

I'm ready to slide the door open and jump out, but we're moving too fast. Max and I both look out the back window, the few small buildings fading behind us. He looks as helpless and frustrated as I feel.

We speed over the fragmented roadways, my body jerking in every direction. The driver's serious about getting to the destination on time.

"Where's Jess's bag?" Max asks.

"I threw it out the window when I realized the driver wasn't stopping," I say.

"You did what?!"

I'm surprised by his reaction. "She needed her money and ID."

Sitting back, Max scowls.

"I was helping her."

He mumbles something and pulls out his phone, typing fast. Then he leans his head back and closes his eyes, done with our conversation. His phone beeps next to him, and I glance over at the text message that flashes on the screen. It's from Jess.

Luke's gone. I'll try to track him down before the next shuttle leaves.

"Still trust him?" Max asks, his eyes closed. It's a rhetorical question.

I don't know what to believe. Max certainly struck a cord

when he confronted Luke about only selling tacos and beers. Was he selling drugs? The restaurant could have been a cover. I've never seen Luke do drugs. And I would know. I worked in the restaurant-and-bar industry in New York. I could always tell when someone came in off their face on Molly or coke or high on weed. I've seen Luke drunk plenty of times, but that's it.

But you don't have to use to sell.

Max's phone pings again. I glance back over at it, unable to help myself.

Sorry I left you alone to babysit. She should be here looking for this asshole, not me. xoxo J

My cheeks blaze as I realize she's referring to me. So that's what Max thinks of me. I'm some child he's babysitting. He and Jess must have had a good laugh about that. Well, fuck them. Sorry, but, really? Babysitting! I don't need him. I've gotten this far. Once we get to Parismina, he can continue on and follow up with his precious story, and I'll find Sonja. On my own.

And once I do, I can finally go home and figure out what the hell went wrong with my life.

Eleven

W ell, this is miserable.

Max and I ride the whole way in silence. I'm pissed—not that he's noticed—he's lost in the music on his headphones, typing into his phone every once in a while. I'm sure talking crap about me to Jess. When we reach the end of the jungle road where the Reventazón River meets the ocean, I can't take it anymore.

"Are you mad at me?" I demand.

Max blinks, his blue eyes looking startled, but he doesn't answer right away, grabbing his bag and following the small crowd off the shuttle behind me. I swipe at the sweat that drips down my forehead. Now that there's no wind from the van, the humidity is attacking me.

"I'm mad at myself." He speeds ahead through the sandy jungle path, and I'm running to keep up.

"Why?"

"For not listening to my gut. I knew Luke was no good."

"Hey! We still don't know what happened," I say as we walk toward the ocean. I assume it's the ocean. The breezy, salty air is getting stronger and the sand thicker under our feet as I follow Max down the path. "His phone could have been stolen from the bathroom. He may be trying to find it. You know how sacred phones are these days."

It's getting harder to keep up with Max as the dirt under our feet turns completely into soft sand. I'm sinking farther into it with each step, and my calves are starting to burn. My cheeks are blazing from anger and the suffocating heat.

"Are you kidding me, Bloom?" Max exhales loudly, exasperation wrapping around his words. "He never lost his phone. It was with him the whole time. He used it as an excuse to get off the van and run away. You really know how to pick 'em, don't you?" We spill out onto the beach, and it looks like every other beach we've been on in Costa Rica and Panama: white sand, palm and mangrove trees hanging over the crystal blue-green waters, surfers and casual swimmers riding the waves, sunbathers under thatched umbrellas sipping raw coconuts and beers. "Just because you like a guy doesn't make him honest."

"I know that, but I don't just like him. We've shared a lot. He was a good friend. What if you woke up next week, and your money was gone, and you knew Jess took it? Would you automatically hate her or distrust her? No. It would be more complicated than that," I say, sweat beads dripping down my back and chest. He goes to speak but I cut in, "Why are you still here? To find more information on this big story? Because it sure as hell doesn't feel like you're here for me." I stop, tired of running after Max.

He turns around when he realizes I am no longer walking behind him. "I am here for you. To help you."

"Well, you suck at it."

His face grows hot, and it's not from the sun. "Excuse me?"

"You say you're my friend, and friends are meant to care about each other and, yeah, sometimes make them face up to hard truths, but you're being a real asshole and completely unhelpful. I get it. I trusted the wrong person, but I don't have a heart of stone like you. I can't just shut my emotions off."

Max takes a deep breath. "I'm sorry, Nat. I am. But haven't you ever had a friend who infuriates you because every time they should go right, they go left? And you want to shake them and yell, 'Go right!' 'Go right!' 'Go right!' until they listen to you. Because you care about them, and you want what's best for them."

His words vibrate truth inside me, and I do have a friend like that, my cousin Beth. She always dated the wrong guys, men who would walk all over her and string her along because she let them. Catie and I would beg her to dump these deadbeats and players, but she always had a thousand excuses for their detached behavior. She never listened to us. It wasn't until she fell in love and discovered the man was cheating on her that she realized she needed to change.

But I don't feel like I'm that blind. I'm not forgiving Luke or letting him off the hook. I just don't want to jump to conclusions until I have all the information. And Max—always sensible—only sees the hard facts and wants to be judge and jury. No matter what he says, it's not helpful. If he wanted to be a good friend, he'd trust me and be supportive instead of questioning my motives and dragging me down. A friend should lift you up.

"I don't want your help anymore. I want you to"—a thousand thoughts rush through my head, but I land on one—"go away. Go find that guy for your story. That's why you're really here. Otherwise you'd be back in Panama nursing Jess from her fake injuries." I stomp past him. "I don't need a babysitter! And I don't need you!"

Does he follow me? Does he tell me he's wrong, and he's sorry? No. He lets me walk away. God, am I Beth in this scenario? Is Max the uncaring asshole who was just using me? But it's not like he was trying to get in my pants. That's what

I wanted, but now I'm not sure I do anymore. I know he's been through a lot, and he's been running from the tragedy of his parents' deaths for years. I know it's why he runs from country to country, and it's probably why he ended up with an army unit in Afghanistan. He's punishing himself or running from the pain of his reality, afraid that if he ever settled down, he'd realize he's alone. Even if he's not.

Thoughts race through my brain, blocking my sense of direction. I have no idea if I'm going the right way in search of the beach Sonja was on. There are a couple of beachside eateries and more thatched umbrellas with lounge chairs under them. If this isn't where Sonja took the picture, then someone should be able to point me in the right direction.

If I do find Sonja, I can prove to myself, and to Max, that I'm right. Or if I'm wrong, then at least I'll know.

As I reach the far section of the beach, I see a man wobbling, trying to balance on something between two trees. I walk closer, and it's the slacklines with the sign that reads *Don't relax, get slacked* next to it. Yes! I found it. I shoot my head around the beach bar and restaurant and then toward the bathers and swimmers on the beach, but I don't see anyone that looks like Sonja.

"Excuse me." I approach the dark-haired girl behind the bar. She looks like most of the bartenders down here: young, pretty, a spattering of tattoos on her arms and back.

"Yes." The girl gives me a half smile.

"I'm looking for a friend of mine. Her name's Sonja." The girl stares. "She's about five five, dark-brown hair past her shoulders, slender. Teaches yoga," I add when the girl continues to stare at me with her cocoa eyes.

"Don't know her."

I exhale, looking for someone else who may be more helpful when the girl adds, "But Amya might. She runs the beach yoga classes. Over there."

Following her finger, I see a large open-air structure about fifty yards into the jungle. I walk down the narrow path, avoiding a trail of leafcutter ants marching across the path, looking like little soldiers carrying chunks of leaves five times the size of their bodies. As I approach the structure, I realize a yoga class is in session. I pause at the top of the platform and scan the yogis. There are six students bent over, touching their toes. Suddenly, they jump their feet back into a plank and pop their heads up as they shift into upward-facing dog.

At the front of the class, the instructor, another young, pretty girl with a sprinkling of tattoos, sees me. She smiles and lifts one of her hands (still holding a perfect upward-facing dog) and beckons me to join. I hesitate for a moment, feeling like a voyeur standing at the back watching all the bodies moving in synchronicity into downward dog. I'm guessing the instructor at the front is Amya. She's several inches shorter than me with dark indigo hair to her chin.

Amya has stopped demonstrating and is walking toward me, telling everyone to continue the *vinyasa* on their own. "Hi," she whispers. "Come in. You can take this spot." She guides me to a green mat at the back of the class next to a pale, freckly guy with short dreadlocks sticking off his head like a hedgehog.

At the front of the class, Amya is back in downward-facing dog, and I bend over, my back cracking at the effort, reaching my hands out in front of me. My calves burn, resisting the stretch they need after practically running over the soft, sandy beach when I was chasing Max.

Oh, holy hell, this is uncomfortable.

My dress slides down my back and around my head. I push it back up over my butt, which sticks up in the inverted position, but when she instructs us to lift our right feet up toward the sky, the dress is back around my head. My choices are to fight with this damn dress all through the class, or take it off and do yoga in my teeny-tiny bikini with my ass hanging out.

No, thank you.

I let my dress stay over my head, exposing my butt anyway, as I bend the knee back and then push the leg through to one of the warrior poses. Warrior one, I think. My dress thankfully falls back down around my body in this upright pose. But then we're back in downward-facing dog, and I'm lifting my left leg, and the dress is around my face.

I'm thankful when she instructs us to lie on our backs and leads the group through several bridge poses. I shove my hips in the air, the dress falling onto my face and restricting my breathing. I puff the light fabric off my mouth and nose. All I want is to ask her a few questions. Hopefully, participating in her class will make her more willing to answer me. Finally, she asks us to lie on our backs, close our eyes, and rest in *savasana*.

When she rings a bell, indicating the end of the class, I snatch the hem of my dress and wipe the sweat off my face and neck. A couple of students thank the instructor, but everyone quickly leaves, and it's only the two of us.

"Great class," I say. It was, even though my body protested at every juncture. "My name's Natalie."

Her hands flutter and then run through her hair self-consciously. "Amya."

"I was wondering…I'm looking for someone. A friend of mine who also teaches yoga."

From the dark wood railing closest to her, Amya takes a folded towel and a spray bottle and goes down the line of mats, spraying and wiping them clean.

"Her name's Sonja. She arrived yesterday."

Amya is bent over one of the mats, scrubbing at a stain. When it's gone, she stands. "I don't know the name. What does she look like?"

"Same build as you, but dark-black hair several inches longer than yours. And a little younger than you. I think." It's hard to tell since I've never actually seen her face.

"A lot of girls look like that." Amya smiles up at me, sweeping the rag over the last mat. She puts the bottle and towel down and picks up two of the mats, draping them over the far railing. I bend down, my calves protesting, picking up the yoga mat next to me and hanging it on the railing next to the other mats. "But it doesn't ring a bell. Did you two get separated on your travels?"

"Kind of," I say, finding it hard to lie.

She stops. "Are you sure you have the right place?"

"Yeah," I say, resting against the railing once all the mats are hung. "She posted a picture on the slacklines yesterday."

"Slacklines?" Amya whips her head at me. "Oh, right. I think they're new." Halfway down the steps, Amya turns, waiting for me, and I hurry after her, slipping my shoes back on. "Sorry I couldn't be more help."

We're walking farther into the jungle, down a packed-sand path lined with small oval rocks, and I'm trying desperately to stand straight and not wince at every step.

What a wimp. Twenty minutes of yoga and I can barely stand straight.

"It's okay. I thought she might have inquired about teaching a yoga class here. That's what she does. She's a yoga instructor. Like you, I guess. Except you run this program, the bartender said."

"Yeah. On and off for about three years now." We reach a narrow path, which leads farther away from the beach toward the river, and Amya stops. "How long are you going to be around?"

"I'm not sure. Probably a day or two. Until I can locate Sonja."

Amya starts down the path, which I now see leads to a small cabin. When she's five steps in, she stops. "Why don't I take your e-mail, and if I see her, I'll let you know."

I give her my address and thank her again for the class. When I'm sure she's out of sight, I limp back to the beach.

My body feels the same as my spirit. Broken. I've reached another dead end. I wanted to find Sonja and find out if Luke was telling the truth about her and about all of it. I need to know.

But in the end, will it change the facts? No. Luke still took my money, and that money is now gone. But Luke has to have some money, even if he lost all of mine. He retired at thirty-five. You don't do that without a lot of money in the bank or stocks or whatever he invested in. If he won't willingly pay me back, then it may be time to look into my legal options.

But if Luke is selling drugs, it could be dangerous.

I walk back into the small village and find the first hotel that has Wi-Fi and sit on the front stoop. I connect my phone and send Max a text asking if he's heard from Jess. I want answers. Real answers.

A moment later, my phone pings with a text. *She found Luke. He's refusing to leave.*

Great. Max was most likely right about Luke.

My phone vibrates, and I expect another message from Max, but my eyes widen when I read the address. It's an e-mail from Amya.

Natalie,

I talked to one of the slackline enthusiasts down by the bar, and he says he met your friend Sonja last night. She told him she was heading to a town farther inland today called Batán.

I hope this helps!
Amya

My head hurts. My calves hurt. My heart hurts. I just want

this to be over. I don't want to get on another bus and go to another town where whomever I'm looking for will be gone by the time I get there.

Against my better judgment—and even though I told him I don't need his help—I text Max back.

Just found out Sonja has gone to Batan.

Batan? There's nothing in Batan!

Well that's where she is! And that's where I'm going!

I feel the need for a lot of exclamation points right now.

Then I'm coming too

No way!

Yes way

"I'm coming."

I practically jump out of my skin at Max's voice behind me.

"How did you...never mind." The sight of him is a relief, but I don't let him know that.

"I'm coming," he states. It isn't a suggestion. And I don't argue.

Twelve

M ax is right. There's nothing in Batán. Certainly not
Sonja. It's a pass-through town with a few colorful
buildings but not a tourist destination. Sonja would have
stuck out like a spider on cotton candy here—especially if she
was planning to stay and teach yoga. There's no one to teach.
The yoga industry is geared toward the backpackers and
tourists who travel through Costa Rica, not the locals. And
this town is all locals.

I don't understand. The bartender in Parismina must have
misunderstood her. There's no way this was Sonja's
destination. Max hasn't said much, letting me writhe in my
own witlessness for even being in this mess. For a moment, I
was pleased Max insisted on coming with me, until I realized
the drug dealer he's interviewing lives close to this town.

"I have about an hour until my meeting," Max says. "The
guy lives about ten miles from here, and I'm not leaving you
in this town by yourself. But..." Max looks at my outfit. I'm
still in the maxi dress and bathing suit. It's become my
unfortunate uniform. Water splashes my ankles and the hem
of my dress as a family of three, squeezed onto one flimsy

bike, glides by. It seems everyone in this town owns a bike. Not even the bit of rain that fell when we first arrived did anything to deter the cyclists. "It's a mile hike through the jungle. We can bike to the trailhead, but the only way to get to his house is by foot or by horse."

I'm not equipped for either mode of transportation. My Toms are flimsy for a hike and will get stuck in the thick mud, and my thighs will be chafed raw if I wear a dress on one of the jungle horses. Across from us is a bright-green storefront with colorfully patterned children's backpacks hanging out front. It looks like they sell everything from shampoo to hammers.

Along the short strip of shops, there's a shoe store, a restaurant with a big chicken over its sign, and a small eatery. That's it. Having no other choice, we go inside the backpack store, which looks the most promising. Max pulls a pair of cheap cargo pants off a rack and hands them to me. I look but can't find any shoes, and the shoe store two doors down had a *cerrado* sign on it. I'm stuck with my flimsy Toms.

"So I guess we're horseback riding." I take the pants to the register and fish out the bit of cash I have. Before I can pay, Max thrusts a handful of bills at the cashier. I don't argue. He's the reason I have no clothes.

Outside, a large cloud overtakes the sun, and I'm thankful for the moment of relief from the hot afternoon heat. I pull the pants on and tie the skirt of my dress in a knot high on my waist.

"You'll need to take it off."

"No way." I am not being jostled around on a horse in just a bikini top.

"The dress will get caught on a branch and rip or, worse, pull you from the horse."

But I refuse. I'll keep it tight to my body and tuck the extra fabric between my thighs, but I am not taking it off. Max shakes his head but doesn't argue any further. It's not like I want to be in this dress. My suitcase was filled with practical outfits and shoes.

"Is this a good idea?" I ask as we come to a store that has a sign offering shuttle trips to different cities. "By the time we find this guy you're interviewing, it's going to be late in the afternoon."

"He may not be there tomorrow. We have to go now. And I'm not leaving you here alone."

"Dammit, Max. I'm a grown woman. I don't need to be minded like a child." I cross my arms as Max approaches the ancient man who sits behind the counter, listening to what sounds like a sportscast in Spanish from a small radio. "I'm not the one who fell in a swarm of jellyfish, couldn't get into Costa Rica, and gets sick on car rides."

Max grinds his teeth, making his jaw muscles flex, and stares at me. His stern look makes my heart race in anticipation of terse words about to be released from his mouth, but instead, he exhales and turns to the man, speaking in Spanish. The short man keeps his eyes on the radio and shakes his head. Max argues, and his voice becomes urgent.

"Spanish, Spanish, Spanish," Max insists.

"Spanish, Spanish," the guy answers back.

"Spanish, Spanish, *Spanish, Spanish, Spanish!*" Max yells.

"*Spanish! Spanish!*" the guy yells back.

They stare at each other, breathing heavily. Finally, Max shoves some money into the guy's hand, and he relents. He yells toward the back, and an older Costa Rican man with a thick mop of salt-and-pepper hair comes out, sipping from a can of Coke. The younger guy explains what we want, and the older man gives us a look that suggests we might be crazy but then shrugs his shoulders and takes the money.

Twenty minutes later, we're saddled up on three horses—which are scrawny and in need of a good grooming—and trotting slowly down the dirt road, our guide leading the way. The sun has fallen behind the buildings on our left and then disappears behind the trees as we leave the village. About a mile out, we turn left into the jungle on an ungroomed path. We're being jostled and jerked around; the horses' hooves are unable to find solid footing on the muddy jungle path; tree roots and fallen branches are scattered across the trail. Not that it's much of a trail. Our guide is off his horse more than on it as he takes his machete and clears the path. An hour into the ride, my thighs ache from gripping tightly to my horse's sides.

"How much longer?" I ask, slapping a mosquito that's sucking blood from my arm. My horse stumbles, and I grip tightly to the reins—a ratty piece of rope—righting myself.

Max speaks to our guide, who is back on his horse.

"We're almost there," Max tells me after the guide answers him. It's the only thing Max has said to me since we left town. Is he mad at me? I'm the one who should be mad. He hasn't turned out to be the most reliable friend. Not since Jess arrived.

We make a sharp turn, and suddenly, the path opens up to a field, several shack houses lining the far side. My horse begins to pick up speed, but before I pass the guide, he grabs the rope from my hands, stopping me. Max saunters up next to my horse.

"Stay here." Max trots ahead, calling over his shoulder, "I'll be back soon." Then he stops, turning his horse to face me. "If you don't see me in thirty minutes, don't come looking. Go back without me."

"No way," I say. I'm not leaving Max in the middle of the jungle with a drug dealer. Ignoring me, Max speaks rapidly in Spanish, stumbling over words, but his voice is insistent and low. Our guide nods to whatever Max has made him agree to, which I'm assuming is taking me back, kicking and screaming if he has to, if Max doesn't return.

What the hell has Max gotten into? Why is this story so important to him? I know he's traveled and reported on stories all over Europe and Asia and a bit in the Middle East, but going off into the jungles of Central America to follow up on a story he hasn't even convinced an editor to print seems crazy.

My heart is in my throat as the minutes tick by. Our guide—whose name I ask, but he ignores me or has no idea what I'm saying—sits in the shade, sleeping against a tree. I'm too anxious to do anything but pace the border of the field. Bending down, I take a look closer at the plants I'm stomping over and suddenly recognize the leaves.

It's a field of cannabis.

This is bad. *So, so, so* bad.

I back away, worried some guy with a machine gun is going to suddenly appear and yell at me for stomping on their precious crops like the scene in that movie, *The Beach*, where the backpackers run through a field of marijuana plants and get shot.

Looking at my phone, which is in the canvas bag I carry, I see it has been thirty-five minutes. Our guide is still asleep, and I don't dare wake him, in case he tries to force me to leave with him. The sun is setting, and the trip back is going to be dark. This guide better be one of those locals that grew up in the jungle and can get us back just by sensing his way.

I chew on my nails, my lip, and the inside of my cheek. Where is Max? My eyes are fixed on the shack he entered. Finally, I see movement. Max appears, and I let out the breath I'd been holding in. He walks across the field, his horse in tow. Really? I'm about to have a heart attack, and he acts like he's sauntering out of a saloon in a Western instead of walking across a field of drugs.

"I told you to leave if I was late," Max says, but his voice is light, joyful.

"I wasn't leaving you."

He blinks and then cracks a smile. "We better wake our guide if we're gonna beat the sunset."

Back on my horse, I don't ask Max about his meeting, but with his mood shift, I'd say he got what he wanted. As the jungle darkens, I can't see more than two feet in front of me, and the horse seems to be having the same problem. He stumbles and trips, and I'm gripping his sides, my palms slick with sweat. Max insists I stay between him and the guide, just in case. In case what? The guide takes off? We get lost? Some psycho comes out of the brush and tries to snatch me?

The blackness circles us fast as any sign of the sun disappears. The sound of my horse's staccato breathing is my only source of comfort. I turn, but I can't see Max behind me. I know he's there because I can hear the *clip-clopping* of his horse, which is suddenly becoming faster. A rush of wind brushes against me, and I realize his horse has galloped past.

"Max!" I yell.

He yells unintelligibly back, his voice far ahead. A noise in the brush makes my horse suddenly startle. He bucks, and the next thing I feel is air underneath me and then the hard ground as I land on the path.

"Oomph." I moan, after landing hard on my right side. I suck air into my lungs, recovering, and realize I'm alone in the dark. Except for the cicadas and the chirping of a creature I can't place—lizard, bird, other?—it is silent. No horse hooves, no heavy breathing, no Max reassuring me.

Then I hear it. The sound that spooked the horses. It's a deep, guttural growling, and I scoot back against a tree, not caring that I'm sinking into watery mud, and make myself small. The howling comes again, closer, and I cover my ears.

Please don't find me. I'm not that tasty, and I can't smell good. I haven't showered, and my clothes are really starting to stink from only being washed in showers and sinks. Move on. Find some other small animal that is much more appetizing. The howling grows nearer, and my heart is pounding so fast I think I'm going to pass out from fear.

My arms wrap around my head and ears, and I sink into

the ground, praying to anything and anyone who will listen, begging that I won't get eaten alive. I'm not that tasty. Really. I know good food. I'm not it.

Something hard brushes against me. I scream, jumping sideways. Instead of curling up in a ball, I should make myself look big and intimidating, but I can't bring myself to stand and stretch my arms out. This confirms that in a crisis, I'm not the fighting kind of girl. I'm not even the flight kind. I'm the curl-up-and-give-up kind of girl. Surprise, surprise.

"Natalie!"

I start at the sound of my name. "Max," I whisper, still worried about whatever creature has been hunting me.

"Speak up. I can't see anything!"

"Max!" I yell as two arms find me and pull me up. I can't see him in the darkness, but I can feel his breath close to my cheek, and my heart immediately unfreezes, beating rapidly. He puts his arm around me and leads me ten feet into a break in the trees, and we step out onto the road. The guide is waiting on the street, looking bored, our horses standing calmly next to him.

I was ten feet from the road? And yet I curled up, ready to be eaten. "Something spooked the horse. And tried to eat me."

Max laughs, but when he sees the fear in my wide eyes, he stops, hugging me closer. "It was howler monkeys. Harmless."

"Tell that to my horse who bucked me off."

"My horse got spooked too."

When I realize Max is leading me back to my horse, I dig my heels in. "I'm not getting back on that beast. I'll walk."

Instead of arguing, he takes the reins from both our horses, and we walk back together. My dress is ripped and caked in mud. I rip off the ruined garment and leave it on the side of the road. Max is startled by my sudden striptease but says nothing.

Once we reach town, Max books a room in a small motel in the village. It's not much better than a hostel, there's a layer of grime on most surfaces, the shower tiles are orange and broken from use, but I don't care. All I care about is the clean shower. I breathe a sigh of momentary joy as the warm water of the shower washes over me.

I pull on the only spare outfit I have in my bag, my mom's navy one-piece swimsuit and the short pink paisley beach wrap. It feels deliciously clean against my skin.

"Did you speak to Jess?" I ask as I emerge from the small bathroom. Max sits on one of the twin beds, his computer on his lap. Max and I aren't traveling back until he can finish his research into this Thomas Carmel story. He won't tell me exactly what he discovered during his interview today, but it must be good. He needs one more day to confirm the kidnapping was a hoax.

"Luke is still refusing to leave, and Jess won't leave him alone." Max snaps his laptop shut. "Luke is Jess's new mission. She's determined not to let him out of her sight until she gets him up here," Max says. I didn't realize she needed a mission, but I guess that's been her life for the past decade. It must be hard to let go.

I can hear the water running as Max takes his turn in the shower, and I lie on one of the beds, enjoying the moment of calm. I try to log on to the Wi-Fi on my phone, but it isn't connecting. Max has one of those devices installed on his computer that allows him to connect to a digital network even if there's no Wi-Fi. I click on the mouse pad, and his screen comes to life.

I move the mouse to open Safari, but one of the e-mails in his inbox catches my eyes before I click off the screen. Catie's name is in the subject line followed by the word *takedown*. I click on the e-mail. It's from Gus, his friend that's an editor at *The Huffington Post*.

Max,

The lead in the Carmel story sounds promising, but I'm not convinced yet.

Regarding the Catelyn Bloom exposé: Was Natalie Bloom bribed or in anyway forced to commit the fraud or was she a willing participant? It wasn't clear from your last e-mail. Do you have any behind-the-scenes photos or footage from the homecoming shoot that could be useful for the story? And you're sure your aunt had no idea? Catelyn worked at her magazine for four years.

Send information as you get it. We're running the piece in a week.

Gus

I have to read the e-mail two more times to fully comprehend the meaning, since my ears are buzzing, and the room is spinning. My hand holds my stomach; I'm feeling sick. So this is why Max came on the trip. To get information. Information for a takedown piece about my sister. About both of us. How could I have been so stupid and naïve? He doesn't care about me. He cares about his career.

What did he do? Sell the story to the highest bidder when he fond out Catie was a fraud? This whole time he's been patronizing me, making me feel silly and naïve for trusting Luke when Max has been lying to me and using me this whole time. How has this happened again? How did I let it happen? What is wrong with me?

The shower shuts off, and I quickly forward the e-mail to

myself and then mark it as unread and dart back to the bed, gathering my few belongings and stuffing them into my bag. Then I run out the door.

Thirteen

I don't get far. There's nowhere to go in this horrible town. I'm walking in circles, unsure where to go. There aren't any more shuttles until tomorrow, and Max and I were staying at the only hotel in town. I nearly toss my phone on the pavement when I realize it's useless without Wi-Fi. Catie needs to know Max is writing a takedown piece about her. She can contact Gillian Kennedy and let her know what her nephew is planning. Gillian can put a stop to it. When a taxi appears, honking to get my attention, I shoot my hand out. The next town east, Estrada, is only ten minutes away. I'll find a hotel and figure out what to do.

If Max writes this piece, it won't just ruin Catie's life and mine, it will hurt Gillian's reputation and all her publications. Gillian will recover, but Catie won't. And I can say good-bye to a career as a prominent and respected chef. All trust would be wiped out. I'd be the girl who helped Catelyn Bloom defraud the American public.

Martha Stewart wasn't perfect, but her fraud had to do with money, not her business or brand. Unlike Catie, who is a very talented interior designer but hopeless in the kitchen or organizing, Martha Stewart really is a domestic goddess. And let's not forget, Catie fooled everyone into thinking she was blissfully married, when in fact she wasn't married. Not really. Yes, America's favorite wife and homemaker is a lie. And I helped her execute the lie. For years. In a very big way. And now it's come back to bite me in the ass. I really thought I was done with it all, but thanks to my blind love for Max, I fell right into his trap.

The realization of this is crushing me, making my eyes water and my heart hurt, because it means Max never cared about me.

When the cab drops me off in front of a rundown motel, I use the emergency credit card my mom gave me to book a room. I thought I was done protecting Catie, but her life keeps seeping back into mine. I connect my phone to the Wi-Fi and call Catie using FaceTime Audio.

"Is everything okay?" Catie asks when she answers. "Max left me an urgent message to call him."

"When? What did he say?"

"Just now. I called him back but it went straight to voice mail. What's going on?"

I tell her about the e-mail I found. There's silence on the other end, but I know she's there because I can hear her breathing quicken.

"That doesn't sound like Max," Catie says.

"Trust me, of all people, I don't want to believe it either, but it was there. In writing." Catie doesn't respond right away. I can hear rustling in the background. "Is Sam there?"

"No. Still in the Alps." She doesn't sound happy, but she doesn't elaborate. "Where are you now?"

"I'm in a hotel in Estrada. I was so upset I ran out of the motel Max and I were staying in and took a cab to the next town. I'll head back to Panama tomorrow."

"What are you doing? Go back and confront him," Catie says. "Find out if it's true. And if it is, and he knows we know, he may reconsider. And if not, we can try to get ahead of the story."

"But if he knows we know, he may print it sooner," I say, sitting on the scratchy comforter of the double bed, the springs squeaking.

"It doesn't sound like him." Catie's voice is garbled as she takes a sip of something. I hear her swallow, and her voice is clearer. "It's not just me. Why would he do that to his aunt? You have to go back and ask him."

My voice goes quiet, and I realize part of me still wants to believe he wouldn't do this. But it was there in black and white. "He's not printing it for another week. Right now our advantage is that he doesn't know we know about it." Suddenly, I remember Max questioning me on the zip line. "He was grilling me about it earlier this week. I thought he was just curious, but he was digging up information." I look out into the night through the cloudy window, the darkness seeping into my already depressed soul. "I forwarded his e-mail to me. Hold on. I'll send it to you. You'll see."

"What did he ask you?" Catie asks. I hear her tapping on her computer keys.

"He wanted to know who else knew about you."

Catie stops tapping and doesn't speak, reading the e-mail, I assume.

"Did you read it?" I finally ask.

"Turn around and confront him." Catie's voice is shrill, panicky. My shoulders slump. I don't think it's a good idea. Sensing my resistance, Catie continues. "Grow a pair, and go find Max. Now!"

"Fine!" I yell, hanging up. Sisters suck. But I don't move. I still think it's better not to confront Max yet. Once Catie and I both have time to calm down and think more clearly, then I'll formulate a plan. I peel off the stiff comforter and place my phone on silent. Then I fall into a restless sleep.

***

I wake up early but there are no buses out of Estrada. The closest shuttle leaves from the next town over. Luckily, cab rides are cheap, or I'd be stuck. Catie hasn't called or e-mailed me by morning, even though it's several hours ahead in New York. I don't call her. If I did, she'd grill me about my confrontation with Max, which never happened.

It's early, and there aren't many cabs out, so I walk about a mile before I find one heading out of town. The cab is dirty, dirtier than the others I've traveled in, and the driver is blasting Bob Marley. It seems a bit early to be jamming to Rastafarian music, and I suspect he may have already enjoyed his first, or fifth, smoke of the day, but it's hot, I'm sweaty, and it's the only taxi I've seen for the last twenty minutes, and I want to get out of this town.

I'm slammed into the back of my seat as he speeds ahead, and I close my eyes. There's no air conditioning, and the morning sun is already scorching. The road is rough and bumpy—like all the roads here—but I relax when we turn southeast, and the sun disappears behind the heavy jungle foliage on either side of the car. The temperature cools slightly, and I'm lulled off to sleep.

When I open my eyes, I forget where I am. The bump, bump, bump of the road jostles my memory, and I look around the cab at my confined surroundings. I blink, but it takes me a moment to realize there's another passenger in the car sitting next to the driver. He has dark hair tied back in a messy ponytail.

His hand is out the window, a rolled cigarette or joint hanging loosely from his fingers. Gazing back, his lazy eyes meet mine, and he nudges the driver, who looks back at me as I come out of my slumber.

"How much longer?" I ask, looking hurriedly out the window for any bit of civilization, but it's jungle on all sides. We should've been to the town by now.

"Not far," the driver says.

I pull out my phone and tap on the home button rapidly, but it's dead. We take a sharp turn down a muddy jungle path that's heavy with overgrowth. My gut tightens, and I yank the door handle, but it's locked. I try to pull the lock up, but it won't budge. The tightness from my gut reaches my throat, and I slide to the other door and jerk the handle. It flies open, and my body tumbles out of the moving car onto the muddy path.

They stop the car and get out, laughing, but instead of coming toward me, they disappear into the jungle. Everything in my body tenses. Where are they? Where am I? I snap my head in the direction we came from and stumble to my feet.

My feet slip in the slick mud as I rush forward. Behind me, the men reemerge from the dense jungle with a woman beside them, and I break into a sprint but fall as I trip over an exposed root. The woman is rushing in front of me, standing above me. She's short and squat, with long, stringy black hair and dark skin. Her clothes are dirty, and she's barefoot. She grabs my arm, hard, pulling me up. She speaks rapidly to me in Spanish, her right hand moving back and forth as she speaks. My throat closes like a Venus flytrap when I realize she holds a knife in her hand.

My eyes lock on to the blade, and for a moment, it's all I see. My ears close up, sound disappearing, but she begins going into almost hysterics, shaking me, the knife coming closer to my chest.

"I…I don't understand. I don't speak…no…no hablo Español." I'm trembling, finding it hard to speak. This woman with the knife is more terrifying than the two men standing back smirking at us. She's pointing the knife at my canvas bag. Not willing to risk my life for the measly contents—a few stinky clothes, my phone, and ten bucks—I hand it to her. She pockets the phone and pulls out the few dollars that are left. She tosses the clothes aside. Holding the emptied bag in front of my face, she takes the knife and rips through the fabric, the tearing sound making bile rise as I imagine the sound of my own flesh ripping apart.

"That's all I have." My voice is a squeak, terrified, and my knees suddenly feel like someone kicked the back of them. I'd collapse to the ground, but she's holding my arm so tight, I can't. Her grip constricts, and I wince. I can already feel the bruises forming. Her voice is rising feverishly, and she shoves me, and I fall to my knees. She beckons the man with the ponytail over and gives him the knife to hold. My eyes are on the blade as the woman's hands start groping me, and I wonder if I'm going to get sexually assaulted by this woman while the men watch. Can a woman do that? I mean, I know she can, but it seems surreal. She shoves her hands under my dress until she finds what she's looking for—my passport.

It was tucked between my breasts. Done with me, she gives me one last shove—to show me who's boss, I guess, as if I didn't already know—and I fall on my face, my forehead hitting a rock.

"Ugh." I wince, my entire body trembling as if I'm outside in zero-degree weather instead of ninety-degree heat.

I hear the not-so-altruistic three musketeers talking rapidly and then the cab doors slamming. Quickly, I scoot to the side of the road as the car turns around and speeds off in the direction we came from.

For several minutes, I sit at the edge of the jungle path, waiting for my heart rate to return to a somewhat normal pace. Blood is trickling down my brow and cheek, and I take the bottom of my short dress and hold it to the cut. When I pull the hem down, it's soaked in blood. Head wounds look worse than they really are, but the thought only comforts me a little.

When I stand to walk, I realize that I twisted my ankle when that bitch spun me around. *Dammit! Can't a girl get a break?!* My ankle is about as tender as my nerves, and my limp worsens the farther I walk. I'm pissed, and I'm tired, and I just want to get the hell out of here.

The path is muddy and uneven. I fall a couple of times, scraping my knees. "Ugh!" I scream at the jungle, as if it's to blame.

My legs and arms are covered in mud by the time I get to the main road. I have no idea where I am, but I walk in the direction of the sun, since it would still be mostly facing east, toward the water.

I hear a car rumbling down the road, and I tuck into the trees, terrified it's the cab driver and his psycho lady friend coming back for more. But I have no more to give. Crouching down, I wait for the car to pass. It's a beat-up truck—there really isn't any other kind of car here; nothing is new in this country; everything is old and battered.

As I clamor back onto the road, my throat becomes sticky with thirst. Keeping my eyes peeled on the underbrush, I look for coconuts that have just fallen from trees. The first two I find are broken open, their sweet liquid long gone. The third one I find is green and hard, and I hear the water swooshing around the inside when I shake it. Finding a sharp rock, I bang the side of the coconut on it. I'm so into my task, which isn't going so well, that I don't hear the vehicle coming down the road until it's almost upon me. Crouching down, I scoot into the brush but then realize it's one of the shuttle buses.

I stand up as quick as I can and wave my hands. It zooms past me.

What the hell? Come on. I know I look like death, but you'd think someone would make the bus stop. It's got to be loaded with backpackers and tourists. I stare after it, feeling scorned and taking it very personally. Then it slows and stops a hundred yards ahead.

Is this a mirage? My hands still grip the coconut as two bodies walk off the bus before it drives away again. As they come closer, I shake my head in disbelief—which aches in protest—but yes, it's them! Luke and Jess! Luke drops his bag and runs to me, gathering me up like a child and laying me in his lap, inspecting me.

"Natalie! It is you! Oh my God. What happened? Who did this? Where are you hurt?"

"Water," I say, but it comes out in a croak.

"Of course!" He hands me a bottle from his bag and looks me over as I gulp the liquid. His eyes are a little wild as he takes in my bloody face, his hand hovering over my cut.

I clear my throat. "Thank you."

Jess stands over me, blocking me from the sun. "Don't drink so fast," Jess says. "Let your body take it in." Kneeling next to me, she checks my vitals and then gently inspects the cut on my head. Tugging the water from my vice grip, she wets the edge of her shirt and dabs the cut, examining it again. "Just a small laceration. You won't need stitches. Head wounds usually look worse than they are. They bleed like a motherfucker."

It's one of the first times Jess has really looked and sounded like a soldier, and I'm thankful for it.

My head rests back against Luke's rock-hard arm, and I see him widen his eyes at Jess and then look pointedly at something below my waist. His forehead creases, and his lips tighten, worry etched all over his face now. I watch Jess take in what he's silently trying to communicate, and then she lifts my dress, scanning my thigh. I realize what's concerning Luke.

"It's from the cut on my head. I used my dress to try to stop the bleeding." The tension in Luke's arm lessens. "I twisted my ankle, but I don't think it's that bad." At the mention of my injury, Jess lifts and prods my ankle with delicate fingers.

"It's probably just sprained," Jess assures me, placing her arm under my left armpit. Luke does the same with my other arm, and we move a little into the brush, so we're protected from the sun.

"What happened?" Jess asks.

I explain the harrowing events, my palms sweating as I get to the part where they drove me down the secluded jungle path and the crazy woman with a knife roughed me up and stole everything. My body starts to shiver at the recollection.

"Is she okay?" Luke is holding on to me tight.

"She's in shock, but she'll be fine." Jess leans forward as she continues her gentle interrogation. "What were you doing out here in a cab?"

"Trying to get out of this place."

"Why didn't you take the shuttle bus?"

"I was trying to, but the town I was in didn't have one." I close my eyes and rest my head against Luke's shoulder.

"Why?"

"Stop grilling her," Luke says. "It's not her fault those guys robbed her."

"Relax, lover boy, I just want to understand." Jess places her hand lightly on my forearm. "I spoke to Max. He said you left suddenly last night. What happened?"

I open my eyes. Jess looks genuinely curious, trying to get to the bottom of this riddle. "I...I just wanted to go home. I'm tired of chasing after money that's gone."

Luke sucks in a quick breath at my last words.

"So, you just left Max? Without saying anything?"

The shade and water and having Luke's strong body behind me is clearing my head, and I sit up. "I just couldn't be there anymore."

Jess eyes me, wanting to ask more, but doesn't. Luke helps me to my feet, and we start walking back on the road, Luke supporting me as I limp along. When we get to Matina, the town that was my destination, we find a small café, and I go into the tiny bathroom and wipe the blood from my face and the dirt from my body. My face is weathered, dark circles under my eyes, ashen skin, and my hair is a tangled mess.

This is what the stress of this trip has done to me. I feel like I've aged five years in the past few days.

Outside the café, Luke sits on a wicker chair, resting his head back, his eyes closed. A glance at the menu reveals plain food in this plain town. I look back at Luke, his chiseled features soften as he relaxes. He looks youthful and reminds me of his boyish charm and carefree approach to life. It's the reason I opened my life and my kitchen up to him. He always made me laugh and never let me take my business too seriously, reminding me it's about the joy of the journey. Not where it's taking me.

When I first met Max during the shoot, he was like that. But I don't think he'd transitioned back into his life after his injuries. The homecoming shoot was an escape for him. Since then, he's much more serious and has lost that carefree spirit I first loved about him. It's still there sometimes, and I love when I catch a glimpse of it.

I've never seen Luke lose his *joie de vie*. Even after running off with the money. Which, compared to Max's story that is about to destroy both Catie's life and mine, doesn't look so bad now.

"Thank you," I say to Luke, in regard to his help on the side of the road. I'm tempted to lean down and hug Luke, a rush of gratitude washing over me, but I'm not sure I'm meant to be friends with him. I don't know who to believe or trust anymore.

Sensing my hesitation, he says, "You still don't forgive me?"

"How can you ask that? You stole more than my money. You stole my dream," I say, sick of it all.

"I didn't!" he quickly shoots back, sitting upright. "I was trying to help. To make it come true."

My head pounds, a million thoughts and disappointments rushing through my mind. "Let's not talk about this now." My tired body falls back against the plastic chair. I look out across the dusty street at the array of colorful shops. One thing Costa Rica does well is colors. No matter how small the town, the buildings are always painted in an assortment of vibrant hues, bringing out a sense of fun and whimsy. Two feelings that escape me now. "Where's Jess?"

"On the phone with Max."

Suddenly alert, I lean forward. Has Catie spoken to him? Does Jess know about the story he's writing? I've been so consumed from the events of this morning that it never crossed my mind that Jess may be privy to the story. She could be helping him, one of his spies. She already knows I was secretly helping Catie, since she was there after Catie confessed to Gillian during the shoot. But she hasn't asked me any questions about it.

The food Luke ordered for us—eggs, coffee, toast—is placed in front of me, but I hardly touch it, uninspired by the food or by my life.

"What did Max say?" I ask when Jess plops down across from us.

"He's on his way to the town where Thomas Carmel was kidnapped." Jess beckons the waiter over and orders a coffee. "I'm going to meet him this afternoon. After this interview, he's hoping he has everything he needs for the story."

I watch Jess, but there's nothing in her eyes or behavior that suggests an underlying meaning. "Did he say anything else?"

"No." Jess slowly sips her hot coffee, and I want to rip the cup from her mouth and ask her more questions. Was Max concerned at all about my well-being after the attack, or has his only concern been getting information out of me for his other big exposé? But Jess only mentions that Max has broken the kidnapping story wide open, and it should be a big story once it's published.

I guess that's it. I nearly die in the jungle, and when Max finds out, he doesn't rush to my side; he asks his not-so-ex girlfriend to join him for the rest of his journey, which she does right after breakfast.

"Let's go," I say to Luke after Jess leaves for Batán to meet Max. All hope has been leeched from my body.

"Where to?"

"Back to Panama. There are some things I need to take care of. And you're coming with me."

"You'll need a passport," Luke reminds me, kicking up loose cement from the broken street.

Oh, crap. I forgot about that.

"There's a travel agent who can help you back in Parismina," Luke says. "When I, um…lost my own passport, it took a few days, but I was able to get a new one with his help."

"You lost your passport?" I ask as we continue down the main road, avoiding cyclists who seem intent not to swerve to avoid us.

"Uh, yeah. About a week ago."

"In Parismina?" I ask.

"Look, there's the bus. Come on." Luke grabs my hand, and we run to it. I'm not missing this shuttle. I just want to get out of here.

After an uneventful shuttle ride, which Luke pays the five-dollar fare for, we're back in Parismina. The breeze of the salty air already makes me feel better, and Luke's right. We talk to the travel agent, and there'll be a new passport waiting for me tomorrow at another travel agent's office when we reach the border town out of Costa Rica. They even had a photo booth to take my passport photo, which no one will ever be allowed to see.

I'm beat down, but when we get back to Red Frog, I'll be able to think straight, and Mom will infuse me with the last bit of strength I need to figure this all out. Luke will come back to New York with me, I'll make sure of that, and I'll get the money back.

I never thought I'd be so happy to leave a tropical paradise for the urban jungle, but all I want is to pull on a pair of jeans, a sweater, and boots and enjoy an overpriced latte in the cool December air as self-important New Yorkers rush past me. Home.

But right now, there's nothing to do but wait. In the morning, we'll catch the bus back toward Panama. I'm eager to know if Catie has been in touch with Max, but I'm not eager to receive her scolding for running away instead of confronting him, even though I still think it's best if he's in the dark about our knowledge of the story.

"Max told me about that scam," I confess to Luke. We sit on two lounge chairs on the beach, drinking rum cocktails, pretending we're on a real vacation. At least, that's what I'm trying to do. But there's a tornado of emotions and regret running through me, making it hard to truly escape. "With the taxi driver robbing tourists. Those guys won't be happy though. I had almost no money."

"They weren't after your money."

"Huh?" I turn my attention from the rough waves beating the shore to Luke.

"They were after your passport."

"Really?"

"It's big money down here."

"How much?" I ask.

"Five thousand bucks," Luke says without skipping a beat.

I laugh out of surprise more than humor, but he doesn't join me. His eyes stay locked on the surf as it slaps the sand, knocking down a partial sand castle two kids have been building for the past fifteen minutes.

I bolt upright as a thought hits me. "Max was right! You were selling something. But not drugs. You sold your passport. And Sonja's too." Luke doesn't answer, but I know I'm right. "That's what you were doing here in this town, wasn't it? That's how you knew about that travel agent."

Then another thought crosses my mind. "Did you steal anyone else's passport to sell?"

"No!" Luke swings his knees around and faces me. "No. After those vendors in Bocas…after I lost the money—some of the money—in Panama, Sonja told me about a guy she knew here who bought and sold passports on the black market. That's why we came."

I'm shocked by this new information, which must be obvious on my face. "You're a real con artist, Luke Hawker."

"No, I'm not!" He takes my hands, his eyes intense behind his sunglasses. "I'm not, Natalie. I just got in over my head. But I did it for you."

I pull my hands out and turn back toward the beach. "So you've said."

"I mean it. I did this all for you. For us. I…" He shoves his hands through his hair and then gently takes my chin with his fingers, turning my face so I'm looking at him.

I shake him off and drop my head. "I can't take much more, Luke. I just want the truth."

Luke slips off his silver aviator sunglasses, and his sharp-blue eyes take hold of mine. The last time I saw him look this intensely at me was when I was lying beside him after we slept together. He wanted to say something to me then, but I rolled away, not wanting to ruin our brief moment of intimacy with truths I didn't want to hear.

He pulls my sunglasses from my face, not letting me run away this time.

"The truth is…" He hesitates, and my heart drops into my belly in anticipation of his next words. "I love you."

Fourteen

I n front of us, the waves take the last of the ruined sand castle out to sea. The two young boys who built it laugh and stomp on the mounds of shapeless sand. I swing my legs back on my lounge chair, crossing my arms over my body and taking in Luke's confession. "You sure have a funny way of showing it."

"I know I fucked it up, but I came here to prove to you that I'm more than just an investor in your business. I wanted you to see I could be like...like him." Luke shoves his sunglasses back on his face and looks out toward the crashing waves that are growing stronger. Dark clouds and wind have rolled in during the past ten minutes.

Him? Is he referring to Max? They never met until the other day.

"I'm not blind, Natalie. Or deaf. You talk about him all the time, all his travels, adventures, near-death experiences. Wonderful, stoic, brave Max. He lost his parents, was almost killed by a suicide bomber, and became a hero rescuing a little girl in Greece." Luke scowls, keeping his face averted. "How can a guy compete with that?"

I had no idea he wanted to compete. There were moments I felt Luke wanted more than friendship, but I brushed them off. During the cooking lessons, he began asking me more questions about my personal life, my aspirations. It's when we grew closer and truly became friends. But he never asked me out. Not properly. We'd often make a meal out of the food I taught him to make, sitting at a table in the kitchen and splitting a bottle of wine.

"Max is a friend. Nothing more." I resist telling him that Max may be less than a friend now. He may be as big of a con artist as Luke. Except, he's never used love to manipulate me.

"Don't do this, Luke. Don't use love to get out of what you did."

Luke squeezes his fists, causing the muscles in his forearms to tighten. "Dammit, Natalie, I'm not lying. I screwed up. I know that, but I was so angry when I saw you two together. I ran away. I wanted to hurt you at first, because I was hurting." Luke takes a breath. "Don't look at me like that. It's a natural reaction to be angry when you realize the woman you love is in love with another man. But I couldn't stop thinking about you. You've consumed me for the past year. It's all I think about. Everything I've done—the cooking lessons, investing in your restaurant, being a part of your life in every way you'd let me—was to bring me closer to you. I love you. I love every part of you. I love your passion for food, your fiery temper when you're angry, your loyalty to your sister. I love it all."

The wind blows my hair around my face, and a raindrop plops on my legs. A chill runs over my body as his words run around my brain like a storm stirring up everything I thought I knew. As the rain increases, I stand, and we hurry into the jungle onto the large covered platform where I took the yoga class the other day.

A crash of thunder roars in the sky, and I jump. Luke rests

against the small stage at the front of the open room. The rain waterfalls around us as it cascades off the flat roof and splatters onto the floor. I move to the center of the room, avoiding most of the downpour.

"So the whole stealing my money and coming down to Panama was meant to win my love?" A hysterical laugh pops out of my mouth, but Luke's expression is so grave, I bite my lip, holding it back. "It's hard to believe."

"In hindsight, I see how stupid it was. But I was in such a state when I saw...when I realized..." Letting out an exasperated sigh, he pushes off the stage and paces the wood floor. "I had to get away. But love makes you stupid. I thought if I could make some money fast and in a way that wasn't just investing in some high-risk, high-reward stock, you'd want me like you want him." Crossing his arms protectively over his body, he looks out at the sheets of rain, water spraying his body. "Your mom made it seem like it was such easy money. Open a restaurant for three months when all the rich expats are in Panama, make a killing on food and alcohol, and come home. Ever since she mentioned it, I wanted to do it. I'd hoped we'd do it together. I was on my way to tell you, when..."

"When what?" Everything he's saying makes sense, and for the first time since I found him, I believe what he's telling me.

He rubs his face roughly and sucks in a deep breath. "Never mind. Forget it. Let's figure out where we're staying tonight."

I cock my head to the side, giving him a not-so-fast-Romeo look.

"Two rooms," he assures me.

The rain has let up, but water still drips heavily from the jungle leaves, soaking my shoulders and the top of my dress, making it stick to my chest and back. A half mile down the beach, we find a lodge with cabins for rent. As with everything down here, it's inexpensive. Since it's a cabin, we only rent one. It's nothing fancy, but it has a kitchen, a double bed, and a small loft with another mattress. Outside, there's a small pool, shared by three other cabins.

The sun has returned, and the air is sticky and thick from the recent downpour. Luke is resting by the pool, and I sit on the small porch watching him, wondering how much of his story is true. The annoying thing is, I believe him. Or maybe I just want to. Who wouldn't want a man to love them so much that he would run off to a foreign country to prove his love and worth to them? It's romantic. Until I remember the whole he-stole-my-money-to-do-it part. But a person in love will do crazy things. I followed Max into the jungle and a marijuana crop. I would have followed him farther.

But what has Max ever done for me? Lied. Used me to expose my sister. Who's worse? Max or Luke? Luke made some awful choices, but he supposedly had altruistic motives. If I'm to believe him. Max pretended to be pure but with selfish and harmful ulterior motives. Anything Max wanted from me has been to benefit him. Even taking care of Bailey. It seemed like a sweet arrangement—time-sharing a dog—but I was only a dog walker when it was convenient for him. I kidded myself into thinking we were co-parenting.

A dog.

How pathetic I must have looked to Max. No wonder he ran out on me when I tried to kiss him that night after the party. He never wanted me. He never saw me as anything more than a girl he could use.

My spirits, which were already below sea level, plummet into the Earth's inner core.

A truck selling fish tacos and other food pulls up, and Luke walks over to it, speaking to the guy behind the sliding window of the food truck. He comes back with a tray of fish tacos and a six-pack of beer. Luke hands me the crisp tonic, and he sits next to me. I drink the whole can in four delicious swallows, immediately feeling the gentle blanket of I-don't-care wrap around my mind and body.

Luke hands me another can from the six-pack he's set on the small wood table next to me, and I gratefully accept.

"How did you pay for these?" I ask.

"I have a little cash."

I slam my beer down. "Dammit, Luke. Show me. Empty your pockets."

Without hesitating, he stuffs his hands into the deep voids of his shorts and pulls out a handful of coins, several small bills, two phones, and his passport. I count the money, but it's not much. Less than forty dollars.

"You've had an iPhone this whole time?" I grab it and press the side button, the screen coming to life. "And it has power. Why would you keep this from me?"

"I wasn't. I swear. Why would I keep it from you?" His eyes are pleading with me.

"Then why have you only used your other phone?"

"I don't have data on my iPhone; it's only good when connected to Wi-Fi. If I need to call someone, I use the local phone." Luke pulls the tacos over. "I promise I'm not keeping anything from you. I've told you everything. To make you understand." My face contorts, still wary. "Eat something. I know you. You get hangry if you don't eat."

A few fish tacos aren't going to make me suddenly forgive Luke, but he's right. I'm light headed and irritable because I'm starving. The mahimahi is gorgeous—lightly grilled with a little bit of salt and pepper and lime juice. I may have to add some fresh-fish tacos to my menu. Nothing fancy. A new chef's biggest mistake can be trying to reinvent something that is already perfect, like a simple fish taco. All it needs is good-quality fish, grilled just right, with a touch of seasoning.

"Tell me the rest of the story," I say. "What did you see that made you suddenly run off with my money to prove your worth to me?"

Luke stretches his long legs in front of him; the blond hair on his muscled thighs and hard calves shimmers in the light of the sun. He does have a fine body. When he doesn't speak, I look over. Luke grips the paper plate, crumpling the thin paper in his hands. He exhales loudly, as if making a decision, and tosses the plate onto the floor. "Okay. But it's a heartrending story that may make you fall in love with me. I've tried it out on a couple of other women, and they immediately wanted to comfort my heartache." He tilts his head, a wicked smile on his face.

"I bet they did." I laugh, his look reminding me of how much I enjoyed teaching Luke in the kitchen. It didn't matter how many times he ruined a dish—burning a steak, congealing fondue, deflating a soufflé—he always laughed it off and wanted to immediately try again until he got it right. It was fun. I laughed a lot during those times.

"It all started a year ago when I was having dinner at my neighborhood restaurant and met the most beautiful, talented chef."

Luke continues his story, most of which I already know, except not his version of the events. Luke did frequent my restaurant. And he seemed to frequent it more once he met me, but I figured it was to impress the girls he was on a date with since he "knew the chef." But he did drop the girls at some point and came in more frequently with friends and colleagues or by himself.

"I brought my dates in to make you jealous and to show you how desirable I was," he tells me. A young couple with their arms tightly wrapped around each other walks past us, and Luke waits for them to pass. The young man's hand is on the girl's butt, and he wraps his other arm around her waist, pressing her to him as they enter their cabin next door.

"But you didn't seem to notice or care," he continues. "You treated me kindly but only as a patron you enjoyed talking to once in a while, nothing more. It's the restaurant business; you had to be nice to everyone. But I wanted more, and I wanted to know you. And I wanted to be someone special. Not just a patron. So I had to do something to stand out."

I remember when he started coming later and later in the evenings and sitting at the bar until the kitchen closed. He'd chat with the bartenders and the other regulars. It wasn't unusual. There's always a group of regulars at any bar that makes it their local neighborhood spot. It's one of the things I love most about running a restaurant. With the right mix, it can feel more like a family, and certain customers are part of that. At that point, Luke had weaved his way into the fabric of the restaurant's kin.

"First, I asked you to teach me how to cook. I thought it would bring us closer, and it did. But it wasn't enough. I wanted more, and when you told me about your dream to open your own restaurant, I wanted to be a part of it."

I remember confiding in him over an apple tart he'd baked, the top and edges burned. We ate around the burnt bits while I told him about my dream of opening my own restaurant. A week later, he proposed investing in my venture. It wasn't unheard of. Owning a piece of a cool restaurant or bar in Manhattan makes these young investors feel special and strokes their egos. And sometimes it pays off.

And he was a businessman, a banker. And by then, he was also my friend. I jumped at the chance for him to be involved and to use his financial knowledge to help me run my business. My failure and past relationship was still hanging heavy inside me, making me question half my decisions regarding the restaurant. Bringing Luke into the fold gave me the confidence that Cole had stripped from me when our relationship was torn apart.

Out of all the scenarios I pictured of Cole and me breaking up one day, his wife was never in them. I didn't think about her. Our relationship was passionate and primal.

I never wanted the white dress and roses with him. I only wanted him. And I had him. But when the stress of the new restaurant he was opening began to take him away from me, I offered to help out.

It was exciting being a part of something like that. The city was buzzing with the anticipation of Cole Merrick's next restaurant, and I was beside him, making it happen. I met with the contractor, inspectors, and designers and reported back to Cole. He was still very much in charge and made all the decisions, but I helped with the day-to-day tasks. Then one Saturday morning, he called and told me he couldn't make the meeting with the city inspector. He had to go to his son's lacrosse game. I was stunned. I never knew he had a child. Cole never mentioned him.

That phone call changed everything.

I couldn't be the reason a family broke up. Never. When my father died, it left a gaping hole in my family. I missed him every day, and my mom and Mamé were a ball of grief. I know divorce isn't the same, but my best friend's parents got divorced when I was in middle school, and it was like a death to her. It was the death of her family. I couldn't do that to someone else's family.

My mind was so wrapped up in this revelation, I hardly remember the meeting with the inspector. He was just meant to meet me outside the restaurant site to discuss the permits Cole was required to get before he began construction, but I let him inside. It didn't occur to me how damaging it would be. The contractor had already begun working on the renovations, and when the city inspector realized this, he was furious. He made Cole stop construction immediately and pay a huge fine.

My mistake put so much red tape over the project, Cole had to shut down the whole operation until he could get everything straightened out and got the inspector back on his side. In the end, I think Cole bribed the guy. I never asked.

Cole was furious at me, and I took the blame since it was my fault. I should never have let the inspector inside. But I was furious too. About his son that he'd kept from me.

After weeks of fighting and hate sex and fighting again, I told Cole it was over. I swore I would never get in the middle of another relationship again. And I haven't. But it shook my confidence. How could I open my own restaurant when I almost shut Cole's whole venture down over some stupid relationship drama? I needed to keep my feet on the ground, and I needed someone who was used to dealing with a lot of money and difficult people and high stress. Luke was the perfect solution.

At least, I thought he was.

"So you invested in my restaurant to get in my pants?"

"That's the cynical way to look at it. But, yes, I did it because I liked you, and I wanted you to like me back. And I'm not an idiot. At least, not typically. Despite my latest endeavors, I'm a very good businessman. I was one of the most successful associates at my company. I took risks, but they paid off because I did my research. I would never invest in something I didn't know every aspect of. Even you. Yes, I invested in your business to impress you, but I didn't go into it blindly. I did a lot of research on the restaurant industry and what makes a restaurant successful, because it's a risky business. Eighty percent of restaurants fail in New York City. But you had the right ingredients. Including a celebrity sister, whose recipes are awfully similar to yours."

I turn my head sharply at Luke. Does he know about my arrangement with Catie? Perhaps it's not as secret as I once thought. If Luke knows, who else knows?

"All my recipes are original," I assure him.

"I know that. I also know that your sister owes you, and she would be very helpful in promoting the restaurant."

"She would have helped me no matter what." Which is true, but her guilt hasn't hurt.

"You picked a great location, you already have a platform through your sister, you're an amazing chef, and you always thought of the bigger picture—a gourmet shop, a series of cookbooks, catering events." A loud squeal makes Luke and I turn toward the cabin the young couple disappeared into. It's followed by several disjointed yelps and a loud moan of pleasure.

Our eyes catch, and a blush crawls up my neck. I look away, the heat rising inside my body surprising me.

"So what happened ne—"

"Then you slept with me," Luke cuts me off. It sounds like an accusation. "I thought that was it. You finally wanted me like I wanted you. But the next morning, you laughed it off. When I said I'd call you, you scoffed at me and told me I didn't have to play that game. You said we'd had too much to drink—I'd barely had anything, by the way—and it was fun, but that was all."

I had drank a lot that night. It was two nights before I headed to Brooklyn and the homecoming shoot where I met Max. I was nervous, and after I'd closed down the restaurant, Luke suggested we go to a bar and have another drink. He knew I was worried about the shoot, and I'd just quit my job as head chef to dive full time into my restaurant endeavor. The next thing I knew, I was stumbling into his apartment.

I ain't gonna lie. The sex was good. Very good. And it certainly kept my mind off the impending weekend. But when he started to tell me he'd call me, I brushed it off, assuming he was trying to be a nice guy and "do the right thing." But I didn't want anything more, and I didn't think he did either. Now I can see how harsh that must have been if he thought that night was the start of something more.

"It wouldn't have been so bad," Luke says. "You went off to the shoot, and I figured when you got back, I would take you out, and I'd let you know how I felt. But then I…I went to your good-bye party at the restaurant. And you were floating on air, and we laughed and danced, and I left the party with so much hope, to the point that I couldn't hold it in. I ran back to the restaurant, but when I got there, the lights were off except for a few candles on the bar, and you were there. Dancing in a tight embrace with him. With Max." He can barely say the name. "The way you held on to him, it was obvious you were in love with him. You'd never held me like that. When you lifted your mouth to his, I felt sick. I'd never felt physically ill from love before."

My heart is pounding wildly in my chest, and I feel guilty, even though I didn't do anything wrong. But to cause someone so much pain, it affects me. I want to reach out and grasp his arm and tell him I understand, that I've been there, but his body is rigid, and he's in the throws of his hurt and anger, reliving the story.

"You'd think I would have been smart and just moved on, realizing I had no chance. But love makes you do stupid things. So, on a whim, I took the money from the account and jumped on a flight down here. No research. No real plan—except to make some fast money. I knew you were worried about the bills that were racking up, and that contractor was really pissing me off. I know you think he's this sweet family man, but he's taking advantage of you."

I open my mouth to protest, but Luke rushes on.

"And then I got here and realized it's not as easy as your mom made it seem. Half the ingredients aren't available or are very limited. The vendors are sketchy at best, thieves at worst. The money's not great. And Panamanians are lazy workers. When they work. After only a month, half the money was gone and the rest was going fast. When Sonja—who had been helping me—told me about the guy she knew that would buy our passports, I thought I could at least get some of the money back before I traveled back to the city to confess what I'd done and how awfully I'd failed."

I shake my head. "That's quite a story."

THE ADVENTURES OF NATALIE BLOOM

"You don't believe me," Luke says, accusing me, his voice hard.

My hand covers his. "Funnily enough, I do believe you. Love makes you do crazy things. I should know."

In a quick movement, he wraps his hands behind my neck and brings my face close to his. I pull back, looking into the intensity of his eyes. His story is rich in my body, wrapping me in warmth. When his mouth covers mine, I don't stop him. His lips are soft and warm, and I'm pulled into the love and comfort in them.

But when I close my eyes, I see Max. The image startles me.

"Stop." I push Luke off.

What the hell am I doing? I'm feeling sorry for Luke and more sorry for myself. I can't do this. I can't lead him on. Even if I wanted to, what does it mean that I would let myself be drawn into bed with a man who has stolen so much from me? No matter what the reason.

"Please don't be mad at me." Luke cups his hand behind my neck, but I pull back, the words making me suddenly angry.

"I am mad at you, Luke. Saying I love you doesn't put the money back in my bank account." I push him off, standing. "Until you give that back, I can never forgive you."

Fifteen

I 'm alone in the cabin.
   When Luke realized his confession changed nothing, he stormed off, hurt and frustrated. Instead of chasing after him, I let him go. He left his phones and passport on the table outside, so I know he'll be back.

My finger presses the button of his iPhone, and I swipe the screen. To my surprise, it's not password protected. Immediately, I connect to the Wi-Fi and check my e-mail. As I suspected, I have several unread e-mails from Catie. And none from Max. My hand hovers over Catie's most recent message, with the subject *Where are you?? Urgent!*

The door jiggles, and I click out of my e-mail and place the phone on the nightstand next to the bed. Luke enters, wearing only his shorts, his body slick from a recent swim.

"Where were you?" I ask.

"I wasn't running away again," he shoots at me, walking into the bathroom. He comes out, a towel wrapped around his taut abs. For a moment, I regret not letting our kiss go any further.

"I know you weren't." I indicate his phone and passport.

"I was thinking about how I can pay you back." Luke sits, his weight on the bed makes me slide closer to him. "I have several stocks I can sell, and for the rest of the money, I can easily secure a loan for you. I'll pay the interest, of course, and then we can forget this ever happened. We can hire a new contractor, if you want, and we shouldn't be that behind on everything. We still don't have the liquor license, which can take forever, so we still have time."

"There's no we, Luke. Just me. No matter what the reason, I can't have a partner who stole from me. I'll never be able to trust you again."

"How can you say that? I just confessed everything. And I told you I'm going to get the money back."

I throw his phone at him. "Then do it. Call your bank, and sell your stocks."

"It's not that easy." He snatches his phone from the rug where it landed. "I have to check the market, see how the stocks are going, if it's a good time to sell."

"You always have an excuse, don't you?" I shove off the bed and grab my bag.

"Where are you going?" His voice is panicked.

"I need to think."

I trek down to the beach and order a piña colada at the bar, greedily drinking it down. A breeze hits my face, and I relish in the juxtaposition of the hot air against my skin and the cool drink sliding down my throat.

"I spoke to my stockbroker." Luke slides onto the barstool next to me, looking wary, gauging my mood.

"Good. What did they say?"

"She's looking into selling the stocks, but it's late, and the market is closed for the day, so I'm going to call her back tomorrow." I don't know much about the stock market, but I do know it closes around four Eastern Time. What's one more day? We're not going anywhere.

Amya, the yoga instructor I met the other day, comes up

the few steps to the platform the bar sits on, carrying a beach towel under her arm, her skin looking darker and more sun kissed since I saw her a few days ago. I wave at her, and she smiles. Her eyes slide to Luke, and the sight of him stops her in her barefoot tracks. Her reaction at the sight of him reminds me how handsome he is—a blond God with the muscled body to match.

"Amya. Hi." I stand and walk a few steps toward her, glad for the distraction. "Join us."

Luke stands abruptly.

"Luke, this is Amya." I introduce them. "She was helping me locate Sonja, and she teaches a mean yoga class."

Her voice shakes in an unsteady laugh, and then she says, "Nice to meet you."

"I'm glad I ran into you. Is that bartender who told you where Sonja went here? The town he mentioned was in the middle of nowhere. There's no way she went to teach a yoga class there," I explain.

"I'm not sure where he is. But I don't think Sonja was staying in that town. He said she was meeting up with a tour group in Batán and traveling with them."

"Oh. Well that makes more sense, I guess. But if you see him, can you ask him to come talk to me. We're staying at the cabins down the beach. Number three."

"If I see him, I'll let him know."

"Thanks. Would you like to join us? I'd offer to buy you a drink, but I was robbed earlier and my money is scarce."

Amya's mouth hangs slack, and she glances at Luke.

"It's okay. I'm fine now. Just a cut on the head and a bit of a sore ankle. And sore ego."

"A sketchy cab driver," Luke explains at Amya's questioning look.

Grabbing the bartender's attention, I order two more piña coladas and hand one to Amya. "Please don't tell me you're one of those super healthy yogis who doesn't drink and only eats vegan."

Amya takes a long sip from the straw. "Absolutely not."

"Sit." Luke steps back, giving up his seat.

"No. I can't stay." Amya slurps the rest of the drink down. "I'm catching a ride out of town for a yoga retreat." She pulls her hair back, the blue dye faded, and steps back. "It was nice to see you again, and thanks for the drink."

"I think she liked you," I say when she's gone. Luke is looking after her. "She was quite taken with you."

Luke sits down and paints his bright-white smile on his tanned face. "Can you blame her?"

I let out a long exhale, not feeling up to any flirty banter. "I'm going back to the cabin, and I'm going to bed. I just want the day to be over."

He looks disappointed but doesn't stop me when I go.

***

The next morning is gloriously uneventful. My passport is waiting for me, and we cross the border into Panama with no issue, making it back to Bocas del Toro by late afternoon. Luke hasn't said much to me, sensing my reluctance to discuss the revelations of yesterday. I heard him on the phone with his stockbroker before we left the cabin this morning, and the trade will be done by this afternoon, and ten thousand dollars will be back in my bank account. For someone who made enough money to retire early, the amount seems small. His portfolio—that's what it's called, right?—should have a lot more money in it. But for the moment, I'll take what he's offering and look into it later.

When we arrive at the Red Frog office in Bocas Town, we walk through the small building and out onto the dock at the back, sliding into the boat that's about to depart. The boat is packed with the latest group of tourists arriving for their holiday, all with red VIP wristbands, which everyone receives when they first arrive.

The motor starts, and I scoot next to Luke, but my mind

goes to Max. The last time I made this trip, he was sitting next to me, and I had so much hope for what lay ahead of us. A woman yelling from the dock for the boat to wait brings me out of my daydream. Thinking about Max is not productive and will bring me nothing but pain and disappointment.

"Hold the boat!" the woman yells again, and something in her voice makes me sit up straighter. My mouth hangs agape when I see the svelte woman, dressed in a long silk sundress and, holding on to the fedora that adorns her head, looking immaculate.

Luke follows my gaze. "Isn't that…"

I gasp as a wave of excitement rushes over me. "My sister."

Sixteen

My mouth is still slack as Catie shoves her way onto the boat, carefully maneuvering her red aluminum Ted Baker suitcase next to her on the empty seat. After she's settled, she lazily scans the boat, her eyes halting when she spots Luke. "You." She shoots up. "Thief! That man is a thief!"

The captain ignores her, revving the engine—as much as the dinky engine can rev on the old boat—and pushes off the dock, sending Catie slamming down into her seat. The rest of the passengers stare at Catie and send curious looks to Luke.

Clamping her eyes on me, she clamors over the few passengers between us and pushes her way into the spot on the seat next to me. "What are you doing here? Why are you with him?" Catie shoots questions at me. "Did the bastard give you your money back?"

"Relax." I place a calming hand on her shoulder, momentarily muting her attack. "A lot has happened since I last talked to you. Luke is transferring some of the money back by this afternoon."

"Why not all of it?" Catie shoots venomous eyes at Luke.

"I'll explain everything," I shout over the wind rushing around us as we speed into the open water.

As the boat soars over the crystal ocean, the engine thundering, I explain—as best I can in the congested atmosphere—why Luke took the money, his confession of love, and that he's paying me back.

"And all is forgiven," Catie says ruefully, grasping her hat to her head against the wind whipping around us.

"It's not like that—" Luke starts to speak, but Catie cuts him off.

"I'm not talking to you. I'm talking to my ingenious sister," Catie says, her last few words dripping in sarcasm.

Luke shrugs off Catie's comments and looks out toward the island of mangroves we're zooming past as we near the marina. The boat slows, and the wind becomes a warm breeze; my skin is still buzzing from the ride.

"Does Mom know you're here?" I need a change of subject.

"I e-mailed her right before I got on the plane." Catie lets go of her hat now that we're cruising into the small dock of the welcome center. "She thinks you're still in Costa Rica."

"I lost my phone."

Stepping off the boat, Luke lifts Catie's luggage onto the dock, which Catie snatches back from him as soon as she's gained her footing on the swaying platform. "I'll meet you girls up there." Luke squeezes past the rest of the passengers and luggage being unloaded and walks down the boardwalk path to the welcome center.

"What are you doing here, Catie?" I've wanted to ask this question since she jumped on the boat, but I didn't have a chance to since her guns were blazing as soon as she saw Luke.

"Didn't you read any of my messages?"

"I lost my phone," I say again.

"Well, you were right. Max is writing a takedown piece

about me."

"You talked to him?!" I stop on the narrow path, the murky water of the marsh underneath us. We squeeze to the side, letting the rest of the travelers pass.

"Yes. Like you should have done when you first found out, instead of running away." We continue walking down the path.

"I was furious and not thinking straight, Catie. I've been through a lot. Besides, I was worried he'd publish it sooner if he knew we knew."

We stop the conversation as we approach the welcome center and Luke. "I've reserved a golf cart," Catie says as she walks to the welcome desk. "Come on."

As we drive up to the villa—was I only here a few days ago, because it feels like weeks?—we have to park at the bottom of the driveway because it's filled with other carts. There's a bustling of activity as we enter the villa. Mom is scurrying from one side of the kitchen to another, peeking into the oven, stirring a pot on the stove, and slamming the fridge door shut with her heel. When she sees us, she throws her arms in the air.

"My girls!" After wiping her hands on her apron, she embraces us. "Thank God, my prayers have been answered. I'm catering a dinner party at the Reeds' in an hour, and I've lost two of my helpers. Help me get this stuff ready."

Catie looks horrified at the thought, but I jump right in, taking the wooden spoon from Mom, stirring what looks like a large pot of crab bisque.

"Catie, you can get all the serving dishes and wares out and ready them to be filled. Then iron my red-silk Nordstrom dress and make several flower arrangements in those small vases by the door from the flowers around the yard."

Those are all tasks Catie is more than capable of.

"What can I do?" Luke asks.

Mom's face screws up in a confused twist as she sees Luke

standing in her living room. You'd think she saw two monkeys swinging from her fan singing "Baby Got Back."

"Help Marty outside on the grill." Once Luke is gone, Mom dumps a pot of linguini in a strainer in the sink and says, "We'll talk about that later."

I forgot how much fun I have cooking with Mom. When Mamé helped Mom launch her catering business, Mamé was too old to do much, so I stepped in and helped Mom after school whenever I could. She never let me do more than cook with her in the kitchen; she wanted me to focus on school and my friends and have a real life. Catie wanted nothing to do with the cooking, but she loved the party-planning side of the business and always found clever new ways to showcase the meals and put together place settings and do all the branding for the business.

Mom's catering business—The Savory Dish—is retired now, but she still takes on small jobs here and there for friends. Like tonight. This brings back many memories of my teenage years, our home filled with the smell of cooking and baking—Mamé was more of a baker and loved making French desserts from her home country—Mom rushing around in a happy frenzy, Catie refusing to have anything to do with the cooking, and me hovering over the activity, giving Mom tips on spices and flavors I thought would add or retract from a dish. It didn't take long for Mom to see I had a knack for cooking, and she encouraged me to go to culinary school instead of college.

"I've got a big piece of meat with your name on it." Marty stands in the entryway with two large serving dishes, one piled high with grilled fish and the other with thick steaks.

Mom laughs at his boorish language—used to it by now—and tells him to put the dishes down so I can garnish the food and arrange them in a presentation that is suitable for the party. Luke's phone sits on the counter, and I snap several pictures of the beautiful food.

It's just under the wire, but we make it to the Reeds' in time to set up before their friends arrive. I forgot how exhausting catering can be; the work's not done until the party's over. Catie helped with the set-up and stuck around, to the delight of the Reeds, and greeted their guests, who were ecstatic to have Catelyn Bloom in their presence. Catie was polite and made it clear she had little to do with the party and nothing to do with the cooking of tonight's meal—it was all her mother, who taught her everything she knows. Then she ducked out graciously, not wanting to steal the thunder from Mom—and she was tired from a long day's journey, I'm sure.

My feet throb and feel twice their size by the time we get back to the villa. We rumble up the paved driveway in the golf cart, holding tightly to all the empty and cleaned serving ware, and park at the top of the drive. Marty comes out when he hears the golf cart and takes the pile of platters from my lap.

"World War III has started inside."

Part of me did worry about leaving Catie alone with Luke while we were at the party. Marty pushes the front door open with his foot; the sound of voices rising in confrontation bombards me. I hurry in and see Catie standing over Luke, who sits on the couch—his arms crossed, his brow creased, and his hands in fists. He's obviously trying to keep his temper in check, but he looks like he's at a tipping point.

"I don't care if that girl gave the money to Mother Teresa; it's Natalie's money," Catie is yelling above him, her face red and sweaty.

Seeing me, Luke's fists loosen, and he relaxes into the couch. "Oh, thank God. Can you please talk to your sister?"

"I'm exhausted." I set a bag of silverware down on the kitchen counter and flip open my laptop. "And she has a right to be upset. She's my sister. She cares about me." I log into my bank account, which I haven't had a chance to do all day. "Did the money go through?"

"It'll take a couple of days, but I've forwarded you a copy of the transfer from my bank."

Catie lets out a loud groan, but I turn my computer to her once I check my e-mail and see a receipt for the transfer to my bank account.

"You still owe her a lot more than that," Catie says.

"And you owe her a lot more than that," Luke shoots back.

Catie's eyes widen in shock. "You told him?" She turns to me in outrage.

"No!" I assure her. "I would never."

"So I'm right. You have been helping Catie this whole time, haven't you?" Luke crosses his arms and looks triumphantly at Catie. Every time they've met, there's been competitive contention between them. Catie will not take kindly to his accusations.

"I'm not the one who stole forty grand from her and ran off and am now trying to manipulate her with shallow words of love," Catie spits at Luke. "That money better be in her account tomorrow. I know people. And I'll make sure you pay for this with more than just money." Disgusted, Catie spins on her heels and stomps to her room, slamming the door.

I have to hold back a laugh, remembering many days of our childhood when Catie raged and then stomped off to her room. Luke looks at me, but I have nothing more to add. His iPhone and passport are on the counter, and I swipe them.

"I'm keeping these hostage in my room until morning. You can sleep on the couch."

After I wash my face and brush my teeth, I crawl into bed. Even if the money comes through, it's not enough to open the restaurant. I still have money coming in from the book I ghostwrote with Catie, but the amount is dwindling.

Luke said he'd get a loan for the restaurant, but I'm not

letting him near it. But I could get a loan. And write the book with Catie that we keep talking about. And watching Mom come alive tonight with the party, I know she misses running her business. She never wanted to retire, but she didn't have the energy to run the business on her own after Mamé passed away. Mom's always jumping at the chance to throw parties and catering her friends' affairs. I bet if I asked her, she'd love to help me with my restaurant.

My insides buzz with adrenaline, and my eyes are wide open with excitement. I can do this. I can get my life back on track. Ideas rush through my head for the restaurant and the gourmet shop I've always wanted to run in conjunction with the restaurant. With Mom's help, we could open a catering side to the business. Fearing I'll forget half the ideas by morning, I look for a pen and paper in the nightstand, but it only has an old deck of cards and a small flashlight. Luke's phone is next to the bed, and I pick it up to send an e-mail to myself with all my notes.

I press it on, and the screen lights up. I type a quick e-mail and then remember the photos I took of the food earlier, before we left for the party. I open his photos and scroll through the dozen shots. When I get to the last one in the series, my finger freezes above the small screen. Two rows up is a series of photos of him on Red Frog Beach with a girl. A girl I recognize. At first, I think it's Sonja—same hair and body—but as the face comes into focus, I realize it's Amya.

I put my finger over Amya's face, and there's no denying it. Amya and Sonja are the same person.

Seventeen

M y instinct is to rush out and shake Luke awake, screaming about what I've discovered. But my blood boils so hot that I'm afraid I'll kill him. I pace the floor, trying to decide what to do. He lied to me. Again. Or, at least, withheld the truth. Am I as naïve as Max said? That's why Amya acted so weird when she met him. But how can she be Sonja? She runs the yoga program in Costa Rica.

I pick up his phone and look at the photo again. There's no denying it. Amya is Sonja. There are photos of them working together on the boat restaurant at the marina. Sonja/Amya is behind the bar, and Luke is serving a dish of grilled fish to an older couple. The presentation is awful; there's no color or variety on the plate, and the fish is burned. No wonder they failed.

I rush out and shove open the door to Catie's room. It's the same room Jess and Max slept in the night of his birthday. An image of them tangled together in the sheets briefly flashes through my head, making me even more angry and hurt. Of course, I didn't witness them doing the horizontal tango, but I know the steps.

"Catie," I hiss into the dark. "Catie, are you awake?"

"Wah?" Catie rolls onto her back, her eyes closed, the light from the portico outside the sheer curtains illuminating her face. Rubbing her eyes, she sits up.

I crawl into the bed with her, sitting against the headboard, my arms crossed, my breath hissing out of my mouth. As she adjusts the pillow behind her, I notice dried mascara under her eyes and down her cheeks.

"Have you been crying?" I ask, my discovery momentarily forgotten. "Is it Sam?"

"No. Yes. I don't know."

"Is he back? Did you see him?"

"The Aussie skier won the whole comp, so Sam traveled with him to Australia to conclude the story." Catie shrugs, trying to act like it's no biggie, but her relationship with Sam is so new and fragile. It's the first time she's let her heart be free to love in years, so I know she's more worried than she's letting on. "We're meeting up at that Valentine's Day gala, but he seems so distant all of a sudden. I know he's busy with work and thousands of miles away. I'm just scared. Now that we're finally together, I'm terrified something's going to happen. Like last time with Chris."

I put my arm around her shoulder and give her a sideways hug, like I did when we were girls. She never accepted full-on hugs, but she let me give her these half hugs, pretending to grudgingly take them, though I know she loved them. I'm surprised when she collapses into me, sobs pouring out of her.

"It's okay, Little Bee." I use the nickname I gave her when we were kids, which rolls off my tongue anytime she's in need of comfort. After our father died, it became more frequent, as did the hugs. It was my way of protecting her. When the sobs turn into sniffles, she straightens, wipes her eyes, and lets out a long breath.

"It's just hard, and our relationship feels so precarious

right now. But it'll be fine." Catie puts on her I've-got-this face, which she uses often with her work, and looks at me, calm and afresh. How does she do that? "Why have you crawled into my bed in the middle of night?"

Blood rushes into my head, making me dizzy with fury and humiliation as I remember the picture of Sonja/Amya and Luke's interaction with her at the bar.

"I'm such an idiot." Catie leans back, waiting for me to continue, not arguing. "You were right about Luke. Of course you were. Max has been in my ear since the start of this journey, telling me not to trust this guy, and I didn't. Not until Luke confessed he loved me and told me why he took the money. He sounded genuine. It's hard to fake that kind of hurt and jealousy. Am I that desperate that I was blinded by his words of love? Was everything he said to me leading up to this moment one big scam? Even saying I love you?"

Taking a deep breath, Catie considers this. "I don't think it's that black and white. Life never is, and love certainly isn't." Catie pushes the covers off, the warmth from our rising emotions causing a heat wave under the blanket. "What happened now that made you question everything?"

I tell her about meeting Amya and introducing her to Luke, who pretended not to know her, and then my discovery of the picture on Luke's phone.

"I'm going to try to not think of Luke as some evil bastard who stole your money and look at this objectively for a moment," Catie says diplomatically. "If Amya and Sonja are the same person, and he really does love you, he may not have wanted to ruin anything now that he's told you how he feels, so he pretended not to know her."

I relax slightly, not feeling as betrayed by Luke. Not that it was right for him to lie, but I can see why he would.

"Or," Catie continues, her face hardening, "he may have been protecting Sonja and didn't want you to go after her for the money."

And my shoulders grow tight again, blood rushing back into my head. "Why? If I'm to believe he loves me, and don't kill me for saying this, but I do believe him, then why would he protect Sonja?"

"He may be in love with you. That may not be a lie. He may just be in love with himself more. And protecting Sonja may be a way of protecting his own interests."

There's a knock on the door. Catie and I look at each other. If it were Mom, she would have barged right in. And Marty would never knock on the door in the middle of the night unless it was an emergency. The knock becomes more urgent. I look at Catie, checking her sleep outfit—a silk tank top and matching shorts—and answer the door. It's Luke, grasping his phone, which I left on my bed in my shock.

"Natalie," his voice is quick and urgent. "I saw your door open and when I looked at my phone and saw the picture"— Catie leans forward in the bed, listening intently—"I might as well tell both of you."

My arms cross, and I raise my eyebrows. "I want to know everything. Now."

Catie is up on her knees, ready to pounce, enjoying the role of sister protector. Luke raises his arms in surrender. "Okay. Okay. It's not as bad as it looks."

"It looks like Amya is really Sonja, and you pretended not to know her, even though she has my money, and she's the whole reason I was in Costa Rica." Saying it out loud makes my blood heat. "It looks like you're protecting her instead of me. It looks like you're still a liar."

"Yes, Amya is Sonja's real name. She changed her name a year ago after some backpacker was stalking her. But she's been running the yoga program in Parismina for several years, and everyone still knows her by Amya there. I'm sorry I pretended not to know her, but she already gave the money to her sister, and I was just gaining your trust. I didn't want to lose it again."

"It's too late for that." I don't care what the reason, what he's done, and keeps doing, is egregious.

"Why was Amya running the restaurant with you if she runs that yoga program in Costa Rica?" Catie jumps in.

"Sometimes she teaches yoga at other resorts up and down the coast to promote her business. I met her in a yoga class here, and she offered to help bartend at the restaurant for some extra cash. When she saw how bad things were going for me, she told me about the passport scam."

"We're going back to Costa Rica and finding her," Catie says.

"She's not there," Luke says.

"Where is she?"

"In Coral Cay."

"That's on the other side of this island," I say, stunned.

Luke at least has the decency to look shamefaced.

"But how? We just saw her yesterday?" I ask. She would have had to leave right after us. But Amya did mention she was leaving for a retreat.

"She comes down here twice a month. That's where I met her."

"You're taking us there," Catie says.

"Now? It's the middle of the night."

"First thing tomorrow."

"Okay." Luke looks at me, his eyes pleading. "Please don't be mad at me, Natalie. I didn't want anything to mess this up." Before he leaves, I take his phone back, my trust for him eradicated.

***

In the morning we take a boat taxi to Coral Cay on the other side of the island, leaving Luke at the villa with strict instructions to Mom that he's not to leave. There are little docks stretched out across the sparkling water with small cabins attached to them. We walk past them after we arrive and trek through the beach and jungle until we find a little hut that says information. The small Panamanian lady behind the hut instructs us to the yoga camp. The first class is about to start, and we scurry forward.

There are about ten students on a large platform near the beach. It's completely open—no roof—but shaded by palm trees. My pulse quickens when I see Amya walk to the front of the class. She smiles, takes a deep breath, lifting her arms above her head, and then freezes when she sees us standing at the edge of the platform. She beckons to a young man in the front row, and he takes her place, instructing the students to place their hands on their hearts and breath deeply.

We follow Amya ten yards down a sandy jungle path away from the class. She's continuing farther into the trees when I tell her to stop.

"It's nice to finally meet you, Sonja. Or is it Amya?"

When I speak her name, her eyes widen in surprise.

"Luke told you," she says, stepping aside to let a young man carrying snorkeling gear and fins pass.

"Yes," I say. "How did you know who I was in Parismina?"

"Luke told me about you, of course. How he'd come down here to make all this money to prove to the girl he loves that he's adventurous and worthy of her and all that bullshit. So when you told me your name and that you were looking for Sonja, I knew immediately who you were." I prickle at the way she makes light of everything with Luke. It's one thing for my sister to do it, but to have this stranger, who stole the rest of the money, do it pisses me off. "Look, I'm sorry I sent you on a wild-goose chase, but I was afraid you were going to ask for the money back. But you can't. I don't have it. I already sent it to my sister. Did Luke tell you about her? Mira's sick and she has—"

"A one-year-old daughter. I'm aware. But that doesn't make it okay to steal. What the hell kind of world do you think you're living in? You're a yoga instructor for God's sake. Aren't you supposed to teach peace, love, and harmony? Or are you just full of bullshit?" The words tumble out of my mouth; I'm annoyed at how blasé she is about the whole situation.

But, despite my anger, I know the story about her sister is true, which is why it's hard for me to stand here and demand the money back. I saw the photos of the little girl. One picture in particular tore at my heart. The daughter is wrapped in Mira's arms while she's lying in a hospital bed with all her hair gone. The smile on Mira's face as she looks at her daughter is heartbreaking. And if you look closely at the photo, which I did, you can see two glistening lines on her cheeks—she'd been crying.

How can I deprive that child of her mother? I've never wanted to slap someone as much as I do right now, looking at Amya, but if someone could have helped my father when he was sick, it would have eased the burden of the medical bills that were left after he was gone. Remembering my mother's face when she got those bills after everything she'd already been through, I know I can't ask for the money back.

My chin quivers at the memory, and Catie grabs my arm, hard. It works. The tears dry up, which I'm sure was her intention.

"I'm sorry about your sister and her family," Catie says, pulling in front of me. "But if you were really worried about that little girl, you'd be there helping them instead of being a spineless bitch who runs away and takes what isn't hers to purge her guilt for being a shitty sister."

"I am helping them." Amya's cheeks burn crimson. "I'm taking every job I can find down here and sending every penny back to them. My sister has an amazing family and friends at home. She doesn't need any more moral support. She needs treatment."

"That doesn't mean you can just steal. What do you do? Go around to everyone's lodges while one of your lackeys teaches your class and take whatever money is lying around?"

"No!"

"Or steal their passports to sell?" I jump in.

"He told you about that?!" The look she gives me is incredulous. Catie and I exchange a glance and we wait as Amya simmers in the already sizzling heat. "And besides, Luke gave me your money."

"If you're lying, I'm marching right in front of that class and telling them exactly what you did," I say. "Did you steal it, or did he give it to you?"

"They'll never believe you," Amya says.

"Does it matter? The accusation will be enough."

Amya's lips purse, and she looks away from us, considering if I'm bluffing. "What do you want?" Amya asks. "I don't have the money. I already gave it to my sister."

"Prove it," Catie says.

Amya taps her phone and pulls up an e-mail from her sister thanking her prolifically for the generous—ha!—donation. Then she continues with information about her treatment and her daughter.

"I want to talk to your sister," Catie says.

"No. I don't want anything upsetting her." Amya's expression is unyielding, reminding me of the look I got on my face when I had to protect Catie when we were growing up.

"Enough," I say, taking Catie's arm. "Amya doesn't have the money anymore."

"This isn't over!" Catie shouts over her shoulder as we walk back to the dock. Catie is eerily silent. It makes me nervous because she'd normally be talking my ear off over what just happened. When we get to the end of the dock where the water taxis drop off and pick up passengers, Catie grabs my shoulders, fury in her eyes.

"Why aren't you more...more...enraged by all of this?! You barely put up a fight back there. You haven't put up a fight to get your money back since you discovered it was gone." Her hands release me, the gesture as harsh as when she grabbed me, and I teeter backward falling hard on my butt, and the dock sways.

It takes me a moment to respond, her words ringing loudly in my ears. "What the hell are you talking about? I flew all the way to Panama to get the money back. I found Luke. I just confronted Amya," I shoot back when words are able to form in my mouth again. "But I'm not going to take money from a dying woman."

"It isn't her money!" Catie shakes her arms at the sky. "That bitch stole it. You should have torn her apart back there."

"You think I should stand up for myself?"

Catie nods emphatically.

"Fine. Why didn't you pay me for the special? I did just as much work as you did, and you never offered me anything except to reimburse me for the vacation I had to cancel." I didn't realize I was holding resentment for that weekend until right now. I bent over backward to help her get through that special without being exposed. Which reminds me. "What happened when you spoke to Max? You said he's doing the takedown piece. Did you tell him off?"

"You bet your ass I did. And I've got legal looking into it. That story will never see the light of day because I took action immediately. But you. Instead of suing Luke immediately for the money, you travel across the continent and try to what? Talk some sense into him. He's a con artist. You don't talk sense into him! He'll just keep manipulating you. And what the hell was Luke even doing with access to your bank account?! That was your restaurant!" Catie pushes back sweaty strands of hair from her forehead. "Do you know why he left his job at Morgan Stanley?"

"He made a lot of money and didn't need to work anymore, so he quit," I snap back at her, pushing up to my knees. I know he wasn't lying about his job. I've been to his spacious office and met a lot his colleagues and clients. Many of them frequented Chez Bella.

Catie nods her head, except it looks slightly manic with its jerky movement up and down. "That's what he told you. But he was fired." Catie waits for this to sink in and then continues, "For fraud."

I'm about to stand, but this keeps me on the ground, staring up at her in disbelief. "What?"

"He was fired for misusing client funds. He was sued by three separate clients. Or the bank was, but he was named as the party at fault. It was all settled internally, of course."

There's the soft rumble of an engine as a boat taxi with peeling blue paint approaches the dock. I stand and step back from the edge. I open my mouth to ask Catie more, but she speaks first.

"If you want to let your dream slip away, fine. But I'm not standing here and helping you anymore. Not when you're willing to trust Luke so blindly and forgive him." Catie turns on her heels and stomps back toward the island.

"You're done helping me?" Rushing in front of her, I collide with the information stand, knocking down several brochures. I snatch them up and then drag Catie to the edge of the jungle path, palms towering above us. "I'm the one who's been saving your ass for the past six years. If it weren't for me, you wouldn't have a career. And what thanks do I get? Half the profits from a book I helped write and that's it. You should have given me more. I deserved half the money from that special. And you keep promising we're going to write the next book together, but you won't talk to your publisher. Don't you dare tell me you're done helping me. You know what? I'm done helping *you*."

The sand under my feet kicks up sharply as I dash back to the dock, leaving Catie alone at the edge of the jungle. The boat captain speaks to me in Spanish and puts out his hand,

and I stumble onto the boat, telling him to take me back to Red Frog. I close my eyes tight as the wind pummels me while we speed through the water.

Catie has never talked to me like that, and I've never yelled at her. I didn't realize how angry I was about our arrangement until this moment. It didn't matter before because I was happy in my job, and I wasn't thinking much beyond it until I decided to open the restaurant. Now that my dream is sinking, I'm seeing my life differently.

Catie is angry too. Angrier than I've ever seen her. But I don't think it's really me she's angry at. Disappointed, but not angry. If Max goes through with his takedown piece, her career is over. She'll never recover. She must realize this.

But no matter her motives, real or misguided, I can't deny the truth in her words. I'm an idiot for believing Luke after he stole the money. And why did I come all this way to confront him? I could have sued him. But that could have cost more than the money he took. So it wasn't completely naïve of me to come all this way. And Max was supposed to be beside me, helping me, confronting Luke with me. But in the end, it has to be me who stands up to Luke. I've been so damned scared of failing, of making the same mistake that sent Cole's restaurant into turmoil. Except, it wasn't really my fault. He should have been there at that meeting with the inspector. Not me. And I should never have given Luke access to my account. Even if I thought he was my friend.

When I arrive back at the welcome center, instead of calling Mom to come get me, I walk the two miles back to the villa, my anger sizzling under the surface. My dress sticks to me from the sweat soaking the skin under my breasts and down my back. My face is red from the hike, and my feet have several new blisters. I trudge up the hill to the villa, and as my hand reaches for the handle on the front door, I hear a voice that sends a cacophony of emotions through me, which land in a heap in the pit of my stomach.

Max.

My chin quivers, and tears pop into my eyes. What a mess my life has become. The man I thought I loved is about to rip my sister's life apart, and the man I trusted with my dreams ripped them to shreds. And when all the pieces land, I'll be left with nothing but a broken heart, an empty dream, and no one to blame but my own pitiful self.

Eighteen

I storm into the villa, ignoring the stares from Max and Jess as I confront Luke. "I want to speak to your stockbroker now. Right now."

"Wha…what?" Luke stammers.

"Call her now."

"I can't. She's not there." Luke looks worried.

"What are you talking about?" Max asks.

I ignore Max and keep my focus on Luke. "Despite your protests, I think you have plenty of money or stocks or whatever to pay me back."

"Is that true?" Max asks. Why is he suddenly so interested? He didn't care this much a few days ago.

"Butt out, Max. I've got this."

"Hey, he's just trying to help," Jess says, placing a hand on Max's arm, which pisses me off.

"Max is just as bad as Luke. I don't want his help."

"Max is nothing like Luke."

All Jess has done is wreak havoc on my life since she arrived. Max and I were meant to come down here, confront Luke, get my money, and leave. But she showed up, and everything fell apart. "What are you doing here?" I skewer the words at her. "You want Max back? You got him. I don't want him anymore."

"I knew it!" Luke claps his hands once in triumph. "You are in love with him."

"Don't you talk to me about love," I snap back. "You know nothing about it. Love isn't sneaky and doesn't play games. It doesn't steal forty thousand dollars and make up lie after lie to save its own ass. I want you gone. Now. I know what happened at Morgan Stanley. I'm going to sue you the second I land in New York."

"But—"

"You heard my daughter." My head spins, and I see my mother standing at the top of the stairs of the entryway, Marty next to her. "Get the hell out of my house."

Luke turns pleading eyes to me, but I walk past my mother and hold the door open until Luke skulks out of the house. I slam the door after he leaves, as a final note of closure.

Mom jumps up and down, cheering as if our team has just won the final match of a long, hard game. "This calls for a celebration. What does everyone want to drink?"

I stop her. "No. Max and Jess aren't staying."

Max's eyes meet mine, and I can tell he knows why. If Catie spoke to him, she would have told him how she found out about his story.

"Can we talk?" Max asks.

"Fine. But not here." I walk outside and down the driveway, away from prying ears. If my mother knew what Max was about to do to Catie, she'd kill him.

I stare down the hill. Luke is just rounding the corner, and I watch until he disappears. I can't help the pang of sadness that seeps in, but I push it away, knowing it's only the remaining vapors of our friendship, and the feeling will soon be gone. My emotions aren't a faucet I can turn on and off when I choose, but I can control what I do with those emotions.

I turn to Max, and my heart goes pitter-patter when his deep-blue eyes take me in, but the love I once felt has been suffocated by the thick blanket of lies and deceit. He scans my face, and his eyes widen in alarm when he sees the bloody scab on my forehead. Self consciously, I dab at the rough skin.

"Are you okay? How did you get that?" Max's eyes shine with concern as he sweeps his fingers to my forehead.

"It's from when I was robbed." I push his hand away.

"Robbed?"

"You know. In Costa Rica."

Anger fills Max's eyes. "What are you talking about?"

"I thought Jess told you."

"No." He spits the word out. "No one told me."

"It doesn't matter now," I say. So Jess didn't tell Max I was attacked. Surprise, surprise. It doesn't change anything.

Max's face skews in anger and alarm. "Did they..."

"No. Nothing like that. It was a woman, actually. She was a little rough, and I fell over on some rocks." As I remember it now, fear bats at my insides. It could have ended a lot worse than it did. "They took my phone, money, and passport. But they left me pretty much unharmed."

"And Jess knew?" Max asks, looking away from me and up toward the villa.

"Yes, but are you really that surprised?" His concern for my well-being is too little, too late. If he were really concerned for me, he wouldn't be about to trash my sister's career and life. "She's been manipulating you from the moment she arrived."

"Why would she do that?"

"She was afraid of a little competition, I guess. Not that she had anything to worry about." My head shakes at my foolishness. It seems like another person who was chasing after Max.

A golf cart comes chugging down the street, and we pause until it passes. On the back of the cart, a mother holds a baby in her lap and grips the seat as the man driving whips them around the corner. The baby sputters a giggle as the mother strangles the metal sidebar.

"Who was she competing with?" Max smiles, brightening his whole face.

"Don't. Your charming little smile isn't working this time."

He drops it. "Was it true what Luke said up there?"

"That's inconsequential now." I turn away, in case he can see any doubt in my eyes. Maybe my feelings for him are still lurking around. Time will wipe them out soon enough. "What I want to know is if you've been using me from the moment we met?"

Before he can answer, my phone rings. Mom gave me an old one of hers until I can replace mine. I glance at the number, but I don't recognize it. There's a bit of static on the other end when I answer, and I move a few steps down the road.

"Is this Natalie Bloom?" I'm startled to hear my name since no one has this number. Except... "This is Mrs. Trivett, Mira's mother."

I sent an e-mail to Mira through her website and asked her to call me in regard to the money Amya sent her, knowing that would pique her interest enough to at least e-mail me back. I won't ask for the money back, but I want Mira to know where the money came from.

I wasn't expecting her mother to call me.

"Oh, hi. What...how can I help you?"

The woman speaks rapidly in a low tone. "I saw your e-mail. I've been managing my daughter's blog while she's recovering from her latest treatment. Cancer treatment. What is this about money from her sister?"

"Yes, uh..." Suddenly I don't want to say anything, but I

219

have to do this. "Well, uh, your daughter Amya stole some money from me and...and sent it to Mira. I just...I wanted Mira to know."

There's a sharp intake of breath and then silence.

"Mrs. Trivett?"

I think she's hung up, but then she speaks again. Her voice is thick with emotion. "Unfortunately, when someone close to you is dying, it makes you do crazy things to try to save them. I'm not going to blindly believe a stranger, but I do know Amya, and she has taken all this very hard. And if she did what you say she did...I'm sorry. But we're not giving the money back."

"I'm not asking for it back, but I wanted Mira to know." My voice falls flat, my skin hot from shame. Why should I be ashamed? I didn't do anything wrong, but it just feels wrong. I keep thinking about my dad. Would I have done something that crazy if I thought it would have kept him alive? Maybe.

"Well, you've told me. That will have to do." There's the high-pitched voice of a little girl in the background. Mrs. Trivett pulls the phone away from her mouth, and I hear her speaking to the little girl, her voice muffled. "I need to go now." There's a sharp click as she hangs up.

My chin quivers, remembering the pain we suffered when Dad was near the end. Every moment was precious.

"Who was that?" Max asks, the slap of his flip-flops approaching behind me. I look at him and realize there's one last loose end I have to tie up before I can start over when I arrive back in Manhattan.

"Why do you care?" I shoot at him, anger still simmering hot under the surface. I'm mad. Mad at myself for not being as harsh on Max as I was on Luke. Standing up to Luke isn't enough. The real test will be to cut everything off with Max.

"I...what do you mean?"

"I am so sick of lies. My life has been woven in lies for so many years that I forgot what the truth feels like. We're done." I wave my hand between our two bodies. "I don't want to be around someone who's out to hurt me or my sister."

Max narrows his eyes, weighing something up. "I'm not out to hurt you. I'm helping you."

"Yeah, right. Why did you come to Panama? Just to use me for your story about Catie? How far were you willing to go? On the beach that night, right before Jess arrived...do you remember?" My voice has risen, and I feel my cheeks growing red as I recall the second time he left my lips hanging for his.

Max is working his jaw and speaks through gritted teeth. "I remember."

"Was it all a game to you? Your way of manipulating a story out of me?"

"I wasn't manipulating you. I would never do that to someone...to a friend." His eyes soften, willing me to believe.

"We're not friends, Max. I can't be friends with a man who would hurt someone I love."

Max shoves his hands in the pockets of his shorts and kicks some loose rocks in front of him. "Dammit, Bloom. You have it all wrong. I wasn't supposed to...I'm not..."— he lets out an exasperated sigh—"Fuck it. Catie's just gonna have to forgive me. I—"

The loud rumbling of the resort truck draws my attention, and I hurry to it, waving the driver down. I'm done listening to excuses. It's time to move on.

"'Ello, Ms. Natalie," Enrique speaks, rolling down the window.

"Are you going to the dock?" I ask.

"Yes. The last boat to Bocas leaves in twenty minutes."

"Can you wait a minute? You're going to have a couple more passengers," I say, and Enrique sits back and waits, turning up AC/DC, which blares from the truck radio.

"You're leaving?" Max asks.

"No. You're leaving." I walk up the driveway. "I'll tell Jess to get your bags, and I don't want to see either of you again."

"But, Nat—"

"No!" I yell. "Enough. I've had enough."

I shove open the door and toss Jess's and Max's bags, which are still packed, out the front door.

"Hey!" Jess is sitting at the counter, looking at her phone.

"Out." I point to the door. "It's time for you to go."

Jess hesitates but quickly scurries to the door when I step toward her. The sound of the door slamming behind another poisonous person that is now out of my life is not as satisfying as I'd hoped.

I collapse on the couch, tension releasing from the tight coil that's been wrapped around my insides. My chest hurts, and tears threaten to spill, but I'm finally free of everything and everyone that has been holding me back from living my life.

Nineteen

"Priiiiince Street. Next stop, Prince Street," the low, rumbling voice of the subway conductor announces.

I lift my head from the metal wall I'm resting against, exhausted after the events of the past couple of weeks. Catie and I landed at 6:00 a.m., and I only managed a couple hours of restless sleep on the plane. The seats were cramped and scratchy on the discount airline, and my mind was working overtime, sorting out my life.

After I arrived back to my apartment, took a hot shower, and changed into fresh clothes, I felt like a new woman, ready to face my new reality. I gathered my mail and sat at the little café on the corner with a large cup of coffee and ripped open the few letters that weren't junk or bills. The confidence that had been building in me faltered when I opened a notice from a small-claims court. Jim, my contractor, is suing me.

With my temporary cell phone—an old iPhone 4 I had lying around my apartment—I called my voice mail, and my balloon of hope deflated even more as I listened to a message from the landlord of the restaurant, notifying me that due to being two months late on rent, he would be evicting me at the end of the month, and would be filing a claim if he did not receive the money he is owed. Then I checked my bank account—both business and personal—and all hope evaporated. I have no money to pay anyone. The money Luke promised never came through. Surprise, surprise.

I called Catie at her office this afternoon—our relationship isn't repaired, but we're trying to find a new normal—and after I told her about the contractor and landlord, she gave me the number of her lawyer to discuss my options and to start the process of suing Luke. I left a message for the lawyer to call me back.

With no money and no job and debt racking up, I have no other choice but to move out of my apartment since I can't pay the rent. Catie has offered to let me live with her rent free for a while. Once my landlord returns my security deposit, I can pay off part of the rent due to the restaurant. It will hopefully be enough to hold him off from filing a claim. Later today, I'll stop by Chez Bella and beg for my job as head chef back. The owner loves me and was resistant to let me go, so I'm at least hopeful I'll have a job.

Walking down Prince Street, I take a right onto Greene Street and go into a small café. I look around, but the only people I see are an older couple looking at a guidebook and a group of hipsters who look like they didn't make it home last night. Unless they always look that greasy. After ordering a large latte, I sit on one of the wooden chairs and watch the door. A young woman in a baseball cap gingerly walks in, looking around with tired eyes. When she sees me, she gives a waning smile and joins me.

"Can I get you something?" I ask.

"I'm fine. I have water." The color drains from her already pale face as a coughing fit takes over her slim frame. When she recovers, she takes a deep breath and sits back in the hard wood chair.

"You didn't travel into the city just to meet me, did you?"

I ask.

After all the bad news I'd received upon landing back in Manhattan, I received an unexpected call this morning from Mira, Amya's sister, asking if we could meet today. I'd suggested I take a train into Connecticut and meet her near her home, but she insisted we meet in the city.

"No," Mira says. "I have an appointment here to be fitted for a special bra for my lopsided chest until I can have my breast operation." Her eyes fall to the left side of her chest where a breast should be, except it's flat. "I had it removed a few months ago. I finished my last round of chemo, and soon I'll have my first consultation for breast surgery to replace it."

"You're finished with all your chemo?"

"Yes. I have more treatment over the next year, but not as harsh. I was lucky, in a way. It was only stage two, and it's not in my lymph nodes. After the treatment, I'll hopefully be on my way to a full recovery."

"My father had cancer," I blurt out. Her eyes open wide, and I give an apologetic smile, unsure why I want to tell her, except to let her know I've been there. In a way.

"How is he?"

"He died."

Mira takes in a sharp breath. "I'm sorry."

"No, I'm sorry. I...it doesn't always turn out badly." Why did I say anything at all? "My uncle had bladder cancer, and he is still happy and healthy at seventy-five years old." I take a slow sip of my now lukewarm coffee. "Anyway, I know you didn't ask to meet me here to discuss the sad C-word."

"You're right." Mira massages her temples. I'm not sure if she's in pain or considering something. "It's about the money my sister stole."

"When I talked to your mom the other day, I wasn't calling to ask for the money back. I mean, I should. But after witnessing what my father went through I...I understand how hard it can be and why people do things they never would have in any other circumstance."

"Oh, my sister would do something like this no matter what. That's why I wanted to see you." Mira unzips her purse. "I'm giving the money back."

I open my mouth to protest but stop. It is my money. "Why?" I ask instead.

"Because it's the right thing to do. And the treatment hasn't been as long or as hard as I'd imagined. From everything my doctor said and everyone I've met with this type of breast cancer, I'll most likely have a long life. It's not as dire as we once believed." Mira smiles, and tears prick the corner of her eyes. "No matter what, it's not my money to keep."

"Thank you."

I'm expecting an envelope of cash, but instead Mira pulls out her phone and, after a few taps on her screen, informs me she's sent the money back to me via PayPal. My phone chimes, indicating an e-mail, and I open it. It's not all the money Luke took from me, since he lost a lot during his fated restaurant venture in Panama, but it's enough to pump a little life back into my dream.

"I spoke to my sister, and she reluctantly told me how you traveled all the way to Panama in search of this money," Mira says. "My friends and family have been generous with their time and money as I've battled this damn cancer, and my insurance is shockingly paying a lot more for the treatments than I first thought they would."

"I'm sorry."

"No, I'm sorry. Please forgive my sister. She's a bit misguided sometimes, but she means well."

"I understand," I say. "I have a sister." This whole ordeal has been a huge pain in the ass, and I'm glad for it all to be over. Mira and I talk for a few more minutes, and then I give her a brief hug, and she leaves. The money won't pay for everything I owe, but it should mean the small-claims lawsuit might be dropped. I'll still have to give up my restaurant and my apartment, but at least I won't be in debt, and my credit will stay clean. I can still apply for a loan and find a new space, once I get back on my feet.

I take out my phone and dial the contractor's number again. This time I'm thankful when he picks up.

***

The past several hours have been humbling. I've begged, pleaded, and swallowed my pride, but Jim has withdrawn his claim, and I've already wired him the money he is owed. He seemed in good spirits by the end of the conversation, but we won't be working together again. The landlord was a much easier call. When I explained the situation, he was surprisingly understanding, and we worked out a payment plan. I still have to give up the space, but he told me if he hasn't rented it when I'm ready to move forward with my restaurant again, he'd happily rent it to me. With the contingency that I'd need a guarantor next time.

Now I'm sitting on Catie's sofa, a glass of white wine in my hand. She sits next to me, not speaking. After our fight in Panama, we've been civil, but there's a big fat elephant wedged between us.

"I meant what I said in Panama. I can't keep helping you, but that doesn't mean I don't support you," I finally say. It's going to be a miserable few months if we don't kick this elephant out. "And I know you've been working hard to have a more honest career."

"Don't." Catie puts her hand on my wrist. "You were right. I owe you much more than just the royalties from the book. I called my publisher, and they were thrilled to start moving forward on the second book. They were surprised when I said I want to coauthor it with you, but I told them that was the only way I would do it."

Emotion wells up inside me, and I bite my lip, holding back tears. It's not gratitude that's overtaking me; it's realizing

227

that I stood up for myself, and I'm seeing the fruits of my effort.

"I've been so caught up in my own life that I never thanked you properly for everything you did for me during the homecoming special and for the past four years. And the few years before that with the blog. Without you, I wouldn't be here." Catie releases my hand and opens her large Stella McCartney tote that's on the floor next to her feet. Catie pulls a small notepad from her bag and scribbles something on it. She hands me the piece of paper, and I realize it's a check. When I look at the amount on it, my mouth drops open.

"What's this for?"

"What you asked for. Half of my fee, including the bonus, from the homecoming special. I'm sorry I didn't give it to you earlier. You're right. You deserve this. If anything, it's not enough for all the work you've put in to help my career through the years."

"You know I was happy to do it," I say. It feels damn good to finally be appreciated. I know Catie never meant to take advantage of me. We fell into a pattern, and the profits I received (and still receive) from the first book were significant, and I was grateful. It didn't occur to me until I started going after my own dreams that I was giving too much of my talent away for free.

"You didn't have to help me," Catie continues. "I know that. Thank you for all the times you've been there for me and my career." Catie squeezes my hand, a smile on her lips.

I grip the check in my hands, tears popping into my eyes again. With this money, I can easily pay the rent on the restaurant for the next several months and continue on the renovations. I won't even need a loan.

"Thank you, Catie," I say again. "And I have a favor to ask. I want you set up a meeting with Patrick for me to discuss freelancing for the magazine as a food writer."

"That's a great idea." Catie's eyes sparkle with excitement.

It will certainly take the pressure off her. "I think Patrick will be relieved to finally have you out from behind the curtain and in the public eye. I should have done it a long time ago."

I give Catie a hug, excitement welling up inside me. When I release her, she glances at her phone. Sam's flight is landing any minute.

"He'll call you as soon as he lands," I assure her. Catie's been a ball of nerves since Sam e-mailed to tell her he was finally done with his cover story and heading back to New York. "Unless he comes straight here to surprise you. He may not be able to wait to see you. Especially since you two haven't…you know what yet."

"Maybe." Catie doesn't sound confident, but Sam has been in love with her for four years. He'll be as eager to see her as Catie is to see him. "I'll see him tomorrow night at the party if not. You're coming, right?"

"Absolutely."

Kennedy Media throws a huge ball every year for Valentine's Day. It's called the Red Ball, and all proceeds go to support children with leukemia. This year it's being held at The Empire Hotel on the Upper West Side. Catie has secured two designer dresses for us from the fashion editor at *Simply Chic*. Now that the puzzle pieces of my life are clicking into place, I'm eager to celebrate.

Since Catie and I weren't really talking on our flight back, I never asked her what happened when she confronted Max. I can't get him and everything that happened off my mind. It's driving me crazy. "Is Max still writing a takedown piece about you?"

Her answer is interrupted by her phone ringing, and her face lights up when she reads the name on the screen, mouthing *It's Sam*. I put my wine glass on the kitchen counter and leave Catie to bask in the joy of listening to her new lover's voice. As excited as I am about the turn my life has just taken, listening to Catie gush on the phone is too hard for my newly bruised heart. Max's betrayal still stings.

I long for what Catie and Sam found, but I know it's not on the horizon for me. I leave Catie and walk out into the brisk night air and try to focus on the good things in my life and not let my mind get bogged down in my emotional sorrows. My dream is back on track, I may have a new job, and soon I'll have my name sitting next to Catie's on what will hopefully be another best-selling book.

If only I had love to go with it. I want to be an independent woman and not need a man. And I don't *need* a man, but I want one. I want someone to love and be loved by.

Shaking off the wisp of sadness, I hug my coat tighter to me and walk around the corner, a sad smile adorning my lips as I think about the start of my new life.

THE ADVENTURES OF NATALIE BLOOM

Twenty

"Catelyn! Over here!"

Photographers snap pictures of Catie on the red carpet leading into the grand lobby of The Empire Hotel. They continue to yell her name, and I stand on the sidelines waiting for her to finish, but she grabs my hand and pulls me on the carpet, telling the photographers I'm her sister. They yell my name along with Catie's, and I laugh, buzzing from their enthusiasm.

We ride the elevator to the rooftop bar and lounge, which luckily is covered since it's twenty degrees outside. There are silver-and-white lights dangling above our heads and cushy red-velvet sofas arranged throughout the large room. The centerpiece is a large fireplace with stools and low tables situated in front of it.

Waiters carry trays of canapés and pink cocktails, offering them to the guests. I snatch a tuna ceviche and pop it into my mouth. It's delicious but nothing compared to the fresh tuna I had on my travels in Costa Rica.

"You're not drinking?" I ask as Catie hands me a glass of sparkling rosé.

"I'm too nervous to drink." Her eyes cascade the party guests, looking for Sam. His luggage wasn't on the plane when he landed last night, and he was at the airport until after midnight sorting it out.

My eyes also scan the party. If Max is here—his aunt does own Kennedy Media, and he works for one of the magazines, so it's very likely—I need to finish our conversation. I still feel unsettled, and I want to know why he did it. Every time I ask Catie what happened when she confronted him, she dodges my questions. I don't understand why she's not freaking out about it. I'm missing something—but what?

Across the dance floor, a lanky man in a loose-fitting black suit twirls a petite woman with an adorable pixie cut. Catching sight of Catie and me, they dance across the floor and stop in front of us.

"Happy Valentine's Day," he says, kissing our cheeks. It's Patrick, Catie's editor. He adores Catie and will do anything for her—even keep her secret for the past two years. Next to him is his wife, Avery. After three years of trying, they recently found out they're pregnant, which explains the glow on both of their faces.

"How was the trip to Panama?" Avery asks, rubbing her still-flat belly.

"Eventful," I say. "Congratulations!"

"Thanks!" Patrick and Avery both beam.

"How's my favorite chef?"

"Great," Catie and I both say together.

Patrick laughs and clarifies. "I meant Natalie. It sounds like you've been through quite an ordeal this past week."

"It's resolved now. But it feels like it's been a year since it all began."

"Hey, Patrick," Catie says, her voice lowering. "What do you think about bringing Natalie on as a part-time food writer?"

Patrick bends over laughing, and I deflate. He recovers,

wiping his eyes. "I'm sorry. It's too good. Poor Natalie. It's almost a demotion. Isn't she basically the full-time food writer?"

Catie frowns, realizing Patrick is making fun of her, not me.

"But, yes, it's a great idea." Patrick slides his arm around Avery's waist. "Come in to the office Monday morning, and we'll talk details." Patrick and Avery twirl back onto the dance floor.

That was a lot easier than I anticipated. I should have insisted on this years ago.

Catie slaps my arm.

"What?" I whine, rubbing my arm. She points across the terrace, and I follow her slender finger until my eyes land on Sam. His tall, lean figure looks dashing in his gray French-cut suit. Through the entryway, two women hurry up to him. One is petite with wavy dark hair, and she speaks urgently to Sam. The second woman is tall and blonde and looks familiar, but I can't place her. Catie excuses herself and glides across the floor to meet him.

I look beyond Catie, and my eyes widen when I see Jess enter the room wearing a teal jumpsuit; her hair is ironed straight and hangs bluntly at her shoulders. When she spots me, she crosses the room.

"What are you doing here?" I ask when Jess stands in front of me. I begrudgingly have to admit that she looks lovely. Besides the stylish outfit, she wears tasteful false lashes and dark-blue glitter eye shadow that makes her eyes pop.

"Looking for Max. I need to talk to him." She gives me a guilty look. "He's avoiding me."

"Why?"

"He's mad at me. For...for a lot of reasons." Jess fidgets with the slim belt on her jumpsuit, twisting it between her fingers. "And he's been consumed by his story over the past forty-eight hours."

"The kidnapping story?" I ask, putting my empty flute down on one of the tall cocktail tables, the sparkles from a disco ball dancing across my hand.

"No, another story he's working on." Jess's face lights up as she motions to someone over my shoulder. I turn, tension rising in my chest when I see Max. He wears a charcoal suit, heather-gray silk shirt, and a gray-and-white striped skinny tie. His broad shoulders and strong thighs fill out the suit nicely. I don't want to admire his physique, but it's impossible not to be impressed. Heads turn as he walks across the rooftop.

When he sees me, his eyes scan my dress, and he pauses at the plunging neckline of the black Vera Wang gown. "Those are beautiful...earrings," he says when he tears his eyes from the dress to my face. He clears his throat and turns to Jess, his face darkening. "What are you doing here?"

"I want to talk to you." Jess beckons him toward the edge of the terrace.

"We can talk here."

Michael Bublé's "Lost" begins to play, and I look over at the dance floor. Catie stands at the side, her face crestfallen as she watches Sam hurry out of the party, the tall blonde leading the way.

"Let's not fight." Jess slides her arm under Max's jacket, but he shakes her off.

"I just had an enlightening phone call. With Gus." He grabs her hand. "Do you want me to tell Natalie what I found out?" He doesn't wait for Jess to reply. "It was you who told him about Catie and her."

Everything in the room stops, and all my senses are focused on Max and Jess.

"What are you talking about?" Jess laughs, but it's tight and false. Her hand reaches out to him, as I've seen so many times.

"Don't." Max steps away. "If you deny it, I'm not speaking to you again."

The sexy little smile drops from Jess's face. "Fine. I told him. But you're the one who agreed to write the story. It was a big scoop. I was trying to help your career."

"No, you weren't. You were jealous of Catie, and then you were jealous of Natalie, and you tried to sabotage them."

Fear enters Jess's eyes. "I'm...I'm sorry."

"Good. You should be. Now get the hell out of here."

Jess's chin quivers, and she shoves through a group of girls in high heels who are spinning across the dance floor. The momentum knocks the girl in the tallest heels off-balance, and she stumbles, falling on her backside. The group of girls collapses onto each other in frenzied laughter at their friend—who's laughing too—and Jess keeps plowing ahead until her sleek bob fades away.

"I know you saw that e-mail about the takedown piece." The music switches to Bruno Mars's "Uptown Funk," and the revelers hoot and holler, swaying to the upbeat music. "That's why you've been so angry," Max confirms. "I never planned to publish it. I was only writing it so Gus wouldn't give the story to someone else, while I figured out a way to keep it out of the press. That opportunity came when I stumbled onto the Thomas Carmel kidnapping story."

"You're not publishing the takedown story anymore?"

"Natalie. I was never writing the story. Not really. Not once I told Gus the kidnapping was a hoax and Thomas Carmel stole over twenty grand from the public when he started a GoFundMe to pay back drug dealers in Costa Rica. And to top it off, his wife isn't even pregnant. She only said she was to gain more sympathy." Max's eyes are pleading; he wants me to believe him, to understand. "I never wanted to write that story about your sister, but Gus contacted me after a source came to him with proof that Catelyn Bloom was a fraud. He wanted confirmation from me, since I'd just done the special with Catie, but I told him to give me a week before we published anything. Gus was a little reluctant;

exposing Catie as a fraud would be a huge story, but once I discovered who his source was—Jess—I convinced him she wouldn't go to anyone else with the story, so he agreed. Gus is a good guy. But he works in a cut-throat world."

I rub my forehead, taking in this new information. "But I saw the e-mail on your computer."

"I had to string Gus along for a bit while I tracked down the kidnapping story. If he didn't think I was serious about writing the Catie piece myself, he would have given it to another writer. I had to keep control of it for as long as I could until I could find a way to make him drop the story."

I breathe out, a bit of hope creeping in, but a lump rises in my throat. Forgiveness is hard. I've been through so much with Luke's betrayal, and I don't know if I can believe Max. The pounding music muddles my thoughts, and I walk to the far side of the large terrace where heat lamps are spread out among lounge chairs and low tables, twinkling lights hanging around the edge of the low brick wall. The lights from the buildings running down the Upper West Side to Midtown twinkle, and snow begins to fall. It would be a magical moment if I didn't feel so sad and conflicted.

Max never wanted to write that story. The whole time he was trying to save Catie—not hurt her. My eyes scan the dance floor inside, and I see Catie sitting at the bar, deflated. I should go to her, but I don't have the energy to deal with someone else's problems right now. I need to figure out my own.

I turn back to the cityscape, and the tight fist of emotion gripping the pit of my stomach breaks apart, accosting every part of my body; a lump presses at my throat again, tears pop into my eyes, and a shiver runs across my spine, despite the heat lamp beside me.

I believe him. And it's a relief to know that Max *is* a good guy. He wasn't scamming me the whole time, like Luke. He was trying to help me. But what hurts is knowing that forgiving him and letting him back into my life isn't enough. I don't want to be his friend again. I want more from him, but he doesn't. I don't want to be around him and not be *with* him.

"What's wrong?" Max's voice causes the emotions that are beating me up inside to freeze. "Why did you just walk away?"

"I needed a change of scenery," I say, keeping my back to him. I don't want him to see the tears or the pain that's skittering through my body like a scared mouse.

"You didn't give me a chance to apologize." Max steps beside me, his warmth burning hotter than the heat lamp. "I'm sure it was a shock to find that e-mail on my computer, but why did you run away? Why didn't you ask me about it?"

I keep my face from his, hoping the cool breeze across the terrace will dry the wet streaks on my cheeks, hiding the evidence of my tears. "What was there to ask? It was there in black and white. I just needed to get out of there. I was sick of everyone's lies."

"Don't compare me to Luke. I was trying to help you, not hurt you," Max spits out. The disgust in his voice causes me to turn to him. "I'm nothing like him."

"I know that."

"Do you?" Max steps toward me, his face close. My eyes catch his lips, and I want to lean in and feel their warmth. Instead, I step away.

"Yes. Everything is very clear." I turn my back to him, not able to look at him as I say the next words. "I don't think we should hang out anymore. I'll miss Bailey, but I'm sure you can find someone else to walk him. There are plenty of services."

"If that's what you want."

"It is."

I take two steps, and then Max stops me with, "Why did you kiss me?"

"You kissed me back," I shoot at him.

"Yes, but you told me it didn't mean anything."

His hand touches my bare arm, and desire drops between my thighs as my breath hitches in my throat. I can't speak.

"Jess thinks you're in love with me." My chin quivers. Why is he torturing me? "I told her she's imagining things. You made it clear to me that morning after the kiss that you don't think of me that way."

"You made it clear to me the night of the farewell party that you weren't interested," I shoot back, my eyes focused on the party spinning behind us. I won't have to see him after this, so I might as well tell him the truth. "Jess is right. I am in love with you, but you kissed me in Panama, and then you chose her. I don't want to be your second choice."

"You were never my second choice."

I stay frozen, looking straight ahead, but my eyes can't focus. All my senses are absorbed in Max. He moves behind me, his warm breath tickles the back of my neck, causing me to shiver involuntarily.

"When you tried to kiss me at your farewell party, I was still recovering from everything that had happened in Greece, and I was trying to get a grip on all the media attention from it. My world was a mess. I liked you. A lot. But I didn't want to start a relationship until my life was calmer, and I knew what I was doing. You deserved better than that."

"And now?" I ask.

"Now I'm hoping you can forgive me. When Gus told me about that story, I was terrified I'd lose you if you ever found out I was involved. It's why I went to Panama and was grilling you about your relationship with Catie. I wanted to find the source to stop the story, and then I hoped you'd never know about it. When you kissed me on the beach, I knew I was ready. For you. For us."

My whole body tenses as he pulls me backward into him, his hard chest pressing against my back. "Don't," I whisper, tears popping into my eyes again. His lips brush against the skin of my neck. "Don't!" I rip away from him. "I'm so tired of the lies and deceit. I can't take it!" I swipe at the tears. "I kissed you! I kissed you and then she arrived, and you slept with her. Of course I told you the kiss meant nothing. What was I supposed to say? *I know you're still in love with your ex, but remember that little kiss on the beach? It meant everything to me.*" I hiccup a breath. "Everything."

"I didn't sleep with her."

"What?"

"I didn't sleep with her," Max says. "I...I was hurt and confused, and I was an idiot."

"But you kissed her."

Max drops his head. "Because I was hurt. Because I couldn't have who I really wanted."

"You're so stupid," I say.

"Excuse me?"

I laugh through my tears. "We're so stupid."

"I was stupid for not grabbing you up that night and telling you I'm in love with you."

I bite my lip, the ringing in my ears drowning everything out around me. If he says it again, I'm not sure I'll hear him.

"I love you too."

We both smile.

"Say it again," I say, stepping toward him, my arms wrapping around his waist, feeling the warmth of him against me.

"No." There's a twinkle in his eyes. "This time I'm going to show you." He scoops me up, his lips enveloping mine, the warmth of his kiss devouring me. There's music pounding and lights twinkling and couples laughing, but I hardly notice.

"Happy Valentine's Day." He smiles, and his lips press to mine once more. When he pulls away, his eyes look intensely into mine. "I love you, Natalie Bloom, and I'm going to show you for the rest of your life."

For a FREE ebook (Ignite: a prequel to The Bloom Sisters series), sign-up for Brooke's mailing list at her website, brookestantonbooks.com

ACKNOWLEDGMENTS

Many locations in this book hold a special place in my heart. In particular, Red Frog Beach on the Isla Bastimentos. Unlike Natalie, I always have a very relaxing and blessedly uneventful time there. It's paradise.

Thank you to everyone who helped bring this book together. Thanks to my team of publishing bandits: Lindsey Nelson, Silvia Curry, Kate Marope, and Daliborka Mijailovic. To Corinne Barlow and my mom, Sue, who always read early versions of all my books. To my aunt, Maris Soule, a romance and mystery writer long before I came onto the scene; she's been an inspiration and generous mentor into this fun and crazy world called being a writer. To my amazing group of moms here in West Palm Beach. I gave birth to my second child in the middle of launching my first book and writing this book. I wouldn't have been able to pull all this off without your love, compassion, and lots of wine. And to my husband, Mick, who makes all this possible with his support, love, generosity, and compassion. I've said it before and I'll say it again - a Domestic Goddess I am not!

ABOUT THE AUTHOR

After her own misadventures in New York City, LA, and London, **Brooke Stanton** now lives in sunny South Florida. She's a bestselling and award-winning author who has contributed to *Natural Awakenings Magazine*, wrote a column for *Examiner.com*, and is the author of The Bloom Sisters series. Visit her website at brookestantonbooks.com.

Made in the USA
Charleston, SC
13 November 2016